Praise for 43 Light Street from Romantic Times BOOKreviews

SHATTERED LULLABY

"Chilling excitement...exquisitely tender romance...the very best in romantic suspense."

NOWHERE MAN

"...a to-die-for hero, chilling suspense and an unforgettable love story."

FOR YOUR EYES ONLY

"Few write suspense like Rebecca York."

FACE TO FACE

"Harlequin's first lady of suspense...a marvelous storyteller, Ms. York cleverly develops an intricately plotted romance to challenge our imaginations and warm our hearts."

PRINCE OF TIME

"Get ready for the time of your life.... Breathtaking excitement and exotic romance...in the most thrilling 43 Light Street adventure yet!"

TILL DEATH US DO PART

"Readers will delight in every page."

REBECCA YORK

USA TODAY bestselling author Ruth Glick published her one hundredth book, *Crimson Moon,* a Berkley Sensation, in January 2005. Her latest 43 Light Street book is *The Secret Night,* published in April 2006. In October she launches the Harlequin Intrigue continuity series SECURITY BREACH with *Chain Reaction.*

Ruth's many honors include two RITA Award finalist books. She has two Career Achievement Awards from *Romantic Times BOOKreviews* for Series Romantic Suspense and Series Romantic Mystery. *Nowhere Man* was the *Romantic Times BOOKreviews* Best Intrigue of 1998 and is one of their "all-time favorite 400 romances." Ruth's *Killing Moon* and *Witching Moon* both won the New Jersey Romance Writers Golden Leaf Award for Paranormal.

Michael Dirda of *Washington Post Book World* says, "Her books...deliver what they promise—excitement, mystery, romance."

Since 1997 she has been writing on her own as Rebecca York. Between 1990 and 1997 she wrote the Light Street series with Eileen Buckholtz. You can contact Ruth at rglick@capaccess.org or visit her Web site at www.rebeccayork.com.

43 LIGHT STREET

REBECCA YORK
Midnight Caller

RUTH GLICK WRITING AS REBECCA YORK

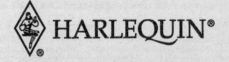

HARLEQUIN®

TORONTO • NEW YORK • LONDON
AMSTERDAM • PARIS • SYDNEY • HAMBURG
STOCKHOLM • ATHENS • TOKYO • MILAN • MADRID
PRAGUE • WARSAW • BUDAPEST • AUCKLAND

ISBN-13: 978-0-373-36070-3
ISBN-10:   0-373-36070-3

MIDNIGHT CALLER

www.eHarlequin.com

Printed in U.S.A.

CAST OF CHARACTERS

Meg Faulkner (aka Meg Wexler)—She came to Castle Phoenix with a hidden agenda. But she couldn't remember what it was.

Glenn Bridgman—He'd do anything to carry out his mission, until Meg Faulkner made him break every commandment in his personal rule book.

Jerome Johnson—Winning was everything, unfortunately for any man or woman who stood in his way.

Hal Dorsey—His health might be fragile, but he had a will of iron.

Tommy Faulkner—He knew his sister Meg would do anything to save his life.

Blake Claymore—Chief of security, and the most disliked man at Castle Phoenix.

Dylan Ryder—If Glenn Bridgman got killed he'd have to take over the Castle Phoenix project.

Tim Lipscomb—Was he into drugs, or was there some other explanation for his behavior?

Terry Shipley—He was in the wrong place at the wrong time.

Leroy Enders—How did he fit into Jerome Johnson's plans?

Chuck Fogerty, Stewart MacArthur, Bill Gady, Edmond Sparks, Duncan Catlan, James Oakland, Bruce Erdman—Was one of them a traitor?

Chapter One

Meg Faulkner felt it like a dull ache—disaster looming around the next hairpin turn of the road. Night had fallen hours ago, bringing with it a chill haze that billowed across the narrow ribbon of macadam winding through the thick pine forest. The mist fogged the headlight beams and turned the landscape into a scene from *The X-Files*.

In the TV show, Meg would be playing the unsuspecting first victim of some unseen menace. In real life, there were plenty of reasons why the analogy didn't quite work. She wasn't an innocent victim. She knew what she was getting into. And now that she was having second thoughts, it was too late to back out.

"Damn Glenn Bridgman's hide!" she muttered under her breath as she hunched over the wheel, straining her eyes trying to see the road ahead. Maybe he hadn't arranged the nightmare driving conditions, but he'd chosen to live in the back of beyond, fifty miles from the nearest town and a couple of well-placed steps from hell. Which was where she hoped to send him, if she ever made it to the front gate of his estate—and managed to talk her way inside.

The car rounded a rock outcropping, dipped into a hollow where the pavement was covered with water, and went into a skid. Jaw clenched, Meg fought to keep from sliding into the wall of rock hemming the right-hand shoulder.

From the trunk of the car she heard a muffled sound like

that of a couple of sacks of oranges rolling around. But she wasn't carrying a shipment of citrus fruit to Mr. Bridgman.

Tires spun on gravel as she surged back onto the road. Breathing a little sigh, she slowed the heavy car, then glanced at the glowing green numerals on the dashboard clock. Ten after eleven. Probably she should have taken a motel room when she'd had the chance and started fresh in the morning.

She'd voiced that observation to Mr. Johnson, after he'd blinked his lights and led her onto the old logging road where they'd agreed to exchange cars. But he'd told her in his gravelly voice that they'd lose the element of surprise if she stopped overnight. So she'd slid behind the wheel of her borrowed vehicle with its special cargo hidden in the trunk. Then Johnson had driven off in her car, leaving her on her own.

Nervous energy and fear had kept her going for the past fifty miles. Not fear for herself, but for Tommy.

Thinking about her brother made her vision shimmer. She managed to fight back the tears, but she couldn't wipe away the mental image of his haunted face, sunken cheeks, and trembling hands. He was going downhill fast—thanks to Glenn Bridgman.

She'd made the mistake of delivering that opinion to Tommy, and the old spark had ignited in his hazel eyes. For a moment she'd been glad that he was still capable of showing some spirit. Then he'd started defending Bridgman, warning her that he didn't want to hear a negative word about the man, since every member of the team had known what they were getting into.

Seeing that the heated defense was draining her brother's strength, she'd clamped her mouth shut and gone into the kitchen to fix sloppy-joe sandwiches—one of Tommy's all-time favorite meals. But even her home cooking hadn't tempted him to eat more than a few bites.

She'd left his small apartment a half hour later, choked with despair and simmering with anger. Over the next few days, the anger had grown into a roiling cauldron of emotions that had left her vulnerable to a devil's proposition. A man named "Mr. Johnson" had been playing the devil. He'd shown up at her Light Street office a week after her visit to Tommy, taken her out to dinner, and made her an offer so tempting that her mouth had practically watered.

Still, she'd politely refused. No way was she getting into anything illegal, immoral and insane.

He'd kept talking—knocking down her objections one by one, making it sound as if it was her patriotic duty to give Glenn Bridgman what he deserved. Even then, she might have gotten up from the table, until he'd pointed out how far a million dollars could go toward defraying Tommy's medical costs.

Johnson must have sensed the moment when she'd gone from confirmed skeptic to would-be convert, and he'd started talking faster. Before she quite knew what was happening, she'd agreed to sign on to his "mission impossible" team.

According to instructions, she'd told her Light Street friends she was just going off on a much-needed vacation. Which meant nobody knew where she was or what she was doing, she reminded herself with a sudden chill as a gust of wind whipped clouds of mist into her path like a fog machine on a Hollywood set. Still, she caught a glimpse of a diamond-shaped yellow sign that said, Falling Rock Area.

Great.

For the hundredth time since the nightmare ride had begun, she glanced at the odometer. Only five more miles to Bridgman's private road. When she got to his estate, the real fun would begin. First she'd have to confront the armed guards. Then, if she were lucky, she'd get an audience with the Big B, as she'd started calling him in her mind. Some luck!

She'd seen a couple of pictures of him. He was tall and dark-haired, with icy, shuttered eyes—the kind of man you'd hate to face in a high-stakes poker game. Unfortunately, that was pretty close to what she was going to be doing.

She found the turnoff in the fog. The small sign said Castle Phoenix. She'd thought the name was pretentious when Johnson had told it to her. And she'd seen pictures of the dark, brooding pile of stone that looked like something out of a gothic novel.

As she swung onto the one-lane access road, she mentally reviewed her prep sessions with Johnson—all the things she was supposed to say in answer to Bridgman's inevitable questions.

Her attention was focused on the confrontation, so that it was several seconds before she realized she was hearing a rumbling noise above her.

Thunder?

The question was answered as a trash-can-size boulder came hurtling down the cliff to her left, crashing through the underbrush and landing with a thud in front of the car. Jamming her foot on the brake, she managed to avoid the obstruction. Unfortunately, it was only the first of several chunks of mountain that had torn loose. They came cannonballing down, slamming into the side and back of the car and straight toward the window beside her head.

A scream tore from her throat. The last conscious thought she had was that she'd bartered her soul to the devil—and he was going to collect on the deal a lot sooner than she'd anticipated.

"IT'S AFTER MIDNIGHT. Get some rest." The words were said quietly, deliberately, like an oft-repeated mantra.

Down on his knees in the dirt, Glenn Bridgman composed his features, glad that he had his back to the walkway. It had been a long time since he'd closed his eyes before two in the morning. Tonight, a kind of charged feeling in the air had made him even more restless than usual. The sensation had been building for weeks—a crawling feeling at the base of his spine that he couldn't define. Yet he'd learned to trust his instincts. Something evil was in the air. Too bad he didn't know what—or when it would happen.

He'd tried to work off the tension with a grueling session in the gym, but the punishing physical workout hadn't settled him down. After a shower, he was more wide-awake than ever. It was too early to check the cell samples in the level-four biohazards lab. So he'd wandered into greenhouse eight and started looking for new growth on the rare cliff-dwelling bushes that he'd brought back from an expedition to Nepal three months ago. A tea brewed from the bark had been used by the natives for years as a headache remedy. A chemical analysis of the active ingredients showed high potential in the treatment of migraine headaches.

The trouble was, he'd damn near broken his neck getting samples of the stuff from rock crevices halfway up a mountainside. The only way he was going to get a stable supply was to propagate the dozen specimens he'd brought into the country.

"Give it a rest," Hal Dorsey repeated, his tone a little more demanding as he jabbed a gnarled finger at the controls of his motorized wheelchair, moving a few inches closer to the edge of the path.

Glenn stood, brushing dirt from the knees of his jeans. He rose to his full six-foot height before turning to stare down into dark eyes that were still as sharp as bayonets. He'd learned that those eyes could pierce his armor as no one else's dared. Still, he kept his voice level. "I was just getting ready to turn in."

"I mean, give the guilt a rest."

"Don't start on that tonight," he answered, hoping the subject was closed.

No such luck.

"Spending the hours between midnight and five in the morning doing penance isn't going to help the men from Operation Clean Sweep."

Glenn gestured toward the low-growing plants with their twisted stems and feathery leaves. "I'm not doing penance. I'm making money so I can keep the main research project going. That will help them."

"Any cash you see from this stuff is years down the road," the man in the wheelchair retorted.

"Not if Mac McQuade at Medizone Labs buys into the research project."

"Chump change. You need to score something bigger."

Glenn might have risen to the bait. Instead, he worked hard to keep his features even. It was starting to look as if he could hit big in the biotech lottery with one of the projects in the main bio lab, but he wasn't going to put a jinx on it by speaking too soon.

"You trust McQuade?"

"I've known him for a long time."

"Everyone has his price."

Before Glenn could respond to the cynical observation, a series of electronic beeps interrupted the discussion. With a little sigh, Glenn pulled a portable phone from his pocket and pressed the receive button. "Bridgman here."

The voice on the other end of the line belonged to Jay Trescott at the communications center, and his tone resonated with suppressed excitement. "We have something on the screen you might want to see, sir."

"Don't call me sir," he snapped. After walking away from the army three years ago, he'd looked forward to being simply Glenn Bridgman, private citizen. Then, in one unforgettable afternoon of carnage, when armed men had stormed Castle Phoenix, he'd discovered that his work demanded a private security force. Most of the guys he'd hired had military backgrounds, which made them tough and loyal. Unfortunately, they had speech patterns that were hard to break. "Just give me a summary," he added more gently, regretful that he was taking out his dark mood on Trescott.

"Uh...sorry. We were monitoring a car heading toward

the main gate—on your private access road,'' he added unnecessarily, since Glenn had made sure there was only one way to get to this place.

He glanced at his watch. Midnight. An inauspicious time for visitors.

''How close is the vehicle?''

''Four point six miles.''

Which meant that either the driver was lost in the woods north of Rome, New York, or he was planning a surprise visit to Castle Phoenix.

''But there's been a complication,'' Trescott said, interrupting his speculation. ''A rockslide along that stretch we've been worried about.''

''The rocks hit the car?''

''Looks like it from what we're seeing on the sensors.''

''I'm on my way,'' Glenn advised. ''Have a fully armed security team ready to leave the compound at once.''

''Yes, sir!''

Trescott was really excited now. Glenn didn't waste the energy correcting his form of address again.

''I take it there's trouble,'' Hal muttered as Glenn slipped the phone back into his pocket.

''Maybe. I've got to check out an accident on the access road.''

''You expecting company?''

''Negative.'' He strode toward the greenhouse door, knowing Hal would wheel himself into the communications center where he could monitor the action from the comfort of his chair—although comfort was a relative term for his old friend.

Three minutes later, Glenn trotted into the garage at the right of the main house. Hell of a night to be out, he thought as he set his medical bag on the back seat and climbed behind the wheel of the lead jeep.

Blake Claymore, the security chief, was already in the passenger seat, a compact machine gun held upright. There were two more jeeps in the small convoy and a van bringing up the rear—all full of armed men. Quite a little military force to investigate an accident—and probably not enough firepower if they were walking into an ambush.

Glenn made a low sound under his breath as he started the engine and pulled out of the parking garage. This could be a trap, but it would take anyone else over an hour—under the best of driving conditions—to arrive at the scene of the accident. Tonight, the roads were less than ideal, and he couldn't leave an injured motorist out there in God knows what kind of shape. The guy could be bleeding to death for all they knew.

Switching on the cellular phone as he headed toward the main gate, he aimed a question in the direction of the speaker. "Any sign of movement at the accident scene?"

"Negative," Trescott answered.

"Let me know if there's any change."

"Yes..."

The gate swung noiselessly open as the lead jeep approached. Then the convoy rumbled into the fog-shrouded night. Glenn felt Blake's tension as the headlights cut a path through the gloom. They both knew this could be another stealth attack by the man who called himself Jerome Johnson, the man they'd dubbed "The Jackal."

Johnson had started with the direct approach—an armed strike force. Only luck—in the form of a freak March snowstorm—had defeated him in his first attempt to break through the Castle Phoenix security perimeter. His subsequent gambits had been more subtle. Johnson had fronted a drug company willing to invest in Bridgman Enterprises. Glenn had put Hal to work, researching the deal. It had taken him six weeks, but he'd finally exposed the scam. Undaunted, the Jackal had switched tactics and sent a representative from a multinational cartel willing to finance one of Glenn's wilderness expeditions.

With the patience of a military surgeon digging hidden shrapnel out of a wound, Hal had unmasked that scheme, as well.

"He could have men on the cliff above the road," Blake pointed out. "He could have men in the woods. The car could be wired to explode when the door is opened. Or—"

Glenn waved him to silence. "I appreciate the insights, but we'll find out soon enough."

"I wish you'd carry a weapon."

"We've been through that," Glenn growled. "I've already killed and disabled enough people."

"Don't be ridiculous. You didn't kill anybody."

"That depends on your point of view."

"You—"

"Drop it," Glenn warned. "Just drop it."

The security chief nodded tightly. They were friends— or as close to being friends as Glenn had permitted. But there was an invisible line neither one of them had ever crossed.

For the remainder of the drive through the midnight landscape, they rode in silence. Finally the beams of the headlights collided with a boulder lying in the middle of the road. Beyond it, metal gleamed in the murky darkness. A car.

Glenn eased to a controlled halt. Behind him, doors were already opening as armed men, some wearing night-vision scopes, hit the pavement. You'd think they were making a raid into hostile territory, Glenn reflected with a sigh as he grabbed his bag.

After medical school, Glenn had gone into research and hadn't worked much with patients until he'd come to Castle Phoenix. But now he was ministering to the security force part-time and making regular health assessments of the men from Operation Clean Sweep while he tried to repair the damage he'd left in his wake.

Blake was moving toward the silent car, the beam of his flashlight playing over the rocks in their path. Glenn switched on his own light as he caught up and passed the other man, picking his way carefully through the debris.

He'd sensed that something was going to happen tonight.

Now he felt as if some unseen force had guided him to this place for a crucial meeting with his destiny. Blake caught up with him. "Stay away from the car until I give you the all clear."

"It's not wired," Glenn said, making an effort to shake off the strange mood that gripped him as he took another step toward the disabled vehicle.

"Now you're a mind reader?" came the sarcastic reply.

"Look at it this way—the Jackal would be pretty stupid to blow me up. He'd be killing the goose that lays the golden eggs."

Blake grunted in reluctant agreement, then barked orders to several men from one of the other jeeps.

Nothing moved in the woods, on the road, or in the vehicle. It was a dark-colored Volvo sedan, as sturdy as a military tank, yet the rockslide had knocked it catawampus halfway across the road and onto the shoulder. The front bumper was wrapped around a large boulder, the windshield was shattered, and an oil slick spread outward from beneath the chassis. The majority of the damage appeared to be on the other side—the driver's side. Blake lifted his flashlight and trained it on the front seat. There appeared to be only one occupant, slumped across the wheel. All Glenn could see in the beam of light was a wild tumble of long golden hair that might have looked sexy, if it hadn't been smeared with blood.

"A woman," Blake muttered. "I don't like it."

"A woman is worse than a man?"

"Depends on her training."

"Let's assume she's a geologist trained to study rock formations." Setting his bag on the bumper, he cupped his hands around his mouth to project the sound. "Can you hear me?"

She didn't answer, didn't move.

"We'd better get the door open," he said, inspecting the large chunk of rock crumpling the side of the car and blocking the exit. It had cracked the window, turning the glass into a misshapen spiderweb of destruction. Both men took an automatic step forward and began to push against the barrier. They might as well have been trying to move the cliff that towered over the road.

After several minutes of frustration, Glenn swore and went to the other side of the vehicle. It was also blocked—by a tree trunk. But he figured there was room enough to squeeze past if he sucked in his middle. Opening the door, he emptied his lungs and wormed his way though the narrow opening.

One of the men was holding a light so that he could see what he was doing. He was vaguely aware that several others were trying to move the boulder. Then he lost track of what was happening outside the car as he slid across the console and reached out to touch the shoulder of the small figure slumped over the wheel.

"Are you all right?" he asked urgently, unnerved by her silence.

Odds were, he didn't know this woman, yet he felt the weight of responsibility hanging over him as he gently slipped his arm under her chest and leaned her back against the seat. Holding her upright, he felt for a pulse in her neck and let out a sigh of relief as he felt the warmth of her skin and the artery beating shallowly but steadily against his fingertips.

Opening his bag, he took out a stethoscope and blood-pressure cuff. Pressure and heart rate were normal, but she didn't stir as he opened the top button of her blouse and pressed the cold metal disk to the creamy skin above her bra. Next he moved his hands quickly over her arms and legs, checking for broken bones, keeping his touch deliberately impersonal.

When he tipped her face up, though, his breath involuntarily caught in his throat. Her skin was like fine porcelain, and her eyes were closed, the lashes several shades darker than the golden hair he'd first seen. Mesmerized, he studied her pale features. They were delicate and feminine, with perfectly arched brows that matched her lashes, a small straight nose, and beautifully shaped lips, the fullness of the lower one hinting at sensuality.

It was a face to stir a man's fantasies. *His* fantasies. And yet, the sensual effect was marred by a half-hidden wound at her hairline. It looked as if she'd been knocked around when the rocks had hit the car. Hopefully, her seat belt had kept the damage to a minimum. But he'd be happier if she woke up.

Something tugged at his memory as he stared down into her still face—a spark of recognition that made him wonder for a moment if they'd crossed paths before.

"So where did we meet—the senior prom?" he asked wryly.

She didn't answer. And he dismissed his speculations, certain that if he had met this woman, he would have a vivid recollection of the occasion, whenever it was.

Opening one of her lids and then the other, he was startled by the vivid green of her eyes, then remembered what he was supposed to be doing—checking her pupillary reflex. He was relieved to see that the pupils were the same size and that they contracted in response to the flashlight.

A wrenching sound to his left made his head jerk up as the driver's door eased open. Blake leaned into the car, shone the light around the interior, and picked up a pocketbook from where it had fallen under the dashboard.

The security chief pulled out a wallet, extracted a driver's license and examined it under the light. "Issued in Maryland. She's a long way from home. This says she's Meg Wexler. Twenty-eight years old. One hundred and twenty pounds. Five-six. Green eyes and blond hair."

Green. Emerald green.

"The description fits," Blake mused aloud, his voice speculative—and hard.

"You sound like you don't believe the face goes with the name," Glenn observed.

"I'll believe it when I get some verification—and hear her pretty little story about what she's doing in the middle of nowhere on a night that would warm the heart of the devil himself."

Chapter Two

Two men arrived with a stretcher from the van, which was equipped like a small ambulance—one of the expensive pieces of equipment that had sucked up the monetary resources of Bridgman Enterprises.

Accompanying them was Dylan Ryder, who ran the medical center. Like Blake, he had been with Glenn since before Operation Clean Sweep.

In low voices, they discussed the woman's medical condition and the steps that needed to be taken.

"She's concussed and there's a head wound," Glenn told the other physician. "If she doesn't come around in the next hour, we'll do a series of skull X rays and a CAT scan."

He lifted her wrists to check whether she was wearing a Medic Alert bracelet warning of some underlying condition that might affect her treatment—or could have caused unconsciousness. If she had any health problems, she wasn't advertising them.

Ryder nodded as the men wheeled the stretcher toward the van, opened the back door, and slid the unconscious woman inside.

"I want to talk to her as soon as possible," Blake said, interrupting the conversation.

"She can't talk to you now," Glenn answered over his shoulder as he climbed into the vehicle.

"Until she proves otherwise, we have to assume she's an enemy agent."

Glenn turned to face the security chief. "Maybe, but we also have to give her responsible medical treatment. And every moment we delay could be critical."

There was a two-second hesitation. "Yes, sir." Blake turned on his heel and moved toward another group of men.

Glenn sighed. The former Captain Claymore tended to see the world in black-and-white terms—which was the kind of mentality that had gotten them jammed up with Operation Clean Sweep in the first place. *Carry out the main mission, and damn the human cost.*

He could hear Blake ordering the car to be towed to the compound. Then he heard him curse loudly when he was informed that the tow truck would be delayed due to a flat tire.

"The equipment is supposed to be maintained on a ready-to-go basis," he bellowed.

"It was, sir. We checked every system thoroughly last week. The tire blew as they were backing onto the road."

"Not an acceptable excuse," the security chief snapped.

Glenn closed the door to the van, making a mental note to ask Blake not to ride the guys so hard.

They reached the main gate quickly. Through the mist and rain, Glenn stared at the bulky shape of the stone castle that commanded the top of the hill, amazed anew that he lived in such a place. It wasn't just that his home was a fortress. It was literally and figuratively a long way from Omaha, Nebraska, where he'd grown up. The main structure had been built during the roaring twenties by an eccentric millionaire who had wanted to raise his family of ten children away from corrupting modern influences.

In the mid-twentieth century, the building had been renovated for use as a health spa. After Hal had bought it, there had been still more modifications—chiefly the addition of various specialized facilities like the communications center, the labs, and the medical wing packed with equipment worthy of a small hospital.

Once inside the emergency room, Glenn and Dylan worked as an efficient team, doing many of the routine jobs that would have been assigned to less highly trained individuals in a big-city hospital.

An hour later they'd ruled out immediate evidence of skull fracture, internal bleeding and brain swelling and had cleaned Meg Wexler's head wound and stitched the cut that disappeared into her blond hair.

Twice as they'd worked over her, Glenn had thought she was struggling toward consciousness. She'd become restless and momentarily opened her eyes. Each time, he'd leaned over her, called her name, clasped her hand, trying to get her to waken more fully.

Instead of responding, she'd squeezed her eyes tightly shut and contorted her face under the bright overhead lights. Then she'd sunk back into unconsciousness, as if she were afraid to awaken—or were fighting to remain detached from her surroundings.

"I guess she's not impressed by your bedside manner," Dylan observed wryly.

Glenn gave a short laugh. "I'm out of practice."

The conversation was interrupted by the shrill ringing of the wall phone.

Glenn snatched up the receiver. "Bridgman."

It was Steward MacArthur, one of the men who had gone out with the midnight expedition. His voice was strained. "Sir, after you left, there was another rockslide. Swift's got a broken leg, and there are some other injuries. We need a doc."

Dylan glanced toward the patient, who was going to need monitoring throughout the night. "You keep tabs on our guest. I'll go back out there."

"You sure?"

"Yeah." He was already striding toward the door. Moments later, Glenn was alone with the woman whose driver's license said she was Meg Wexler.

Under the revealing emergency-room lights, her skin color looked better, but she lay still and silent, her lashes closed over those remarkable green eyes.

The notion stole into his head that she might be Sleeping Beauty, come to his stronghold. Except in the fairy tale, it was supposed to be the other way around. The princess was the one doomed to slumber in the castle—until a prince strong and brave enough fought his way inside to rescue her with a kiss.

He was certainly no prince, he told himself with a snort. Yet the admonition didn't stop his gaze from lingering on the curve of her lips. He was bending at the waist when he stopped with a jolt. He'd started spinning fantasies about this woman the moment he'd set eyes on her. Fantasy was one thing, though. Taking liberties with an unconscious accident victim was quite another.

God, he must be losing it. To distract himself, he focused on the white bandage that covered her stitches. Reaching out, he lightly touched the surgical tape, then rearranged some of her long hair, smoothing it to the side, hiding the evidence of her injury. She didn't wake, but his fingers lingered on the golden strands, feeling their silky texture.

Her lips parted slightly, giving him the uncanny feeling that she'd picked up on his thoughts of kissing her.

Pulling his hand away, he made his voice stern.

"Dylan will be back, with injured men. They were out tonight because of you," he said, trying to remind himself why she was lying unconscious in his E.R. "Did you come here to breach my defenses?"

She didn't enlighten him as he pushed the gurney down the hall to one of the empty patient rooms.

She was still wearing her disheveled clothing, and the collar of her blouse was stained with blood . One foot was clad in a bone-colored pump. The other shoe was missing.

"We have to get you into a hospital gown so you don't

contaminate our sterile environment. Too bad I'm the only nursing staff available,'' he said, his voice too loud in the small room.

Quickly he snatched off her remaining shoe. It was the easiest part, although his hands lingered appreciatively on the delicate instep of her small foot. The toenails were cut short and straight across. No polish. No nonsense.

After tossing the pump onto the floor, he unzipped her skirt and pulled it over her hips, trying to remain impersonal as he lifted her nicely curved thighs, cradling their weight. Detachment became impossible as he rolled down her panty hose.

''Glad I don't have to stuff my body into these things,'' he muttered. ''Probably Eve's punishment for giving Adam the apple in the garden.''

And *this* was his punishment for his own past sins, he thought, as the sight of her long legs with their slender ankles made his stomach muscles tighten. His eyes traveled upward to silky, cream-colored panties. At the juncture of her legs he could see a triangle of blond hair.

Sucking in a breath, he held it until his lungs began to burn. He was already way past turned-on, and he hadn't even gotten to the hard part. Teeth clenched, he slipped her arms out of the sleeves of her ruined blouse, noting with as little emotional involvement as possible that her bra matched her panties.

Rolling her slightly to the side, he worked the clasp on her bra, wondering what would happen if she woke up now. As he removed the garment, her generous breasts spilled out, drawing a strangled exclamation from deep in his throat. God, had he ever seen such gorgeous breasts? They were creamy and coral-tipped; the sight of them made him rock hard.

He was a doctor taking care of a patient, he reminded himself sternly. He had seen plenty of women with their clothes off. But that didn't stop him from staring appreciatively at this particular woman. She was in very good physical shape. Well muscled and centerfold gorgeous. Or maybe it had simply been too long since he'd consorted with the fairer sex. That was why she was affecting him so strongly, he told himself. Nothing personal.

His body didn't believe that for a minute. With a low curse, he covered her provocative chest with the gown, then worked her arms through the short sleeves and tied the tapes in back. Only after he'd pulled down the hem to cover her hips did he reach underneath to grasp the elastic waistband of her panties and pull them down her legs.

He balled her clothing into a wad, and started to pitch it toward the trash, then decided that Blake or someone else might want it as evidence. So he stuffed everything inside a plastic bag.

When some of the blood in his body had worked its way back to his brain, he transferred the patient to the bed, then covered her with a sheet and a soft blanket before taking her vital signs again. Her respiration was good. So were her heart rate and her blood pressure.

As he was removing the cuff, her eyes fluttered open, and he went completely still, silently thanking God that she'd waited until he had her dressed. The thought brought a flood of heat to his face.

He cleared his throat. "Meg? Meg Wexler?"

She only stared at him, as if her vision were fuzzy. "Hmm?"

"Meg. Talk to me."

She looked confused and worried as she gazed into his face. "Head hurts."

"Yes. You were in an automobile accident," he said. "A rockslide hit your car."

"And you saved me," she answered, the words carrying absolute conviction.

"I was with the rescue team."

Her hand fluttered. "You don't have to be ashamed of being kind and compassionate."

He made a low sound, trying to read her expression. "Are you putting me on by any chance?"

Her eyes clouded. "No…" She seemed to be thinking it over. "Why would I do that?"

He was instantly sorry he had challenged her. She had just survived a very nasty accident. She was in his care. Of course she'd want him to be someone she could trust.

When she started to raise her hand toward the sutures in her head, he grabbed her fingers.

She clung to him, staring into his eyes, asking for something he wasn't prepared to give. "Your hands are strong," she murmured, her thumb stroking over his flesh.

"What are you trying to do?" he asked gruffly.

"Get closer to you."

"Why? Is that your assignment?" he retorted, reminding himself that he should be using her vulnerability to pry loose some information.

A jolt of mixed satisfaction and regret went through him when panic filled her eyes.

"Do…do I have an assignment?" she quavered.

"Do you?" he countered, his question rough and quick, as he tried to keep her off-balance.

Her expression clouded. "You'd be happier if you trusted…people."

The advice was too dangerous to take. Especially from her. "Trust you?" he pressed.

She gave the barest of shrugs. "I don't know. Is that why you didn't tell me your name?"

"It's Glenn."

"Glenn," she repeated. "I like it. Like the forest. Peaceful. Strong. Enduring."

His laugh was meant to hide the sudden twisting in his gut. "What are you, some kind of poet?"

"I don't know." Once again, panic filled her features. "I don't know," she repeated, trying to sit up, her eyes wild as they darted around the room.

He pressed gently against her slender shoulder, holding her in place. "It's okay," he reassured her.

She fought him with surprising strength until the burst of energy faded as quickly as it had come. With a sigh, she sank back onto the hospital sheet.

"It's okay," he repeated.

Relief swept across her face like a strong wind blowing away thunderclouds. "If you say so." Her lashes fluttered. "I'm tired."

"I know. But don't go to sleep. I have to—"

"Watch over me. My guardian angel," she finished for him, her voice carrying deep conviction as her lids fluttered closed.

"Meg?"

She stirred. "Stay with me," she breathed. "I need your...protection."

"From what?"

"From all the bad things that hide in the dark," she murmured, the words fading as she drifted off.

Her features smoothed, like a trusting child's, and he found himself promising, "I'll stay as long as I can."

A smile flickered on her lips. Moments later, she was sleeping deeply, and he studied her face, seeing only innocence. Maybe that was what he wanted to see.

Annoyed by his reaction, Glenn turned and left the room. Pausing in the bathroom, he leaned his elbows on the sink and stared at himself in the mirror, trying to figure out what she'd seen in his features. He'd never thought of himself as easy to read, and particularly not by a woman waking up after a concussion.

With a grimace, he splashed cold water on his cheeks and dried off with a paper towel. Heading for the lounge, he poured a cup of coffee and gulped it down hot and black, jolting his system with caffeine. Feeling a little more in control, he cleaned up the E.R., before returning to the patient.

"What am I going to do with you?" he asked in a gritty voice as he checked her blood pressure again.

She didn't answer, and he leaned closer, studying her face, his gaze lingering on each peaceful feature. When he found himself reaching to adjust the blanket across her breasts, he pulled his hand back. They'd had five minutes of disjointed conversation during which he'd learned nothing about her. Either she was damn good, or he was going soft in the head. Was she good enough to have faked her half of the conversation?

He was saved from further speculation by the phone. This time it was an exasperated-sounding Blake.

"More problems?" Glenn asked, his fingers tightening around the receiver.

"The road's blocked by the mother of all boulders. I have to clear it out of the way before I can get the car back there—or the men. I can't give you an estimated time of arrival."

"I understand."

"Is our uninvited guest awake?"

"Negative."

"The element of surprise could be crucial. If she wakes up, try to get something out of her. She'll be disoriented and vulnerable. Use that."

Too late.

Before Blake could issue any more pointed instructions, Glenn hung up and turned back to the sleeping woman.

After studying her face and sexy little figure with as much detachment as he could muster, he asked sardonically, "So, are you a gorgeous spy? Or are you just a gorgeous door-to-door magazine salesperson sent to practice your persuasive techniques on the reclusive Dr. Bridgman? Come on, answer me so I can give Blake some information."

The only answer was the sound of her gentle breathing.

After hesitating for several seconds, he settled down in the easy chair a few feet from her bed, telling himself that he was simply following sound medical procedure by hovering close to her. If she didn't come around again in the next few hours, they'd have to do more tests.

A cup of strong coffee might be sloshing around in his system, but as soon as he'd kicked off his shoes and leaned back into the cushions, exhaustion claimed him. As if weighted down, his lids refused to stay open, and he gave in to the luxury of closing his eyes.

The next thing he knew, he was jerked awake by a strangled sound. Springing out of the chair, he bent over the narrow bed. "Meg?"

His heart leaped when he saw that those startlingly green eyes were open again. This time the soft focus was gone. This time her expression was full of nameless dread—until she saw him leaning over her.

The change was like a light going on in a dark room. She breathed out a little sigh.

"It's okay," he said.

When she tried to sit up, he laid a gentle hand on her shoulder. "Everything's fine," he said. Of its own accord, his hand began to stroke her reassuringly.

"Is it?" She watched him as if the answer might determine the course of planets moving through the solar system.

"Yes."

Her features relaxed, and she closed her eyes, drifting.

"Don't go to sleep," he said quickly. "Stay with me. I need to talk to you."

"Anything you want," she replied in a dreamy voice.

God, what *did* he want? he wondered.

She gazed up at him and waited a beat before asking, "What…happened?"

"A rockslide hit your car."

"I…" Her voice trailed off, and her features contorted. "What?"

She shook her head, and grimaced. "I can't remember."

He wasn't surprised. Most people with a head injury experienced a loss of memory surrounding the event—and the condition could last for several hours. He'd treated accident victims who required numerous repetitions of the same information before it finally sank in.

"You're going to be all right. Don't be afraid," he said, because he sensed how much she needed reassurance.

Then he realized he was doing it again—forgetting she could well be the enemy.

"What were you doing on the road to Castle Phoenix?" he asked.

Her mind seemed to be turning over the question. After several seconds she answered slowly, "I...don't know. What's Castle Phoenix?"

"My house."

"You live in a castle? Are you a king?"

He laughed. "Hardly."

She was looking into his eyes as if she were probing for long-buried secrets. Every instinct urged him to turn away before it was too late, but the intensity of her gaze held him. Then she lifted her hand and touched his face so softly that her fingers might have been the flutter of a bird's wings against his skin. She brushed the stubble of his day's growth of beard, sending a shiver through him. When her fingers touched his lips, he worked to block any further reaction. He wanted to tell her to stop. That would mean moving his lips. So he only stood there, waiting for her to set him free.

Eons passed before her hand dropped away. When she spoke, her voice was low. "Who are you? Are you my friend?"

The question brought a sharp stab. No, they weren't friends. They could never be friends.

"I—" She stopped short, a look of confusion crossing her face.

"What?"

"I don't know. Someone told me—" She gave a frantic little shrug. "I was going to say something. Then...it wasn't in my mind anymore. What's wrong with me? Why can't I remember?"

She sounded sincere, yet she could be faking the vapid response, faking the intimacy of her touch.

"A certain amount of memory loss is routine after a head injury."

Her face told him she had snatched at the information like a drowning sailor grasping a lifeline.

"Why are you so sad?" she asked, her voice wistful as she turned the conversation back to him again.

He blinked, swallowed hard, didn't reply. "I'm not sad."

"Well, you look like you…" She paused, searching for the right words. "Like you have a lot to worry about."

Mercifully, another phone call saved him from having to dredge up an answer. This time it was his portable ringing, which meant that the business was urgent rather than routine. Snatching the instrument from his pocket, he flipped it open as he stepped into the doorway.

"Bridgman."

"Better get up here," Blake advised. "To the parking area outside the garage."

"What's wrong?"

"Maybe you'll have an opinion."

"Okay. Give me five minutes."

"I'd hurry if I were you."

Before he could ask for details, the line went dead, and he shoved the phone into his pocket, wondering what had gone wrong now.

"Meg, I have to—"

He broke off when he saw that her eyes had closed again and her breathing had become slow and even.

Quickly he went through the procedure of checking her vital signs once more. Normal. He sighed, pleased, then wondered why he was investing so much emotional energy in this woman who had no business on the access road to his estate—or at least, no authorized business.

Before he left the medical wing, he dialed the security office and arranged for a guard. No one was available immediately, but he supposed a fifteen-minute delay wouldn't hurt anything. She wasn't going anywhere.

When he stepped outside, the darkness had faded to gray, and a chorus of birds chirped unseen in the trees. Following the driveway to the garage area, he saw Blake and several security officers standing around the Volvo. The trunk was open, and someone was peering inside. Several men were huddled in a little group talking in low-pitched voices, and another man was sitting on the damp ground, his back against a tree and his head lolling to one side. His body was trembling violently. Dylan was crouched beside him.

It was Tim Lipscomb, one of the men who had signed on six months ago.

"What happened?" Glenn asked as he trotted up. Blake put a restraining hand on his arm. "Don't get too close."

Glenn whirled toward him. "Why not?"

"He went crazy. Decked a couple of guys."

"Oh yeah?"

"He and Peterson were supposed to be guarding the car. Peterson had to take a leak. When he came back, Lipscomb leaped at him screaming obscenities. It took four guys to take him down."

Glenn stared at the young man on the ground, hardly able to believe the assessment. He'd checked out Lipscomb himself before signing him on. He was a rock-solid kind of guy. Stable. Reliable.

Dylan stood and joined them.

"Drugs?" Glenn questioned.

His colleague shrugged. "His heart rate and blood pressure are high. He claims he was standing beside the car. The next thing he knew he was sitting on the ground."

"He doesn't remember attacking anyone?"

"No."

Behind them, Blake cursed. "I don't like it. If he's on something, I want him out of here."

Dylan nodded. "We'll do a thorough physical and a complete blood workup."

Behind them, a low hum of conversation came from the knot of watching men. Then a voice pitched itself above the rest. "He was on his damn feet all night. Maybe he just got so tired, he wigged out."

Blake whirled, his gaze scanning the group of spectators. "Who said that?"

Nobody answered.

When he started forward, Glenn put a hand on his arm. "It's been a long night. Let it go."

There was a tense moment of silence; then the security chief nodded his agreement.

Dylan returned to the man on the ground. "How do you feel?"

He gave the doctor a pleading look. "I don't know what happened to me. Honest."

Glenn shook off Blake's restraining hand as he crossed the driveway and knelt beside the kid. Maybe he'd been out of control, but the spell had passed. Now he looked young and scared and unhappy to be the center of attention.

Touching his shoulder, Glenn asked, "Can you tell us what happened?"

"I was doing my job," he replied in a tight voice. "I don't take drugs. I swear."

"I guess you had a pretty frightening experience," Glenn said reassuringly. "What's the last specific thing you remember?"

The young man relaxed a little. Closing his eyes, he thought for a moment, then began a rambling recitation. "We were beating the bushes out by the accident. It was raining, and I was getting wet. Then we came back here, and I was pissed 'cause I drew guard duty." He glanced up at Glenn, squinting. "Then I was sitting down over here. With a splitting headache. That's it. If I hurt somebody, I didn't mean it. I don't even remember doing it."

Glenn patted him on the shoulder. "We'll figure out what happened."

The kid looked grateful—a point in his favor. If he were on something, he'd want to avoid detection.

Standing, Glenn turned back to Blake, and their gazes met. The security chief gave a little nod, then motioned Glenn several steps away. "What about our other mystery? Did Mata Hari wake up?" he asked in a low voice.

"Briefly."

"What did you get out of her?"

"Not much. At the moment, she's woozy."

"You questioned her?" Blake prompted.

"She's not admitting anything," he answered evasively, glad the conversation had been private. "She has some memory loss."

"Or she's faking it."

"I don't think so," he said, offering his professional opinion.

"That's just great. Maybe we're having an epidemic of amnesia flu. Did she get violent, too?" the security chief demanded.

"No. And what she's got isn't catching," Glenn replied, watching a stretcher team arrive and bend over Lipscomb.

"I can walk!" he insisted.

"I know," Dylan soothed. "But let's check you out first."

When there was no further protest, Glenn turned back to Blake. "What about the guy with the broken leg?"

"He's in the van. Sedated. We were getting ready to bring him up when Lipscomb went berserk. The rest of the injuries were minor."

Glenn nodded and went on to another topic. "Did you check out the car?"

"The trunk had some kind of special lock. We had to use a crowbar to get it open."

"Anything valuable inside?"

Blake hesitated for a moment. "She was carrying a load of plants."

"Oh yeah?" Turning, Glenn hurried toward the back of

the sedan, noting the nasty gouges in the metal. It looked as if someone had attacked the rear of the vehicle with malice.

The edge of the trunk lid was bent out of shape, but the inside was unharmed. A quick inspection told him the cargo area had been wrapped in an extra layer of latex foam. A well at one side held a plastic tray filled with neatly planted specimens that he couldn't immediately identify. "Take them to the lab," he said. Had Meg Wexler come to the castle to bring exotic flora specimens that she thought would interest him? That could explain her unannounced arrival. She'd come without calling first because she'd known it would be harder for him to say no to her in person than over the phone.

MEG'S EYES BLINKED and drifted closed. With an effort she forced them to stay open. Uncertainly, she took in her surroundings. Plain green walls. Stark wood furniture. A metal bed with side railings.

She was in a hospital room. The same room as before? Or had that been a dream? Lying very still, she listened for sounds. Somewhere in the distance she thought she heard voices. Maybe that was only her imagination. Or maybe they were coming for her.

Who?

She didn't know where she was, or who was out there—except for the man with the face full of sadness. He'd said his name was...

All at once, recalling his name became the most important thing in the world. But it wouldn't come to her, and panic rose in her throat.

Then the sound of his voice wafted through her memory. He had said... He had said he was Glenn, she remembered, relief flooding into every cell of her body.

She was safe. Glenn had told her she was safe, yet she felt her heart begin to pound. Somewhere at the edge of her consciousness, she knew there was an important fact she needed to remember. But it was too hard to think about it. Maybe later.

The decision to let it go brought a profound sense of peace. She wanted to sleep—or at least float like a leaf drifting in the current of a lazy stream, far from shore, where it was safe.

But her head wouldn't cooperate. It ached, throbbing with a rhythm that matched the beating of her heart.

Gingerly she slid her hand to her forehead, feeling the bumpy texture of a bandage. He had said…what?

An accident. He had said she'd been in an accident. She tried to think about their conversation. It was a mistake. Thinking brought a stab of pain—and fear bubbling to the surface of her mind.

Something dangerous hovered at the edge of her awareness, ready to grab her if she let down her guard. So she tried to drift again, letting the current take her, letting it rock her to sleep.

Sometime later, a noise at the other end of the room made her eyes snap open. Filling the doorway was a large man, standing in shadow where she couldn't see his face.

Silently, they regarded each other. She was the first to speak.

"Glenn?"

"No." He gave a low laugh before taking several steps closer. "So you're on a first-name basis. That was quick work."

It wasn't him. It was someone else—a hard-faced man whose voice made the hairs on her arms tingle.

"Leave me alone," she managed.

"Now, that's not very friendly." He took a gliding step toward her, his shoes soundless on the tile floor. "I don't think you're in a position to make demands."

She cringed back against the pillow, her eyes darting first one way and then the other as she assessed her chances of escape. Not good. He was between her and the door, and she wasn't sure her legs would support her if she tried to climb out of bed.

He came closer, filling her field of vision. Then, to her overwhelming relief, a noise in the hall made him whirl around.

As quickly as he had appeared, he vanished, leaving her wondering if he had been a bad dream.

Chapter Three

Glenn was still thinking about the plants in the trunk of the car, when he heard the crunch of wheels on gravel. Glancing around, he saw Hal's chair coming down the path.

"Leaving me out of the loop?" he asked, his voice implying high crimes and misdemeanors.

"I thought you'd gone to bed."

"Not a chance." Hal's skin was gray, but his eyes were bright as he looked from Glenn to Blake. "I assume we've got some personal identification on our visitor."

"Her wallet's in her purse, but there's not much in it. Two hundred dollars. A driver's license, one credit card."

"Give me her ID and I'll start a computer search," Hal said.

Blake retrieved Meg Wexler's purse and handed it to the older man. As Glenn watched the exchange, he struggled to stay objective. He wanted her to be what she seemed— an innocent young woman with no ulterior motives. Yet he knew that if there was dirt to be dug on her, Hal would find it.

THE MAN WHO CALLED himself Jerome Johnson was an early riser. After pouring a cup of Kona coffee from the hunt board in the dining room, he strolled to the broad terrace that ran along the back of his comfortable summer home in the Hamptons. From that vantage point, he had an excellent view of the extensive gardens that spread toward the water. He loved flowers—their vibrant colors, their seductive scents, their soft petals. In winter he had to be content with the specimens that could be grown in a greenhouse. In warmer weather he had all outdoors to indulge his taste for lavish displays. The huge beds of tulips that grew in the rich soil he'd had trucked in were only a pleasant memory now. But red, pink and white peonies were still in bloom. And soon the rose garden would be at its glorious height.

A servant appeared with a basket of sweet rolls, and he selected an almond croissant. After he finished breakfast and read the *New York Times* and the *Washington Post,* he could wander down there to pass the time, he thought. Yet he knew he wasn't capable of enjoying his flowers at the moment—or any of the other pleasures great wealth had brought him.

He was too focused on Glenn Bridgman. The bastard who had cost the Johnson Exchange millions of dollars in lost revenues. That alone was reason to screw him to the wall. But somewhere along the line it had become personal.

The Johnson Exchange had been the world's premier arms dealer. His company was still tops in conventional weapons. And his technology team was working with some very grateful nations on nuclear capability. But then he'd failed to deliver on a chemical-weapons shipment to Latin America, and the client had been very upset.

Jerome had given him back the down payment. Then he'd set about discovering why the virus he'd planned to steal was missing from its secret production plant.

The trail had led to the U. S. Army. Then to Glenn Bridgman.

The pain of teeth grinding against each other snapped Jerome's mind back to the present.

It was too early to expect any word from Castle Phoenix. Still, he couldn't stop himself from imagining what was going on behind the stone walls and razor-wire fence that guarded Bridgman's fortress.

He hated the uncertainty of not knowing. As he felt his blood pressure climb, Jerome closed his eyes and took several deep, calming breaths. Bridgman wasn't going to defeat him. Not this time.

He'd launched his career with money from the trust fund his grandfather had left him. And he'd plotted every step of his climb to wealth and power—putting the lie to his father's prediction that he would never amount to anything.

Take this operation. He'd even picked a week when the weather was supposed to be ideal for his purposes. But he had learned a long time ago that you couldn't control every variable.

Like the rockslide. His jaw tightened again, and he deliberately forced his muscles to relax. He was afraid the result had been just a tad more destructive than he'd intended.

Was Meg Wexler alive? She'd probably been knocked around a good deal when the boulders crashed into the side of the car. But the accident had been a necessity, extra insurance that Bridgman would bring her inside the gates.

Well, she was in and he'd have to wait until he got some word from inside Castle Phoenix.

As soon as he returned to the medical center, Glenn started toward Meg's room, brushed past the guard sitting in the hall, and came to a halt beside her bed. She was sleeping again, her face as untroubled and serene as a choir girl's. And yet, one of his men had just gone berserk while guarding her car. That could be an unfortunate coincidence, but until he knew for sure, he'd proceed on the assumption that she was dangerous.

Still, she was a patient in his facility, and the other doctor was busy with injured men. After doing a quick status check, he called her name, then shook her gently.

It was several seconds before her lids blinked open. The

change in her was dramatic. Gazing at him with unfocused eyes, she pushed herself as far away from him as she could get, her breath coming in sharp gasps as she tried to heave herself from the bed.

Automatically, he clamped a hand on her shoulder. With a muffled whimper, she struggled to wrench away.

"Meg, it's Glenn Bridgman. It's okay," he soothed. "You're all right."

"Glenn?" She sounded relieved, yet not entirely reassured, as her eyes darted to the door.

"Has anyone else been here?" he asked, the question coming out low and gritty.

"The man!"

"What man?" he demanded.

"I don't know. He—he scared me."

He gazed down at her pinched face, little doubting that she had been frightened by something or someone.

"Who?" he asked again.

She shrugged. "He was here. In my room."

Had it been a bad dream, or was she hallucinating—showing symptoms of brain injury that hadn't manifested themselves earlier? He'd have to order more tests.

"Is your headache worse?" he asked.

"No."

"Good," he answered, hearing the relief in his voice even as he went on to consider other possibilities. An off-duty guard could have come to get a look at their visitor. Or maybe the security detail had frightened her. He'd check on that as soon as he left.

"Did he do anything to you?" he asked, trying to keep his voice steady.

"He…"

The sentence trailed off before it started, and he leaned closer, gripped her shoulder. "Did he hurt you?"

"No."

He let out the breath he'd been holding. "What did he look like?"

"I didn't see his face." She swallowed and was silent for several moments. He thought she was drifting off to sleep again until she said, "Don't leave me."

"I can't stay."

"Please."

"I have to go," he said firmly, making it clear that he wasn't taking orders from her. "The guard won't let anybody bother you."

"'Guard'?" she repeated, the question coming out high and strangled.

He nodded, shifting his weight from one foot to the other. "I'm going to order some tests. One of the staff will come to take you to the lab soon."

"No. Stay with me," she begged, melting his resolve.

Before he made a fool of himself, he shook his head, then turned and fled.

She's probably a spy. Or worse, he told himself sharply as he barreled down the hall. *Stop letting her twist you around her little finger.*

He thought he'd hardened his heart, until it started to drum as he stopped for a brief conversation with Logan, the man who had been assigned to watch the room.

"What time did you arrive?" he demanded.

"At 0630," Logan replied smartly.

"Did you see anyone in the medical center?"

"Negative."

"Were you on duty the whole time I was gone?"

The man looked uncomfortable. "I got a cup of coffee about forty minutes ago."

Glenn nodded. He'd done the same thing himself. "Did you go into the patient's room?" he asked.

"No, sir," Logan answered.

"But you looked at her from the hall."

The man nodded.

"You didn't speak with her?"

"No, sir."

Maybe it was the truth. Maybe not. At the moment, there

was no way to find out. Leaving the young man looking vastly relieved, he headed for the E.R. to tell Dylan they'd better do another CAT scan on Ms. Wexler, just to be safe.

Then he escaped to the blessed solitude of his quarters. Setting the alarm, he gave himself four hours to recharge his batteries, then sank into welcome oblivion.

Twenty minutes before the alarm was due to sound, a dream grabbed hold of his mind. He had fled from Meg Wexler, but his subconscious had brought him back to her. They were together in her car, on the road to the castle. He was driving. She was staring at him with those eyes so impossibly green that they must belong to a wood nymph. He was aware of everything about her—the scent of her body, the curve of her breast, the rapid cadence of her breathing that seemed to have tuned itself to his.

Neither of them spoke. Yet, when she gently stroked her finger along the line of his jaw, he knew they had come to a silent understanding. Pulling off the road into a clearing sheltered by tall pines, he turned and reached for her.

He lowered his mouth to hers, and she made a small sound of wanting deep in her throat. Then her lips opened under his, and he devoured her essence like a starving man invited to a feast. There was no finesse about the kiss; only a hard, desperate hunger that consumed him—drove everything else from his mind. His whole body burned with it, throbbed with a need so great that it shook him to the core. She should be afraid of a man so desperate, he thought in some tiny corner of his mind, yet she met the onslaught with a passion that drove him to new levels of arousal.

He lowered her to the seat, which had magically grown to the size of a double bed. Wrapping his arms around her, he fitted himself to all her sweet enticing curves, absorbing the tantalizing feel of her. And when he adjusted his hips so that his erection could press into the cleft between her thighs, she surged against him, causing a deep groan in his chest.

Outside the car, thunder rumbled. He tried to ignore it,

tried to concentrate on the fevered melding of their bodies, but the sound grew louder, roaring in his ears.

"Rocks. It's the rock! Don't leave me," Meg gasped, clinging to him. In the next moment, she was pushing at his shoulders, trying to twist away, and he knew she had finally figured out that he was the enemy.

It's too late, Bridgman. A voice in his head echoed the rumble of the boulders.

He knew it was true. Too late. Chunks of the mountain were raining around them, hitting the road, hitting the car. He curved his body around hers, trying to protect her. But the rocks crashed onto his head and shoulders, the pain so intense that he screamed—and woke with a fine sheen of perspiration covering his skin.

Lying among the twisted covers, he remembered the dream, the blatant eroticism and the anguished finale.

Too late. It was way too late for him. He'd known that since the team had come back from Operation Clean Sweep.

A muscle jumped in his jaw as he heaved himself out of bed. By the time he'd showered and shaved, he was feeling almost human. Quickly he dressed in a dark knit shirt and khaki trousers.

The smell of brewing coffee wafted toward him from the dining area, and he cursed softly under his breath. There were only two men who would open the door to his private quarters and make themselves comfortable. Betting on which one it was, he carefully arranged his features before stepping through the bedroom door. He wasn't surprised to find Hal with his wheelchair pulled to the dinette table, sipping from a large mug.

"You're not supposed to be drinking coffee," he snapped. "Caffeine is contraindicated for—"

His visitor cut him off ruthlessly. "Listen, sonny, it doesn't matter what I ingest, I'm not going to get any better. So let me enjoy the java."

Glenn sighed. Technically, Hal was right. Unless they

came up with a miracle cure, his rheumatoid arthritis wasn't going to improve. So he might as well indulge.

"My new gizmo is paying off," Hal said, changing the subject.

"Yeah?"

They'd argued about spending Bridgman Enterprises money on a T1 line to give them instant access to the Web and certain private databases. But since running the intelligence-gathering operation for their joint venture was keeping his friend alive, Glenn had let him have his way.

Until failing health and Operation Clean Sweep had speeded up his retirement, Hal had been a general in the army, and Glenn had been under his command. Early on, they'd clashed over personnel risks versus mission fulfillment. Hal had pushed for sending special forces into dangerous situations where the chances of success were marginal. Glenn had counseled caution. But they'd agreed on the solution to the Clean Sweep fiasco. Hal had used his personal fortune to purchase the castle and make many of the initial improvements. Glenn's projects kept it going.

"I've got some interesting information on Meg Wexler." Hal tapped the folder in front of him with a gnarled finger.

"You sound pleased." Glenn shoved his hands into his pockets. Feeling trapped, he worked to keep his face from reflecting his inner turmoil.

"If I go on a hunting expedition, I like to bag something," his friend said with satisfaction. Reaching into the covered basket beside the folder, he pulled out a blueberry muffin and took a bite.

Glenn wasn't sure he wanted to hear about the size of the kill, but he knew he didn't have much choice. To give himself time to prepare, he strode to the coffeepot and poured a cup. Rooting through the muffins, he found an orange-cranberry one. His favorite. He wasn't very hungry, but he took a bite.

"Meg Wexler isn't her name," the general said.

"What is it?" he demanded, feeling unaccountably like

a bridegroom who'd just discovered his new wife wasn't the virgin she'd pretended to be.

"I don't know. I only know the driver's license is a good fake. There's a Meg Wexler registered in Maryland. But her picture doesn't match our visitor."

Glenn nodded tightly.

"The car registration is interesting, too," Hal continued avidly. "It belongs to a limo service. Their records indicate that the vehicle was rented to a James Taylor."

Glenn snorted. "Probably doing a concert gig up here."

"And Ms. Wexler is his girlfriend traveling incognito." With a satisfied smirk, Hal polished off the muffin before continuing. "Then we have her clothing. The manufacturer's tags are cut out."

"That doesn't prove anything," Glenn retorted.

"Negative inference."

Glenn sighed. "The bottom line is that you think she's up to something."

"What do you think?"

Glenn shook his head. He hadn't wanted it to be true. But it was looking pretty bad for Meg Wexler's credibility.

"When we get this cleared up, you should take a vacation," Hal said. "Go to some nice hot island in the Caribbean where you can get your ashes hauled and come back here ready to work."

It was a good suggestion. In fact, he'd gone that route in the past, letting off steam with a no-strings-attached affair in some vacation paradise. This morning he knew that it wasn't so simple.

"She used her one credit card to charge a hotel room in Westchester last night," Hal continued, switching back to topic A.

"And?" he asked, hoping his casual tone didn't give away the pounding of his heart inside his chest.

"The account was opened two weeks ago. There are no charges before the first of June."

Glenn pursed his lips. "You're saying that's when she became Meg Wexler?"

"If you come up with a better explanation, share it with me," Hal grated. "Or better yet, use the old Bridgman charm and get her to confide in you."

SHE WAS DRIFTING in the stream, letting it carry her where it would, making no demands on herself. You could do it for a long time, she'd discovered, if you kept your eyes closed and your mind in neutral.

She slipped into the comfort of sleep again, then woke when she felt hands on her body. A man's hands. Large, strong, but very gentle—and very personal—pulling the covering away from her body, touching her skin, pressing something hard between her breasts and moving it around on her chest.

She tried not to react, tried not to let him know she was unnerved by his touch. A millimeter at a time, she lifted her lids, letting her lashes screen her eyes. It was him. The doctor who was taking care of her. Last night he'd been dressed in jeans and a knit shirt and his face had told her he cared about what happened to her. Now he wore a white coat and a hard expression. He was listening to her heart.

She couldn't hold back an involuntary little shiver.

"You might as well stop pretending to be asleep." He pulled her gown into place, gazing down at her with unnerving impersonality.

"You woke me up."

"Uh-huh."

When he said no more, she asked, "How did the tests come out?"

"Fine. You remember going to the lab?"

"Yes."

"Does your head still hurt?"

"Yes."

"More than before? Not as much?"

"Not as much," she answered, licking her dry lips, seeing him watching the movement.

"Do you need a drink?"

"Yes." She sat up, dragging the sheet with her so that it covered the front of her thin gown.

Bending, he worked the controls that elevated the head of the bed. When she was settled in the new position, he handed her a glass with a bent straw, watching her while she sucked in water. The water tasted wonderful. His scrutiny was disconcerting.

When he took the glass, she tried giving him a little smile. "I remember you. But I'm sorry, I can't recall your name."

"Glenn Bridgman," he said, as if he expected it to mean something. She tried and failed to dredge up an association.

Pulling up a chair, he sat down beside the bed.

"What happened to me?" she asked.

He gave her some basic information, then demanded, "What do you remember?"

He had posed the question she so desperately wanted to avoid as she'd lain with her eyes closed, letting herself drift. A tide of cold fear rose in her chest, threatening to choke off her breath. She felt as if she were standing at the edge of a bottomless pit—with the ground shifting out from under her feet. She was going to cry, and she didn't want any witnesses. Especially him. When she turned her face into the pillow, he crooked his finger under her chin and slowly turned it back so that she had nowhere to hide—from him or from herself.

She watched him through a film of moisture, her lower lip quivering as she struggled for control.

"Meg, it's okay," he said, his voice gritty as he stared down into her eyes. "Whatever it is, we'll deal with it." His hand found hers, clasped her chilled flesh firmly, and yet there was the hint of an underlying tremor in his touch. "I can imagine what you were told about me." His Adam's apple bobbed. "We won't have to go to the police. If you're just straight with me."

"The police—" Her voice hitched.

His fingers tightened over hers, and she clung to him with all the strength she could dredge up. "Just say it," he urged. "You'll feel better if you tell me."

"Tell you what?" God, what was he expecting her to say?

He gave a little sigh. "Tell me why you hatched some elaborate plan to get into Castle Phoenix."

"Castle Phoenix." The name meant nothing. With a gulp, she forced herself to confront the dark, bottomless chasm of her fears. "I don't know!"

His eyes had turned hard as flint. "Are you working with The Jackal?" he demanded.

"Who?"

He made an exasperated sound. "Sorry. Johnson."

"No. I mean…I don't know. Who is Johnson?" When he didn't speak, she continued in a halting voice. "I don't remember…anything. Except a few things from last night."

"Do you expect me to believe that?" he snapped.

"It's the truth," she said simply, sitting forward in the bed, stretching out her hand toward him and letting it fall back. "If you want to know the honest truth," she whispered, afraid that if she spoke louder, she would dissolve in tears. "I've been lying in this bed, afraid to let myself think. Because…because I can't come up with anything personal. You called me Meg. Meg what?"

"Meg Wexler."

She shrugged. "I can't remember that name. You said I'm in a place called…Castle Phoenix. I can't remember that place. You expect me to know something about you. And someone named Johnson. I don't know him. I don't know you, even by reputation. Last night I think you said I was in an accident and that I was unconscious."

"That's right."

"Well, all I have to go on is what you've told me."

The long speech exhausted her energy, and she sank back against the pillows. There was more she wanted to say, but she wasn't sure it was safe to take the chance. She was in this man's power, and she didn't know what he planned to do with her.

His eyes never left her face, and she found herself waiting for his verdict like a criminal at a judicial hearing.

"All right."

"All right, what?" she managed.

"A blow to the head can cause memory loss."

"For how long?" she whispered.

He shrugged. "It could be temporary. It could be of longer duration."

She wasn't sure what that meant, and she was afraid to ask.

"What country is this?" he suddenly asked.

"The United States."

"And who was the first president?"

"George Washington," she answered, feeling a kind of relief. Her mind wasn't a total blank.

Then he went back to something that might be relevant in her life. "What kind of car do you drive?"

She gave a little shrug, defeated once more. "How do you know I drive a car?"

"Most people have cars. You came here in one." He stood. "Let's see if your effects trigger any memories."

"Okay."

He opened a closet door and brought out a suitcase—the kind with wheels and an extension handle so you could pull it like a cart. Not the smallest model, she thought. Medium-size, which meant that she had memories of suitcases, but not of her own life. How odd.

She moved, tucking up her legs to make room on the bed. Awkwardly, she opened the suitcase. Inside were knit tops, blouses, casual skirts, slacks, a pair of jeans, silky underwear. By the way some things were pushed to the side it looked as if the interior had been searched. The clothing was nothing flashy. But apparently she liked sexy fabric next to her skin.

At the bottom were sandals and a pair of sturdy hiking boots. A flowered case held toiletries. She smelled the shampoo. Citrus. The toothpaste was mint-flavored. The supply of cosmetics was limited to the basics.

She touched the personal items, as though some magic might transmit an association from her fingertips to her mind. Try as she might, though, she could dredge up no feeling of connection, no sense that these things might belong to her.

"Do you want a mirror?"

The question was asked in a casual tone, yet she caught an underlying edge in his voice.

"Yes."

He turned to the dresser on the other side of the room, opened a drawer, and pulled out a large hand mirror. Taking it from him, she wrapped her fingers around the handle in a death grip, saying a little prayer in her mind.

Please, God, let me recognize my own face.

Then she raised her eyes. She was staring at a blond, green-eyed woman who would have been attractive, she thought, if dark smudges didn't mar the skin under her green eyes and if her hair hadn't been matted and stringy.

Her nose was small and straight. Her lower lip was larger than the top one. Her eyes were set fairly wide. She looked for more details and saw that her brows were neatly plucked.

She cataloged all that, but she *didn't know* the woman in the mirror, and she had to clamp her lips together to keep from making a strangled sound.

When she raised her eyes, Bridgman was looking at her expectantly.

Her throat was so dry, she knew she couldn't get any words out. Snatching up the glass of water, she took a long gulp. "I don't recognize the face," she finally whispered.

Chapter Four

Glenn's stomach muscles tightened as he watched the play of emotions on Meg's face. She was struggling not to cry. If she was faking panic, she was damn good.

She set down the mirror and turned back to the suitcase to sift through the contents. Silently she lifted a shirt and put it down, then pulled a strand of blond hair from the hairbrush and twisted it around her fingers. Laying it carefully back on the surface of the brush, she felt in one of the bag's side pockets and pulled out a pair of earrings in a small plastic envelope. They were little gold rings for pierced ears. Raising her hand, she fingered her earlobe and toyed with the small gold stud she found there.

She said nothing, and a new thought occurred to him. Maybe this suitcase full of stuff was as bogus as the recently issued credit card. Maybe the contents had been assembled with the intention of creating a specific impression. Plain clothing. A minimum of makeup. Sexy underwear. A woman who promised more than the surface impression.

Finally, when he couldn't stand either her tension or his own, he asked, "Does any of this help?"

Her eyes remained fixed on the objects. "I can infer certain things," she said in a low voice, using the same word as Hal. "Nothing makes me remember anything specific."

"Too bad," he retorted.

She flinched as if he'd slapped her, and he silently admitted that if she really couldn't remember anything, she was in a pretty frightening situation. She looked shell-shocked, like a refugee who'd been allowed to take one suitcase of personal belongings. And when she'd opened it, she'd found the possessions of a stranger.

A swift knock at the door made him turn. "Yes?"

Jay Trescott stepped smartly into the room. He came toward Glenn, but his gaze flicked to Meg, who gathered the covers against her chest. Her eyes were wide as they took in the young man's neatly pressed khaki uniform and the holstered weapon at his waist.

"Do you have a reason for being here?" Glenn asked.

Trescott's face went a revealing shade of red. "Sir, you wanted to be informed immediately when we had the access road completely cleared."

"Yes."

"The rocks have all been removed."

"Thank you."

"Dr. Ryder said to tell you he'd have something soon on the plants," the kid continued, obviously trying to prolong the exchange. Probably a dozen guys were waiting for him to describe the woman who hadn't emerged from the medical facility since her midnight arrival.

"Thank you, Trescott."

"Sir." The boy turned like a Prussian officer and left.

When they were alone again, Glenn saw Meg swallow. "Who was that?" she asked.

"One of my security men."

"He had a gun."

Glenn nodded. "The security force is armed."

A shiver rippled over her, and she slid her hands up and down her arms. "What kind of place is this, exactly?" she asked in a low voice.

He considered the query, tried to imagine what she was thinking. If she'd really lost her memory she'd be frightened by Trescott, all right. And if she already thought she knew the answer to her own question, then maybe he had a chance to correct some mistaken impressions.

"I do medical research here."

"With armed guards?" she asked, her voice rising on the last word of the sentence. "Is this some kind of government operation?"

"No. This is a private research facility. I gather plants from around the world and test their medical potential," he said, watching her reaction. She was listening carefully. "Some of my projects lead to commercially valuable discoveries. There have been serious attempts to steal some of my work before it could be brought to market. So you can imagine that we're wondering about your unexpected arrival."

"I see."

"It's quite unlikely that you would have wandered in here accidentally, so it would be helpful if you could tell me the purpose of your visit." He waited for some response.

She offered a look of genuine apology. "I'm sorry. I wish I knew."

Neither of them spoke for several moments.

"You're a physician?" she asked.

"I graduated from medical school—Georgetown. But my interest has always been research. I've gotten more into clinical practice because I do periodic health assessments of the men from Operation—" He stopped. "Of men accidentally exposed to a biological-weapons agent."

She nodded.

He shifted from one foot to the other, waiting for her to ask more questions. When there were none, he said, "You'd probably feel more comfortable if you got dressed."

He moved toward her, touched the bandage on her head. "I'll take this off, so you can shower. Pat the stitches dry when you finish." He carefully peeled away the bandage and inspected the wound.

"How does it look?"

"Good. I'll wait for you down the hall in the lounge."
He started to turn, then heard her make a small noise.

When he raised a questioning eyebrow, her chest gave a
little heave.

"You said amnesia could be of long duration," she whispered. "Does that mean I might never remember who I am
or why I came here?"

"Let's not manufacture worst-case scenarios." Unable to
stand the look of anguish on her face, he turned and fled
the room.

MEG GRABBED THE BAG of toiletries, pulled some clothing
from her suitcase, and dashed into the bathroom. After locking the door, she cradled her head in her hands. According
to the man who said his name was Glenn Bridgman, she'd
been on the road to his armed camp of a medical research
facility when a rockslide had hit her car. She'd been
knocked out and had awakened with amnesia. She shuddered. It could all be true. Or it could be an elaborate story;
he could have drugged her and was holding her against her
will. That would fit in with a place like this, wouldn't it?
But then why would he have admitted so much?

The questions spinning in her brain made her knees
weak. God, she was scared. But she wasn't going to turn
into a pool of jelly. She was going to figure out what to
do. Her eyes scanned the room, taking in details. She was
in an ordinary bathroom with white fixtures. The only window was small and high on the wall at the top of a small
shower stall. Behind the sink was a medicine cabinet.

The normality of the room made her feel a little more
confident, until yet another sickening thought grabbed her
by the throat. What if she had lost her mind? What if she
were a patient in a mental hospital, and Dr. Bridgman
hadn't shared that information with her yet?

Would a doctor do that? Maybe, if he thought it was in
the best interests of the patient. She felt tears of fear mixed

with frustration blur her vision. Waking up with no memory in this place was like being trapped in a nightmare. Only she knew she wasn't sleeping.

Raising her eyes, she gazed into the mirror, hoping that something had changed in the past few minutes. But the face that stared anxiously back at her still meant nothing.

Turning away, she started toward the shower, thinking that she'd feel better once she was clean and dressed. Then she glanced at the window again. If she could get a view of the outside, she might have a better idea what kind of place this was.

But that wasn't going to be easy. The window was some eight feet above the floor and set at the back of a deep ledge.

She might have simply abandoned the idea, but a stubborn spark of determination wouldn't let her give up. Purposefully, she looked around the room and spotted a white terry robe draped over a towel bar. Pulling out the belt, she tested its strength before making a loop at one end. Then she climbed on the toilet seat and tossed the loop upward toward the casement window's handle. It took about six tries to get the range. Finally she was able to snag the handle.

Sweat was already beading her brow, and she stopped to drag in several deep breaths. She was in no shape for acrobatics, and the thought of giving up crossed her mind. Instead, she braced her back against the tile on one side of the shower niche and her feet against the other, cautiously making her way upward, using both her body and the belt. By the time she reached the wide ledge at the top, she was panting and dripping with perspiration. Turning, she rested her arms on the ledge, and yanked on the crank until it finally turned.

As the window swung open, she was rewarded by a view of a wide lawn, interrupted every so often by outcroppings of gray rock. To her surprise, it appeared to be late afternoon. So much for her internal clock.

She was in a ground-floor room, which didn't exactly give her a panoramic view, but by easing to the side, she could see that the building lived up to its name. It was a large stone castle that looked as if it had been transplanted from—

She stopped, searching her mind for a reference. To her relief, she came up with several—from a Hollywood-movie set, and from Europe.

She was about to close the window and lower herself again when she saw four uniformed men like the one who had spoken to Bridgman come up the driveway.

Several others joined them, and they all gathered under a low-hanging tree. After looking around to see if they were being observed, they started talking. From their posture, it was evident that they wanted to keep the conversation private. One positioned himself so that he could watch a door about fifty yards to their right. When a tough-looking broad-shouldered blond man stepped outside, the group immediately dispersed.

The newcomer's face was set and his posture rigid. Finally, he turned abruptly and went back into the building, leaving Meg wondering who he was and why the other men were afraid of him.

The strain of keeping herself at the window ledge was making her muscles tremble. After cranking the window closed, she inched back down the wall. When she reached the shower floor she collapsed in a heap, breathing hard. Glancing up at the window, she shook her head. What was she in real life—a movie stuntwoman? Or had desperation given her strength?

With a snort, she pulled off the hospital gown, then suddenly stopped. She hadn't even thought about the implications of the gown. Now she realized that while she'd been unconscious, someone had taken off her clothes and re-dressed her. She hadn't seen any nurses around this medical center. That left Dr. Bridgman. Somehow she knew it had been him.

A little shiver traveled over her skin, making her nipples tighten as she imagined the feel of his hands on her body. For several seconds she stood without moving, then slowly pivoted toward the full-length mirror on the wall and looked at herself. The body that met her frankly curious gaze had high, generous breasts, a narrow waist, and long legs. Not model-thin, but a pretty good shape. *No, be honest,* she told herself. A very good shape. And in excellent physical condition, she added as she raised her arms and flexed her muscles, then turned to get a look at her firmly rounded rear. Either she worked out on a regular basis, or she had great genes.

Somehow she didn't think Bridgman had kept his mind a blank when he'd undressed her. Or maybe she was projecting her own emotions onto him. Unwilling to examine those emotions too closely, she turned on the shower. After adjusting the temperature, she stepped under the water and tried to blank out everything but the feel of the hot spray beating against her skin.

TOMMY FAULKNER PUT DOWN the phone receiver and slumped against the pillows. This wasn't one of his better days, and he'd been hoping that Meg would bring him dinner. But she didn't answer her phone. She hadn't returned his call yesterday, either. And now he was starting to think that she wasn't home. Vaguely, he could remember her telling him something about her being away for a while. Or was he making that up? He used to be really sharp. These days, his mind was playing tricks on him, so that he couldn't always tell the difference between reality and his imagination.

It meant he was getting sicker—with that disease the army wouldn't admit he had.

He squeezed his eyes shut, trying not to think about the future. Instead, he uttered a silent prayer that Glenn Bridgman was going to come through for him and the rest of the guys. Glenn was working on a cure for this damn syndrome that was sucking the life out of him and his buddies. Any day now, he'd call to say they were going into clinical trials.

That was what he had to keep thinking, because it was his only hope for a normal life. Glenn had told him to hang on until it happened. Some days he still believed in getting well again. Other days, he was too tired to bring hope into focus. Today, he needed Meg. With Dad dead, she was his only relative—the only person who cared about him, except Glenn. But Glenn had a lot of other guys to worry about, too. Tommy couldn't go pestering him every time he felt down.

Maybe he'd dialed Meg's number wrong. No, that wasn't it, because he'd gotten her machine and left a message. But she hadn't answered. Maybe she was on one of her trips. He glanced at the corn-husk doll on his shelf. From—he paused and thought for a moment—from some place in the Andes where the Incas used to live. Next to it was a little cat statue from Egypt. Meg had brought those things to him.

Dad had trained his two kids in every outdoor skill known to man. Meg had never liked hunting, but she'd killed game to live on when they'd been wilderness camping. And she was good at fishing.

She'd gotten into adventure travel. She took people hiking and rock climbing and camping in neat places all over the world.

He looked at the phone again. Maybe he should call her office—Adventures in Travel down at Light Street. Or one of her other friends, like Erin Stone who ran that charity organization. She'd told him he could contact her for help anytime.

They were all a great bunch of people. They wouldn't act like he was bothering them. But maybe he should wait until tomorrow. Yeah, he'd wait. No use letting them know that poor Tommy Faulkner was having trouble thinking straight.

BY THE TIME MEG HAD washed her hair, being careful of the stitches, she was feeling more human—but not exactly calm. Any way you looked at it, she was Bridgman's captive. And the vivid image of him undressing her only made things worse.

After toweling her body dry, she pulled on the underwear she'd brought from the suitcase, noting that it fit perfectly. Then she used the hair dryer beside the sink and finished getting dressed. Again the clothing seemed to have been selected for her. Yet, none of it seemed at all familiar.

Experimenting with the makeup, she used a little blusher, eyebrow pencil and lipstick, and decided that she liked the effect. What would Bridgman think?

She wasn't doing it for him, she assured herself; she was simply building her own confidence. Delaying her departure from the room, she studied the way she looked in her navy slacks and knit top, trying to decide whether the light blue of the top was good with her skin tone. But finally there were no more excuses. She had to face Bridgman again.

Her room was near the end of a short corridor with soft apricot-colored walls and recessed overhead fluorescent lights.

At the other end was an open area furnished with plastic sofas and chairs, kitchen appliances and several tables and chairs.

Bridgman was absorbed in a phone conversation, which gave her the perfect opportunity to study him. Dressed in a dark knit shirt and khaki pants, he was sitting at a wooden table, a folder spread in front of him as he talked with the receiver wedged between his ear and shoulder.

Not wanting to move into his field of vision, she strained to hear what he was saying, but his voice was too low for her to pick up more than a few scattered words.

Covertly, she studied his profile, his posture, using this unexpected opportunity to try and figure out what kind of man had rescued her from a car wreck and brought her to his castle. She guessed he was in his mid-thirties—and that responsibilities were weighing heavily on him. His face was strong, as if he'd learned several painful lessons in self-reliance. And yet, there was something about him that made her want to take him in her arms and rock him, give him the comfort he didn't think he needed. That observation brought a little sound to her throat. For a woman whose past life was a blank, she was coming up with outrageous insights into someone else's character.

Alerted to her presence, he looked up, stopped talking and stared at her, his gaze moving over her as if he were trying to reconcile the woman from the car wreck with the one who stood a few feet away. Then he seemed to recall the folder spread in front of him. After a quick look in her direction, he snapped it closed.

"GLENN?" BLAKE SAID through the phone receiver. "I've got her on the monitor. See how she reacts to temptation."

"All right," he muttered, not liking the idea of setting a trap. But his chief of security was right. They needed to find out more about Ms. Wexler's motivation.

Hanging up, he stood, crossed to a sideboard, and stowed the folder in one of the top drawers.

"That grim expression you carry around. Were you born with it, or was it acquired?" she asked when he turned around again.

"I have a lot on my mind," he answered.

"I can tell."

She sounded sympathetic, and he didn't want her sympathy. "How are you feeling?"

She considered the question. "The pain in my head is almost tolerable. My brain's retrieval system is still blocked."

"Don't push yourself to remember. It will come," he replied in the soothing tones of a physician reassuring an anxious patient. "I can give you an analgesic for the headache," he added. "It's in the dispensary. While I'm there, I'm going to make a couple of calls. So make yourself comfortable. There are magazines on the table." He crossed to the door, leaving her alone as he hurried down the hall, punched in the security code, and pulled open the locked door.

Sixty seconds later, he had joined Blake, who was staring intently at a TV screen that showed the recreation room in the infirmary.

"Anything?"

"Not yet."

Glenn went over to the monitor, which gave him a good view of Meg Wexler. She was still standing where he'd left her, but then glanced quickly over her shoulder. His heart started to thump in his chest as she moved toward the drawer where he'd left the folder containing her dossier.

Before she reached the drawer, however, she stopped. For several seconds, she stood facing the sideboard, then crossed to the opposite wall and began to riffle through the magazines on the end table. *Sports Illustrated. Field and Stream. Playboy.* Probably not her usual reading matter.

"She didn't go for the bait," he said, hearing the relief in his voice.

"She's too smart," Blake retorted.

"Or too honest."

"Too bad we can't prove anything by negative inference," the security chief growled.

Meg's hand went to the *Field and Stream.* Sitting down on the couch, she began leafing through the pages and stopped at an article on the reintroduction of wolves to the Yellowstone area, apparently absorbed in the material.

"I've got to get back. Turn off the camera."

"I don't think that's a great idea."

"I'll be more spontaneous with her if I'm not being watched."

"You don't have to be spontaneous. You have to be on your toes."

"Turn it off!"

After Blake complied, he exited before the other man could voice any further opinions.

On the way back he made a call to the kitchen and ordered some dinner. Entering the lounge, he came around to look over Meg's shoulder at the magazine. "You're interested in wolves?"

"This information is fascinating."

He drew her a glass of water, then offered it to her, along with two pills. After she'd swallowed the medication, she remained sitting where she was, not making eye contact.

"Dinner's on its way up."

She nodded, but said nothing for long seconds. Finally she inquired, "Did you undress me?"

He felt color creep into his cheeks and thanked the Lord that he'd insisted on turning off the surveillance system. Keeping his voice brusque, he answered, "Yes. Somebody had to, since I couldn't put you into a clean hospital bed in your clothes. Why are you bringing it up?"

She took another sip of water, then opened her palm in a helpless gesture. "I've lost control of my life. I don't know where I came from. I don't know who I am. I don't know why I'm here. The things that have happened after the accident are the only information I've got."

"I can appreciate the difficulty."

"Can you? I doubt it. I don't even know if you believe me about the memory loss. I don't even—" She stopped, fixed her gaze somewhere above his left shoulder as her teeth clamped down on her lower lip.

"What?" he prompted.

"It looks like I don't have much impulse control," she blurted. "A thought comes into my mind, and it's on my lips before I consider the consequences."

He saw moisture film her eyes, saw her fighting hard against letting tears fall.

"A head injury will do that," he said softly, reading the panic she was trying to hide. However you looked at it, she was in a hell of a fix, and he felt his heart contract as he tried to imagine what she must be feeling.

"Meg?"

She remained sitting there, huddled into herself. And he understood all too well how she felt. He had never lost his memory, but he knew what it felt like to be hemmed in by circumstances, frustrated, blocked from any effective course of action. He also knew it was imperative that he keep his perspective where she was concerned.

That didn't stop all the dangerous emotions he'd been fighting against from surging inside him. Without making a conscious decision, he found himself crossing the distance between them and sitting down on the sofa. Once he was there, it was the most natural thing in the world to reach for her.

"Meg," he said again, his voice thick as he turned her toward him. She felt delicate in his arms, fragile—but that was only on the surface. Below the vulnerable exterior was strength that drew him as much as the fragility. His arms came up to cradle her—first one and then the other—as he fought against surrendering to the tender impulse. He was lost when she let her head drift down to his shoulder; when she made a little noise halfway between a sob and a sigh.

MEG WONDERED IF HE KNEW how much she needed to be held, needed to know that someone was on her side. She couldn't tell him, couldn't speak. The sound of her anguish was wedged in her throat. He pulled her closer, held her gently. She kept her eyes closed, kept her face pressed against him, shutting out everything else as he began to rub his hand across her shoulders and over the tense cords at the back of her neck.

Don't trust him, a voice in her head warned. Yet she was helpless to deny herself what he was offering.

Words welled from deep inside her, words she shouldn't speak. "I feel so lost and helpless," she whispered, breathing in the scent of his body, feeling the coiled strength of his muscles. In a world where nothing seemed real, he was as solid as the rocky promontories she'd seen through the window.

"That's natural. But underneath you're a strong woman."

"How do you know?"

"Maybe the same way you know I've got a lot on my mind."

She clung to that as he stroked her and murmured low, reassuring words. His voice soothed her as much as his hands, his tone a warm gentle caress that made her think everything had a chance of turning out all right. Helpless to stop herself, she leaned into him and let her body melt against his.

She thought she felt his lips skim her hair, knew for sure when he found the tender edge of her temple.

Again she told herself she should take nothing from him, demand nothing. Yet she couldn't block the inexplicable feeling that the two of them stood together against a hostile world, and that the only thing that would save them was the combining of their strengths.

As if to test that bond, she raised her face, bringing her lips close to his—oh, so close.

For an endless moment he didn't move, and she regretted the forwardness of her invitation to the depths of her soul. She had let a tempting fantasy sweep her away—and now she must pay the cost of her folly.

Then, in one quick motion, his lips lowered to hers, and everything changed. With a groan deep in his throat, he took her mouth.

There was a moment when she could have wrenched herself away. She stayed right with him as he angled his head, slanting his lips over hers in an act that could only be taken for possession.

She might have been afraid, should have been afraid, but the wildness caught her, and she gave him what he demanded. Her mouth opened for him, tasting him, drawing on him as if he could satisfy all the hungers of the world.

At that moment, he *was* her world. She said his name, the syllable lost in the mingling of her breath with his. Her head spun as he combed through her hair, finding her skull and holding her still so that he could ravish her mouth. But there was no need to hold her with any force besides the potency of his lips on hers.

Then he pulled her more fully against his body so that her breasts were pressed against the hard wall of his chest. She moved against him, feeling the heat generated by the intimate contact, feeling frustration at the layers of fabric that separated his flesh from hers.

Before she could translate frustration to action, the heat was replaced by the cold air of the room. He had let go of her and slid over to the end of the couch.

She sat swaying, staring up at him, trying to collect her scattered wits.

"I'm sorry," he said in a gritty voice. "It was unforgivable, taking advantage of you that way."

"You didn't take advantage." The breathy denial was about all she could manage.

"You know damn well I have no business kissing a woman who can't remember her own name." He ran his hand through his hair, shook his head as if to clear his thoughts.

She wanted to reach for him again, but she knew it was the wrong thing to do.

"It wasn't your fault," she whispered, determined to carry the blame. "I practically begged you to kiss me."

When he didn't answer, she touched his arm. "My major excuse is that I'm in a pretty needy situation—and you're my only point of human contact."

"All the more reason for me to control myself. It won't happen again."

She would rather not have heard the reassurance. But she could see that losing control had shaken him badly. They needed distance—something else to focus on besides each other. "Uh, did you say something about having a meal sent up?" she asked.

He looked both grateful and relieved that she'd remembered the food. Turning, he strode toward the doorway and disappeared into the hall. When he returned, he was pushing a cart holding several covered dishes.

One of the staff must have brought it. She hoped it had been sitting in the hall for a few minutes and that no one had looked in on them.

Pushing the cart beside a dining-room table, he uncovered the food. There was a basket of whole-grain breads and several kettles of soup. One looked like potatoes and cheese, but it gave off a strong Southwestern aroma. The other was blander—chicken soup for the invalid.

Well, she'd worked up too much of an appetite for bland. "Is it okay for me to have the one with cheese?" she asked.

"It's one of the kitchen's specialties. The guys like it hot. So start with a little and see how your stomach reacts," he advised.

She served herself a small portion and buttered a thick slice of dark, whole-grain bread to go with it.

He took the same. They each set their food on the table and sat down, neither looking at the other. Probably he wished he'd get an emergency phone call so he could leave, she thought, covertly studying his abashed expression.

She took a few spoonfuls of the soup. It was thick and creamy, with a flavorful blend of cheese and green chilies. And the heat was tolerable. "It's delicious."

"I made sure we acquired a good cook."

She spooned in more, watching him, wondering how he'd react to questions. "For your security force?" she finally asked.

Another voice answered the question—a voice that came from the doorway. "It's not a good idea to go into details."

Meg turned her head and froze, the spoon poised in mid-air several inches below her mouth. Standing and watching her with narrowed eyes was the blond man she'd seen outside—the man who'd scattered the little knot of guards with nothing more than a pointed look.

Chapter Five

Meg's glance went from the newcomer to Bridgman as she lowered her spoon.

"I'd ask you to introduce me," the man in the doorway said, his voice edged with flint. "But from the look on Ms. Wexler's face, I'd say she already knows who I am."

Meg shook her head. "I beg your pardon. We've never met."

"Sweetie, your anxious expression says otherwise. You know exactly who I am. So you might as well come clean with me."

"The only thing I know about you is what I saw through the window," Meg answered in a low voice.

He gave a sharp laugh. "Nice try. But there are no windows in the rooms over here."

"There are—in the bathrooms. At least, in my bathroom."

He tipped his head to one side, studying her through glacier-like eyes.

"Right. You've got a tiny bathroom window eight feet from the floor. Not exactly accessible."

"I climbed up to have a look outside."

"Oh, you did. What exactly did you see?" he challenged.

"I saw wide green lawns dotted with rocks. I saw that this building is a gray castle. I saw men in khaki uniforms. Some of them were standing in a group under a tree and talking. One of them looked like he was keeping watch. When you came out of the building, he whispered a warning and the group broke up. You stood there staring at them with the same expression you're using on me,'' she finished, giving a pretty full account of her brief observations.

Though he kept his expression impassive, his color deepened. "Well, Glenn, it looks like our Ms. Wexler has mountain-goat genes."

She gave a little shrug. "You have me at a disadvantage. You seem to know me. I don't have a clue who you are."

"Have it your way. I'm Blake Claymore, chief of security."

Under the circumstances, it didn't seem appropriate to say, Glad to meet you. The first thing this man had done was accuse her of lying. Slipping her hands below the surface of the table, she clasped them tightly in her lap.

Claymore turned to Bridgman, and a look of understanding passed between them. Bridgman might be running this place, but apparently he was ready to defer to his chief of security when the need arose.

Claymore studied her. "I guess if you can climb up to that window, you're fit enough to answer some questions about your background. So are you in training for the Olympic gymnastics team? And how does Castle Phoenix fit into your schedule?" he asked, his voice edged with sarcasm.

She was still trying to come up with a suitable answer as he strode to the table, pulled out a chair and joined them. Up close, he was even more formidable, with piercing blue eyes and the roughened skin of a man who'd endured a bad case of adolescent acne. Probably that had helped cement the chip on his shoulder.

Probably he was a bad choice for an enemy—which was obviously the category he'd assigned to her.

Sitting up straighter, she tried to keep her fear from showing. "I can't remember anything about myself," she said. "It's very frustrating—and unnerving. Maybe you can help."

He gave a sharp laugh. "*You* need *my* help?"

She shrugged. "It seems that you and Dr. Bridgman are the only links I have to my past."

"We're not part of your past."

Clenching her hands, she tried another tack. "But I was coming to this place. At least I was on the road here. Are you sure you can't tell me why?"

His gaze went from her to Bridgman and back again. "I can tell you what we've found out since you arrived."

"Thank you," Meg whispered.

"Hold the thanks until you've heard the details," Claymore told her. "You have a Maryland driver's license issued in the name of Meg Wexler. But it's a fake."

She raised startled eyes to his face. "How do you know?"

"One of our associates was able to make that determination. So that's one dead end we have. Then there's the car you were driving. It was rented by someone named James Taylor." He went on to tell her about the only credit card she was carrying. And about the real Meg Wexler who lived in Baltimore—who had slept in her own bed last night.

"The only conclusion I can draw from the above is that you didn't want us to be able to trace you. What would *you* conclude?" he asked sharply.

Her mouth had gone too dry to answer. To put some distance between them, she paced to the kitchen area, then turned and leaned against the counter for support. "Did you take my fingerprints while I was unconscious?" she asked in a gritty voice, half serious, half mocking.

"Of course. Unfortunately, they're not on file with the FBI. So I assume you don't have a criminal record. In fact, there's no record I can find of you. Every path I've checked leads to a dead end."

"Maybe I'm part of an alien invasion force getting ready

to take over the earth. And this is a test case to see how we do in a controlled environment.''

He gave a bark of a laugh. ''Well, that's one thing we know. You have a sense of humor.''

''Do you have any other hypotheses about me?''

''You won't like my avenue of speculation.''

''Let's drop it,'' Bridgman interjected. ''She's been through a pretty rough time. She needs to rest.''

''No. I want to hear his theories,'' Meg insisted.

Claymore gave her a dry smile. ''I think it's highly likely that someone thought very carefully about the kind of woman who would attract Dr. Bridgman, then sent her in here to get his cooperation—or hold his attention.''

Her gaze shot to the man in question, but his expression gave away nothing beyond a slight tightening of the jaw.

Claymore pressed on. ''I think they decided to put her in danger so he would be sympathetic to her. Let's assume it was our friend Mr. Johnson, since he's the most likely candidate. He has a bad habit of disregarding the safety of his employees. This time he went too far, and his secret agent ended up without her memory. Or she could be a very good actress, pretending that her past is a blank.''

''No!'' Realizing she was pressed painfully against the counter, Meg made an effort to straighten.

Claymore shrugged and continued as if she hadn't interrupted. ''On the other hand, I could be wrong about the stealth attack. Maybe you're not employed by Johnson. You could be working for a small company that knows about Dr. Bridgman's research, and you wanted to make him an offer. But the outfit's cautious, and they don't want him to be able to research them until they're ready to show their hand. If that's the scenario, you've come to sell him something he doesn't need, or you want to go into some kind of partnership.''

The recitation hung in the air between them.

''None of that is very flattering,'' she managed. ''At least

I passed the folder-in-the-drawer test.'' Her eyes locked with Claymore's. "Was it his idea or yours?"

"Mine."

"Good," she answered, then was sorry she'd given away her feelings.

Claymore continued to scrutinize her. "Too bad you find my assessment of your motives unflattering. I'm not paid to hand out bouquets. I'm paid to protect this place from a variety of threats—including an invasion by a beautiful spy."

"Then maybe the best thing for all of us is for me to leave here."

He tipped his head to one side. "If you're telling the truth about your missing memory, where would you go?"

That simple question sent a wave of cold sweeping over her skin. She had no idea where she would go. Her driver's license said she was from Maryland. If it was a fake, it didn't prove anything.

Holding his gaze, she asked, "If I said I wanted transportation to the nearest city, would you give it to me?"

There was no hesitation in his response. "No. I have to keep you here as our guest—for the time being."

Her eyes swung to Bridgman. "You agree?"

"Yes."

"So he's the one in charge?"

"No," he corrected her, his expression so neutral and his voice so flat that it was hard to believe he was the same man who had kissed her passionately a few minutes ago.

"I'm in charge," he continued, "but I hired Blake to do a vital job here. It makes sense to defer to his judgment where security is concerned. Besides, I don't think leaving would be in your best interests."

"Why not?"

"You made me responsible for you."

"How?"

"By coming here. By getting caught in an accident on my property."

"So now that your security chief has given you a fantasy account of my background, you want to protect me," she retorted.

His gaze never wavered. "Think about it this way. There were some pretty serious boulders rolling off that cliff. If someone arranged for you to get injured in a rockslide, they were playing fast and loose with your welfare. A little bad luck, and you could have been killed. So I think it's a good idea to keep you here—for your own protection."

"You're just guessing!" she objected, yet she could feel perspiration forming on her brow.

"Do you want to risk your life on betting that I'm wrong?"

"Are you saying I have no choice but to trust you?" Easing her hand behind her, she gripped the countertop.

"There are always choices," Claymore said, breaking into the exchange.

"Like what?" she demanded, trying to keep her voice even. She needed to sit down, but if she let go of the counter, she was afraid she might fall over. So she stayed with her hand clamped to the hard surface.

The security chief continued to study her as if he didn't believe a word she'd been saying. "You seem intelligent. I'm sure you can figure out what's in your best interests."

"How can I convince you I'm telling the truth?" she asked.

His answer was prompt. "You can start with a lie-detector test."

She gulped. "I—"

Before she could finish, Bridgman jumped in. "No! As her doctor, I think that would be too much of an ordeal at this time."

The two men locked gazes.

"We could go with sodium Pentothal."

"Out of the question in her condition. She's recovering from a concussion, remember?"

"Are you sure?"

"She didn't fake unconsciousness."

Meg fought the sudden ringing that had started in her ears. These two men were acting as if she had no say in what happened to her.

"There are more important considerations than her health," Claymore growled, his voice coming to her as if from a great distance, like the roar of breakers crashing on a beach.

"No," Bridgman countered.

Meg tried looking from one to the other, but she felt her vision going fuzzy, her knees turning to jelly as she slipped from consciousness.

TOMMY WOKE WITH A START, his body covered with sweat, his gaze darting around the room. He had fallen asleep in the easy chair in front of the TV, watching an old *Godzilla* episode. That must be where the nightmare had come from. It had been about his little sister, Meg. She'd been running through a forest with monsters chasing her.

Leaning over the side of the chair, he pulled the phone up off the floor, set it on his lap, and dialed her number.

He got the answering machine. He thought he'd gotten it before, but he wasn't sure. She should be home from work by now. Unless by some chance she was out on a date. He hoped she was out with some guy, having fun. She hardly ever dated, and he knew it was partly because of him. When she was home from her trips, she was always over at his apartment, bringing him food and fussing over him. That didn't leave too much time for relationships.

He'd told her to get a life. She'd put her hands on her hips and said she was old enough to make her own decisions. Fine! But one day she was going to wake up and discover she was too old to get a guy.

He knew she loved him. He also knew she was using him as an excuse, even if she wouldn't admit it to herself. Dad had been really strict with her, drumming it into her head that guys were out to take what they could get from a girl with a great body. She hadn't bought it at first. Then she'd gone away to college and had a couple of bad encounters that had convinced her good old Dad had been right. Like the time she'd been in the library stacks and heard a couple of guys discussing her body. Or the night a drunken fraternity brother had cornered her in the music room and started pawing her.

Too bad stuff like that had made her supercautious, because she deserved to settle down with some nice guy who would love her and give her the kids she longed to have. But so far, he didn't see it happening.

Maybe when he was dead. That wouldn't be too far in the future. Some days he imagined hurrying the process along. His eyes flicked toward the drawer where he kept his service pistol. The image of his lifeless body on the floor was followed by a picture of the stricken look on Meg's face, and he knew he couldn't do that to her.

FROM SOMEWHERE FAR AWAY, Meg heard Bridgman's voice as he steadied her, shifted her in his arms so that her head slumped against his shoulder. "Meg, are you all right? Meg, answer me!"

"I...think so," she managed, pulling herself back to consciousness.

"And I think we're finished with the interrogation," he growled, the comment obviously addressed to Claymore.

"Convenient!" the security chief retorted. "I think she's faking so I'll stop pressing her."

Meg couldn't focus on the rest of the exchange, only the sound of their angry voices, and the feel of Bridgman's hands holding her up. She pressed her face into his shoulder, trying to block out everything but the physical contact.

When he swung her up off the floor and cradled her against his chest, she gave a little sigh. Striding out of the lounge, he carried her down the hall to a small examination room where he laid her on a narrow padded table.

When he switched on an overhead light, she closed her eyes against the glare.

"What…happened to me?"

"You fainted." He picked up her wrist and pressed his finger against her pulse. Through slitted eyes, she watched him check his watch.

"I felt dizzy…then…fuzzy. Then…you were holding me."

"Does your head hurt?"

"No. The stuff you gave me worked."

"Good."

He was already busy fitting a blood-pressure cuff around her arm. She tried to relax while he took the reading.

"What is it?"

"One-twenty over sixty."

She kept her eyes away from his face as he found the hem of her knit top and rolled the fabric out of the way, exposing her skin to cool air before he pressed the stethoscope against her chest.

"Take a deep breath."

She complied. He was just a doctor giving her a quick exam, she told herself; he wasn't a man looking at the way her breasts filled the cups of her lacy bra. But she knew that after the way he'd kissed her, it was impossible for either of them to be completely impersonal.

"Normal," he said, his voice a little thick as he pulled the shirt back into place.

"I'm not the kind of woman who likes being weak and dependent," she whispered, unable to raise her eyes to his.

"How do you know, if you can't remember who you are?" he challenged.

She managed a tiny laugh. "There's the window. How many women would have scaled the bathroom wall?"

"Not many," he admitted. "But it wasn't such a smart move. What if you'd blacked out then?"

"I didn't."

"Look at me, Meg."

She did, staring up at him questioningly. "I'm going to check your pupils," he said, as he switched on a small flashlight and shone it into her right eye, then her left. Afterward he had her follow the movement of his finger.

"Normal," he reported again. "I think you were just reacting to stress."

She managed a small laugh. "You mean Mr. Claymore's interrogation? Or the disturbing fact that my past is a blank?"

"Not knowing who you are would be frightening."

"Then you believe me?" She reached for his hand and folded her fingers around his, holding on tight.

"I...want to."

"But you don't trust me," she clarified, letting her hand drop back to her side.

"This isn't simply about you and me. A lot is at stake here."

"Yes. Your research. It's important to you."

"It's not just a personal whim. A group of sick men is depending on me."

She gave a little nod, closed her eyes and struggled for calm. She wanted to hide from him—from herself. But there was nowhere to disappear in this little room. "You really think it's not safe for me to leave here?"

"Not until you remember why you came."

"Now who's putting on the pressure?"

"Sorry."

She looked into his gray-blue eyes, wanting more than the compassion she saw in their depths. Once again, she found it impossible to censor her thoughts. "Was he telling the truth about the kind of woman who would attract you?"

She saw him swallow. "I think the two of us already answered that question."

She studied his eyes. He was trying hard not to reveal any emotions that would make him vulnerable to her, and she realized that was how he probably lived his life—blocking his feelings. She guessed that someone or something had hurt him terribly, and she longed with all her heart to heal him, to change the very fabric of the way he lived. But she was afraid he wasn't going to let her get close enough to do it, unless he knew who she was and that she hadn't come here for nefarious purposes.

A shiver went through her.

"What?"

She might have ducked the question, except that the only thing she could give him was her honesty. "I'm scared."

"I understand."

"No, you don't. I'm scared that when I find out who I am, I won't like that person. I mean, what if your macho chief of security turns out to be right? What if I came here to…to hurt you in some way?"

"I don't know," he answered, and she heard her own doubts reflected in his voice.

Somehow, that was the worst part—the fear that she had the power to damage him.

She swung her legs to the side of the table and lowered herself to the floor, testing to make sure that her knees would support her. She stood only a few inches from him, and it would be so easy to reach out and pull him close, to lean into his strength the way she had a few minutes ago. But she couldn't afford the luxury. Until her memory came back, they couldn't have anything meaningful together.

That should have made perfect sense. But how could it—in a world where the only truths in her short memory were the feelings that drew her toward this man? He was her protector and her captor, yet the relationship was a lot more complicated than that. In the short time they'd known each other, something out of the ordinary had transpired between them.

She couldn't stop herself from raising her face toward his. He stood unmoving, warning her with his eyes that she'd better not overstep the boundaries again. Yet she felt the heat coming from his body, felt her own body heating, felt the awareness simmering between them like a flow of charged particles. If she moved only a fraction, her breast would be pressed against his arm. Her pulse quickened as she imagined the intimate pressure of his flesh on hers.

"What if Claymore has it wrong?" she asked, her voice thick and husky. "What if I was sent here because I'd be attracted to you?"

She saw him swallow, saw his gaze drop to the front of her top where her nipples rose against the knit fabric. "Do you like to engage in sexy little sparring matches with men? Is that part of your personality?"

She considered the question honestly. "I don't think so."

"Why not? That's certainly a provocative question."

"Yes," she whispered. "It is. But I'm doing things and saying things that embarrass me. I don't seem to be able to stop myself. It's a strange feeling. The lack of control is scary, but it's exciting, too. Maybe it's the only freedom I have at the moment."

"You've picked a dangerous game."

"Have I?"

His gaze remained steady. "What do you think?"

"I think danger is better than fear."

"Don't count on it."

"Are you sure?"

One part of her mind was amazed at what she was doing—pushing and provoking him this way. The other part understood that the verbal provocation wasn't basic enough. Before she could consider the consequences, she rose up on her toes and brushed her lips against his. He didn't move, and she accepted that challenge, as well.

She didn't kiss him the way he had kissed her earlier. She closed her eyes and rubbed her mouth back and forth against his, marveling at the softness of his lips and at the instant fire she could generate with such a simple caress.

It was a risky experiment—one that spiraled out of her control in the space of a heartbeat. Flames licked at her nerve endings, making her breasts ache and sending urgent messages traveling downward to the center of her body. And she was only touching him at one contact point.

Was it the same for him?

She heard him make a strangled sound deep in his throat, which told her that he was trapped by the fire. Yet his hands stayed stiffly at his sides. And she kept hers the same, partly to prove to herself that she could refrain from touching him, partly to prove that they didn't need more than this mouth-to-mouth contact to excite each other beyond endurance.

She wasn't sure how long they stayed that way, lips brushing, nibbling, grazing. She only knew that the kiss deepened by slow degrees until they were tasting each other, taking huge delicious mouthfuls the way one might gorge on the sweetness of a ripe peach. Yet this was so much better—because the taste was of Glenn Bridgman.

She wanted more. She wanted his hands on her, touching, arousing, driving away all the uncertainties that hovered at the edge of her mind. When his palm clamped over her shoulders, a small sigh of wanting eased out of her. His fingers dug into her flesh, and she thought for a moment that he would pull her heated body against his. Instead he lifted his mouth from hers and gently widened the gap between them.

"You know this has to stop," he said hoarsely.

She knew it—in some part of her brain. As she stared into his eyes, she saw that the warm blue had deepened, overwhelming the cool gray, and she knew he wanted the same things she did, even if he couldn't tell her yet.

"I think we're a lot alike," she said.

"How?"

"Afraid to ask for what we need. But here we are, in never-never land together—where none of the rules apply."

His eyes took on an almost-innocent eagerness, before he masked the look of longing. "You're making too many assumptions. This isn't a fairy tale. It's my reality."

"Of course that's true. But it's not like everybody else's

reality. You're a sorcerer who's hidden himself away in a magic castle.''

He gave a bark of a laugh. ''Is that how you see me?''

She nodded gravely.

''Don't get too wound up in fantasies. You don't know what I want. You don't even know yourself.''

''I know a lot about you.''

''From some dossier you read?''

''Do you really believe that?'' Before he could answer, she went on. ''Your eyes give you away. And the way you kiss me. You *wish* this were never-never land. Just for once, you want to lay down the burden you're carrying around on your shoulders. But you can't admit it, even to yourself.''

''You're making that up.''

''Am I? I don't think so. Strange as it sounds, I think that in one way amnesia can be an advantage. I don't have a lot to go on besides feeling and intuition. About myself— about the man who saved my life.''

He made a dismissive sound.

Ignoring him, she continued. ''I'm getting to know who I am. Not the facts,'' she said quickly, ''but the emotions.''

''The facts are relevant,'' he argued.

The harsh reminder jerked her back to reality. Suddenly they were playing by his rules again. She raised her chin. ''Okay. When a person has lost her memory, what does she do to get it back?''

''You can't force it. It just has to happen.''

''There must be something.'' She swallowed. ''What about hypnosis?''

''I wouldn't recommend it. For the same reasons I wouldn't recommend a lie-detector test until you've had a little time to get your equilibrium back.''

''Catch-22,'' she whispered.

''Yeah.''

''So what are my other options?''

''Familiar surroundings can help.''

"What else?"

"Pinpointing the reason for the condition." He looked like a man balanced on a razor's edge, a man who could fall off either side and topple into an abyss. "Memory loss can be associated with a blow to the head. It can also be triggered by a shock. Something could have happened that your mind wants to block. A frightening incident. Or—"

"Or what?"

He shook his head. "I wish I knew."

Chapter Six

His gaze remained steady, and she had the feeling that he was still waiting for her to give him answers.

She had none, so she plowed ahead on the only course open to her. "Okay. Let's work with what we've got. If I can't step into my familiar environment, I can have a look at the car I was driving."

He thought about it for a second, and she held her breath, wondering if he was going to refuse.

When he said, "All right," she breathed out a little sigh.

"Will you take me there?"

His hesitation made her chest tighten.

He looked at his watch. "I have some things I have to do. Give me an hour."

After murmuring her thanks, she let him show her back to the room where she'd spent the night. Slipping off her shoes, she lay down with her clothes on, expecting to spend the interval staring at the far wall. In fact, she quickly drifted off to sleep.

Sometime later, a noise from the doorway made her eyes flick open. Bridgman was standing there watching her.

She swung her head in his direction, trying to read his mood, but his expression was shuttered.

"You found out more about me?" she asked.

"No." His face hardened. "I found out that Lipscomb,

the guy who was guarding your car, got a powerful dose of a hallucinogen combined with knockout spray.''

"Oh," she breathed.

"I don't suppose you know if the vehicle was booby-trapped," he said evenly.

"No. I'm sorry," she added ineffectually, then pushed herself up. "I guess you're not going to let me examine the car after all."

"You'd be taking a chance."

"You don't know it had anything to do with what happened to the man!"

"That's right," he retorted. "Maybe it was a colossal coincidence."

Obviously he didn't think so.

"Let's go see if we can find out," she returned evenly, swinging her legs to the floor. God, was this another test? she wondered as she slipped into her sandals and followed him out of the room. Every time she thought things might be going all right, something else happened.

"The vehicle's in the garage," he said, as they crossed the lounge area where they'd eaten—where they'd kissed. Watching the rigid set of his shoulders, she wondered if any of that had really happened.

She felt as if the walls were closing in around her, and yet she managed to ask, "Can we get there from outside?"

He gave only a tight nod. Then, opening a door, he stepped aside to let her pass and gestured toward a flight of stairs. At the bottom of the steps was a wider hallway with a vaulted ceiling and dark paneling. Probably the original medieval-style interior, she thought, as they passed through a stone archway where a young man in khaki sat at a wooden desk.

"Sir." After snapping to attention, he hurried to open the door.

"Thank you."

She felt the guard's eyes on her. He was curious; she could tell that. And hostile. What had he heard about her?

It was a relief when Bridgman marched her out the door and into waning afternoon sunshine. She trailed several paces behind him, wishing that they weren't in such a hurry as they crossed the wide lawn and skirted a rock outcropping.

What if the car triggered a memory, and she didn't like what she uncovered?

Bridgman turned to give her an inquiring look. The expression on her face must have given her away. "You've changed your mind?" he asked.

"I—" She cleared her throat. "No."

His eyes never leaving her, he came slowly back to where she'd stopped in her tracks. Unable to meet his gaze, she glanced down, studying the lawn. Up close, it was spotted with patches of crabgrass and clover.

A memory ticked at her brain as she stared down at the small shamrock shapes. Sinking to her knees, she ran her hand through the closest patch, moving the low stems, making the leaves ripple against her fingers. It felt good, familiar. Comforting, even. Closing her eyes, she tried to go deeper into the tactile sensation, letting it lead her where it would.

She was close to something—a memory that tickled her brain cells the way the leaves tickled her fingers.

"What are you doing?" Bridgman asked, breaking into her trance.

"Looking for a four-leaf clover," she answered in a husky voice, keeping her face turned toward the green carpet.

"For luck?" he asked, coming down beside her, his own hand beginning to comb through the mass of greenery.

"I need some," she whispered, trying to recapture the feeling of connection to her past that had snapped when he'd spoken. She wanted to ask him to give her time to do things in her own way. But she didn't even know what that way was. Almost frantically, she shifted the low-growing plants, searching for but not finding what she wanted.

"Here," he said, startling her with a small surge of hope. "No," he quickly amended. "I thought I saw four leaves, but one of them is from another plant."

The disappointment was palpable. "That happens," she murmured. "You think you've found one, and it turns out to be an illusion."

"You remember that?" he asked.

"I...don't...know." She made a low sound of frustration in her throat. "I have this image in my mind of a little girl looking through a clover patch. I don't know if it's really me—or a scene from a book or a movie."

"Are you alone?"

She might have said yes. At the moment she felt so totally alone that tears blurred her vision. Yet, in the tantalizing snatch of memory—if that was what it was—there were other people. "My father is with me. And my brother," she whispered, keeping her face tipped down so he couldn't seen the pain in her eyes.

"Can you see their features?"

"No. They both have their heads turned away. Probably a psychiatrist could make something of that. It's not real. Or I'm blocking the important part."

"What color is their hair?"

"Blond," she managed in a husky voice. "But the father's is getting thin on top. He doesn't like it, so he combs his hair to the side."

"No mother?"

She shrugged, turning back to the clover, her hand moving faster as she searched for a magic set of four leaves. Surely, on the grounds of a place called Castle Phoenix, there should be magic. "I don't know. But the father's the one who takes the kids into the woods and teaches them stuff."

"What stuff?"

"Camping. Fishing. Hiking. Do you think it's true?" she persisted, wanting him to give her that much. If he were kind, he would do it, she thought, willing him to reassure her.

Instead he asked, "Do you?" And she understood that he was being ruthless—with both of them.

"I wish I knew. I wish I knew it would all come back—or even if I'd ever found a four-leaf clover." In frustration, she tugged at the ground cover, pulling the leaves free and then letting them drift downward. Unable to cope with the sense of loss, she pushed herself up and looked around. Aware of her surroundings again, she felt a stab of embarrassment as she saw a group of men about fifty yards away, watching her. She couldn't really see their faces, but she imagined disapproving, narrowed gazes.

"They probably think your uninvited female guest is wacko," she muttered. "She's crossing the lawn and all of a sudden she sits down and starts playing with the clover." Her hand swept toward the watchers. When Bridgman shot a glance in their direction, the group immediately began to disperse—either hurrying into the gray stone buildings or drifting across the lawn. "It must be nice to have that kind of authority," she observed.

"What kind?"

"You turn your head toward them, they jump."

"I wouldn't put it that way," he retorted.

"How would you put it?"

He shrugged, looking uncomfortable, and she gathered that he didn't particularly enjoy being the leader of a paramilitary force, or whatever you called the squad of men who guarded his castle.

"You'd live your life differently if you could, wouldn't you?" she asked.

An unfocused look came into his eyes, but he banished it before she was sure she'd seen it. "There's no point in answering hypothetical questions. We should go to the garage. If you still want to do it."

She studied his set expression, but he made no further

comment. Apparently he wasn't going to discuss his life-style with her.

"After you," she murmured.

They crossed the lawn and descended a flight of stairs to a paved area flanked by six garage doors.

Rock music drifted through a smaller door to the right. Just inside the entry, another guard sat at another desk—positioned beside a rack of rifles.

Meg studied them. Winchesters, she decided, then wondered where that piece of knowledge fit into her background. Somehow, she didn't think she was going to share the insight with Bridgman. Not this time.

The music was coming from a small radio that sat on the blotter in front of the guard. When the young man saw Bridgman, his face went rigid and his hand shot out to lower the volume. "Sorry, sir."

"It's all right. As you were, Shipley."

"Yes, sir."

Meg glanced around the garage. There were no other guards, only an assortment of jeeps, vans, cars and other vehicles.

"Over here," Bridgman called, his voice hard-edged, and she realized that he was as nervous about this inspection as she.

When she slid him a sideways glance, she saw his face was carefully neutral. Determined to prove something to both of them, she followed him toward a black Volvo. Her palms grew damp when she saw the caved-in driver's door and the damage to the front end. It looked as if the vehicle had plowed into the side of a mountain—and she'd been inside when it had happened.

Unconsciously rubbing her hands against the sides of her slacks, she stared at the car, trying to bring back memories of terror, of what it felt like to be trapped inside with rocks raining down around her, blocking the road.

But there were no memories. Nothing. And the void in her mind was devastating. Terrifying.

"I can't—" Suddenly unsteady on her feet, she reached out to brace herself against the black metal. When the contact sent a jolt through her, she snatched her hand back.

Bridgman was at her side, his arm coming up to steady her. "What?" he asked in a strained voice. "Did you remember something?"

"No," she whispered. "But it made me feel—" She stopped abruptly.

"What?"

"Bad." The syllable oozed out of her like dirty oil oozing from a broken crankcase. The steady beat of the music made her nerves vibrate, and she wanted to scream at the guy called Shipley to turn it off. But she managed not to direct her fear and frustration at him.

"'Bad'?" Bridgman questioned, his eyes drilling into hers. "Tell me what you mean."

She forced herself to focus on the feeling, to articulate. "A bad sensation. Evil," she added with a catch in her voice. "This car is evil." Realizing what she'd said, she blinked.

He was looking at her, expecting more.

"I...I...don't know what I mean, exactly," she stammered.

The muscles flexed in Bridgman's arm as he gripped her, and she felt clammy sweat gathering at the back of her neck and trickling down her spine. "You said I had plants in the trunk?"

He nodded.

"Can you open it?"

"It's unlocked." He strode to the back and pulled up the door. She stared at the thick carpeting inside—and saw nothing familiar.

"Do you remember?" he demanded, and she knew he'd been hoping for more. She was only hoping for escape. But that wasn't an option.

"No." She turned her back on the gaping cavity of the trunk.

"Maybe if you sit behind the wheel." It was more an order than a suggestion.

She wanted to refuse. Instead she moved to the driver's door and started yanking. It wouldn't open, and she looked questioningly at Bridgman.

"We had to get you out from the other side."

"Why didn't you tell me?" she demanded, her voice high and sharp. So this *was* a kind of test. He was trying to find out if she'd slip up and reveal she already knew that little fact—reveal that she was lying through her teeth about her memory loss.

Grimly putting one foot in front of the other, she circled the car again.

A sudden noise made her jump, and she looked up to see that Bridgman had pressed a series of buttons that opened the garage doors.

"More light," he said.

"Thanks." Before she could chicken out, she pulled open the passenger door and sank onto the leather seat.

As she raised her eyes and studied the spiderweb of cracks that marred the windshield, she felt her throat close. The texture of the leather against her flesh made her skin crawl, and she wanted to leap from the vehicle. She might have done it if she hadn't been so aware of the man watching her every move. When his portable phone rang, she jumped. Couldn't they blow their noses around here without consulting him?

Scowling, he pulled the instrument out of his pocket and jabbed at the receive button. "I'm busy. This had better be good," he snapped.

She heard a voice jabbering on the other end of the line, loud and excited.

Bridgman glanced at her, then moved away from the sound of the radio. "Speak slowly. I can't understand what you're saying. What about the dogs?"

Apparently he couldn't hear the answer, because his face contorted in frustration.

"I'll be right back," he called to Shipley, then stepped into a small glass-enclosed office and shut the door. Turning his back, he hunched over the phone.

Through the cracked windshield, she and the guard exchanged uncertain glances.

He took a step toward her, pitching his voice over the radio music. "You'd better wait over here where I can keep an eye on you."

"Okay," she agreed, glad of the excuse to climb out of the sedan. Over Shipley's shoulder, through the open garage doors, she caught a glimpse of a low, dark shape streaking toward them across the blacktop parking area.

Eyes narrowed, she focused on the blur. As it came closer, it resolved itself into a whir of churning legs, a snarling face, bared teeth. It was a dog. A very large dog with a demonic look in its eyes that made her skin go cold.

Rabid.

Seeing the expression on her face, Shipley whirled, then drew in a startled breath as he fumbled for the gun in the holster at his side. But he wasn't quick enough. Before he could free the weapon, before Meg could scream, the animal gave a mighty leap through the doorway. What looked like a hundred pounds of crazed canine flesh struck the man in the chest, knocking him to the ground.

Shipley made a high, frightened sound as his hand came up to ward off the viciously snapping mouth. The foaming jaws clamped themselves to his arm and began to chew.

Taking a running step in the direction from which she'd come, Meg made it around the desk in seconds and snatched a rifle from the rack. It felt heavy, but the weight was reassuring in her hands. Coolly, as if she were watching herself from somewhere beyond her body, she checked the action, then slid a shell into the chamber. Out of the corner of her eye, she saw Bridgman materialize from the office where he'd been talking.

"Meg!"

His view of Shipley was blocked by the desk, but he'd

spotted the weapon in her hands. Stopping short, he stared at her, anger and confusion warring for control of his features.

"Put that down," he commanded.

He thought— It didn't matter what he thought.

"No time," she managed, even as she saw him scrambling toward the desk.

Animal snarls, punctuated by a scream, reached them, cutting off whatever he was going to say. As if in slow motion, she moved to the side to give herself a clear line of sight, her gaze focused on the man and dog where they writhed together on the concrete floor of the garage. The big dog was on top, his body covering the man from neck to knees.

For a split second she hesitated. Then some force beyond her control seemed to take over. Raising the weapon and bracing it against her shoulder, she sighted down the barrel, aiming for the animal's head.

With a jerky motion, she pulled back the trigger.

Chapter Seven

In the confines of the garage, the blast was deafening. The ejecting shell startled Meg, and the weapon's recoil knocked her back, making the shot go high, whizzing far above its target.

Take it easy, girl, a voice in her head warned. *Easy does it.* The words were part encouragement, part gruff warning.

She clung to the advice—and to the sound of the familiar voice—though her heart threatened to pound its way through her chest as she cocked the weapon and slid in another round. Again she aimed carefully and fired—this time prepared for the recoil. The blast came almost simultaneously with the sound of another shot from behind and to the right. The double burst of gunfire made her stiffen, even as the dog went limp, its body collapsing on top of Shipley.

Bridgman ran forward, past her, a pistol in his hand. He hadn't been wearing one; it must have been in the desk, her dazed brain decided. He'd shot at almost the same time she had.

She squeezed her eyes closed, desperate to recapture the voice of the man who had helped her shoot. It had evaporated—like a figment of her imagination.

Reality was a man gasping in pain. Snapping her eyes open, she saw him writhing on the cement floor of the garage.

Bridgman knelt beside him, grabbing the dog's muzzle with two hands and prying apart the vicious-looking teeth.

The deep bite-marks in the man's flesh made her stomach turn over. Shipley's face was drained of color, and he rolled to his side, drawing his legs into a fetal position. When he moved, Meg saw blood pooled on the concrete.

"Is he going to be all right?" she gasped, her hands clenching and unclenching on the rifle.

"We have to stop the bleeding," Bridgman said, yanking off his shirt and using it to press against the wound. Immediately, blood soaked the makeshift bandage. "There's a first-aid kit in the bottom-right desk drawer. Get it!"

Realizing she was still clenching the rifle, she fixed the safety catch, then set the weapon on the ground before running back to the desk. For a panicked moment she didn't see the kit. Then her eyes found the red cross on a dull metal box. Yanking it from the drawer, she dashed back to the men.

"Open it," Bridgman commanded, both hands clamping down on the wound. "Get me a large bandage. And tape."

Shipley lay very still, his skin beaded with perspiration, his breathing shallow.

"Am I going to lose my arm?" he whispered.

"Not if I can help it, Terry," Bridgman answered as his trained hand kept up the pressure. His voice sounded more like that of a reassuring father with an injured child than a commanding officer with a wounded soldier.

Meg fumbled in the kit, finding the requested items and handing them to him.

He made a sound that might have been meant as thanks as he worked, focusing all his attention on the young man.

"It hurts."

"I know. I know," Bridgman answered in the same low voice. "But you did fine. You kept him away from your throat."

Across the lawn, feet thumped toward them. They belonged to men with guns drawn—some of them pointed at the dog, some of them pointed at Meg.

Her breath frozen in her lungs, she stared at the circle of hostile faces. God, did they think that somehow *she* was responsible for this?

"Put the guns away," Bridgman ordered. "The dog's dead. The danger is over."

"Yes, sir."

As the weapons lowered and the men's postures relaxed a fraction, Meg remembered to breathe again.

Bridgman kept issuing orders. "Tracy, call a medical team."

A man headed for the wall phone.

"Larock, Graham, Peterson, Hastings, secure the area."

They snapped to follow the command.

"What happened?" one of the remaining men asked.

"Columbo went crazy," a distraught voice answered.

Meg's gaze swung to a short, muscular man, whose face held a mixture of bewilderment and self-accusation as he stared from the wounded young man to the body of the dog. "He was fine. I tell you, he was fine when he did his shift this morning. Then I opened the cage to feed him and he knocked me down and took off."

"He'd had his rabies vaccination?" a new voice asked, sending Meg's gaze darting to Bridgman's fingers. He'd had his hands in the dog's mouth. If he had a cut or something—

Before she could finish the thought, the handler snapped an answer. "Certainly he's had his vaccination! That's standard procedure."

The knot uncoiled in Meg's stomach, but Bridgman wasn't going to take the man's word for it. "I'll want to see his certificate," he demanded. "And get blood and saliva samples to the lab right away." Still on the ground, he turned to the injured man. "You're going to be okay. Everything's okay," he said in a calm, reassuring voice. Still, she saw the relief on his face when two men ran forward with the stretcher he'd requested. He helped move Shipley to the stretcher, then leaned over him, still talking quietly, and she knew that taking care of the injured man had become his top priority.

"The excitement's over," a hard voice announced. It came from Claymore, and the crowd began to disperse. "Who shot the dog?" the security chief asked.

"I did," Bridgman and Meg both answered.

The chief's gaze waffled between them.

"I got off a shot with the Beretta in the desk drawer. Right after she got him with a bullet from the Winchester," Bridgman clarified.

Claymore looked from Meg to the rifle lying on the ground. "So you know how to handle one of these?"

She spread her hands helplessly. "All I know is that I saw the dog leap on him and knock him to the ground. It was only a matter of time before he went for the throat. So I—I grabbed a rifle. I guess I know how to use it."

"Yeah," Claymore replied, his narrowed gaze sweeping over the dead animal.

Meg looked away—in time to see Bridgman running to catch up with the stretcher, then disappear behind a door at the other end of the garage.

Her throat went dry as she realized she was alone with Claymore—and a circle of hostile men. When she saw another flicker of movement, she whirled to face the new threat.

It was a man, coming toward them—an older man in a motorized wheelchair.

He stopped the chair about three feet away, eyeing her with interest. "Meg Wexler."

She gave him a tight little nod.

"Hal Dorsey. I've been anxious to meet you." He didn't offer his hand, which was red and gnarled, the fingers painfully deformed. Her gaze dropped to his legs, which were set at an uncomfortable angle. When the older man saw her staring at his twisted flesh, he tightened his jaw and turned his head toward Claymore. "What happened?"

"One of the dogs went crazy, sir," the security chief answered. From his demeanor, it was obvious which one of them outranked the other. Dorsey might not be able to walk, but his physical infirmities didn't dilute his power. For all she knew, he outranked even Bridgman in the hierarchy here.

Claymore gave a concise account of the incident, emphasizing Meg's expert use of the Winchester. She wanted to interrupt and ask if he would rather have had Shipley chewed to death. Instead, she stood with her hands pressed to her sides and her knees locked.

The man in the wheelchair studied her, his face hard and uncompromising. "Is that right?"

She gave him a little nod, then managed, "I need to sit down."

"Yes." He cocked his head, studying her, then barked an order to two of the men. "Bring her to the security center where we can have a nice, comfortable chat."

She made a strangled sound as two men moved to cage her between them. Claymore came into formation behind them. God, had he arranged the dog attack to create a medical emergency so he could get her away from Bridgman? Was he capable of tactics like that?

"This way," one of the guards ordered.

If she didn't go quietly, would they drag her? Stiff-legged, she allowed herself to be escorted through another door and down a flight of stone steps. When they reached a metal door, one of the guards produced a key, metal clanging against metal as he worked the lock.

They stepped into a damp corridor, and she jumped as the heavy door slammed behind them. After that, she tried to make her mind go numb.

"Room two," Claymore directed.

Another door opened, and Meg stepped inside. She had

expected to find herself in a cell. Instead there were three wooden chairs and a battered table.

Claymore gestured for her to take the seat near the far wall. Stiffly, she complied, grateful that her legs had carried her that far.

Moments later, Dorsey wheeled through the door and dismissed her escort.

"Well," he said with satisfaction as he saw her grip the arms of the chair.

She tried to take in a steadying breath, but her heart was blocking her windpipe.

"I want information," he growled.

She gave the barest shrug. "So do I."

"Well, you can't fault her for guts," Claymore murmured, his eyes hard. If Bridgman was the king of Castle Phoenix, then Claymore was the ogre. Or maybe the troll under the bridge.

She kept her fairy-tale insights to herself and her eyes on Dorsey.

"I hear you claim to have amnesia," he said, tersely.

"I do. You have to believe me," she said, detesting the pleading sound that had crept into her voice.

The old man tipped his head to one side, watching her. "There are ways to establish whether you are telling us the truth," he said, his tone mild.

"You mean sodium Pentothal?" she managed.

He gestured with a gnarled hand. "I agree with Glenn that drugs might not be a good idea at this time. I think a polygraph test would offer a reasonable alternative."

She could have protested. Instead, she raised her chin and answered, "All right."

Claymore looked surprised.

"I'm telling the truth. The sooner you believe me, the better."

"A practical woman," Dorsey said. He turned to the security chief. "How soon can you get set up?"

"I have the equipment ready to go. And a list of questions prepared. We can start in fifteen minutes."

Fast, super fast, Meg thought. Maybe he hadn't set the dog on Shipley, but he'd been waiting for an opportunity to get her away from Bridgman.

He stood and left the room, and she could suddenly breathe easier. "Is he going to do it?" she asked.

"Yes."

She swallowed.

"You don't like him?" Dorsey asked.

"And you don't like me," she observed.

"It's nothing personal," he said, speaking more gently than before, his eyes softening several degrees.

"You'd stand with Glenn Bridgman at the gates of hell."

He gave a bark of a laugh. "That's right."

"So would I."

"After a few hours' conversation?" he challenged. "That's express-lane loyalty."

She shrugged. "I'll tell you the same thing I told him. Having amnesia is a strange experience. With nothing to go on but your immediate impressions, you get a pretty quick reading on people. If I had to personify duty and honor, I'd pick Glenn Bridgman."

He didn't answer, only studied her intently.

She swallowed. "Actually, I may have phrased my earlier comment incorrectly. I'd say Glenn Bridgman *is* standing at the gates of hell. And he needs somebody to pull him back."

"And you're volunteering for the job?"

She flushed, looked down at her hands.

The man across from her shifted in his seat. "I should be preparing you for the procedure. Are you familiar with the polygraph?"

"No. It just sounds like something out of a police state."

"You've probably heard of the police using it. But it's also employed extensively in private industry."

"It's not admissible as evidence in a trial, is it?"

"No. But in the hands of a skilled operator, it's very effective. And Blake Claymore is very skilled."

"Oh, goody," she replied.

A smile danced at the corners of Dorsey's mouth before disappearing. "Let's stay on track, shall we? Basically, the polygraph measures the body's physiological changes—respiration, blood pressure, pulse rate and something called galvanic skin response—that are all triggered by emotional responses to specific verbal questions. You'll be hooked up to apparatuses that record these changes."

She gave a tight nod, as Claymore reappeared in the doorway, looking like a candy freak who'd been given the keys to the jelly-bean factory. "Ready. Come this way."

For a moment, she was paralyzed. Then she managed to make her body work so that she could move around the table and across the few feet to the door.

GLENN ROLLED THE CRAMPED muscles in his neck and shoulders. "I want an autopsy report on the dog as soon as possible."

Dylan Ryder nodded. "Parker already has some of the blood work done. It looks like he was given a massive dose of atropine."

Glenn swore. "That would have made him psychotic, all right. No wonder he bolted from his pen and attacked. Poor Shipley was in the wrong place at the wrong time."

"Yeah."

His eyes narrowed as his mind turned over various unappealing possibilities. "So how did he get it? The same way Lipscomb was drugged?"

"Blake is working on it."

Glenn nodded, remembering that the phone had rung several times while he was patching up Terry. He'd declined all calls. "I want Shipley to see a plastic surgeon and a neurologist," he said.

"Is that necessary? You did a superb job of stitching his arm."

Glenn scowled. "A workman-like job. I want that arm to look normal and function normally. I don't want that kid's life ruined because he signed on to work at Castle Phoenix."

"I'll make the arrangements. We can have him airlifted out of here to New York City within the hour."

"Do it," he ordered as he tossed his white coat into the laundry bag.

He'd kept his mind off Meg while he worked. Now a picture of her snapped into focus—Meg handling a Winchester rifle like Rambo.

"What happened to Ms. Wexler after I left?" he asked.

Dylan busied himself putting instruments in the autoclave. "Blake took her to security for questioning."

"What? You knew that, and you didn't tell me?"

"We got a phone call from Hal. He approved it. You were busy stitching up the kid. I didn't want to interrupt you."

"Approved what?" he growled.

"A polygraph test."

Glenn cursed under his breath.

"It makes sense."

"She's in fragile shape. She doesn't need the stress."

Dylan was looking at him. "She's in fragile shape because she invaded our territory."

"Right," Glenn retorted, but he was already on his way to the door.

CLAYMORE LED MEG TWO doors down the hall to another room with what looked like a window covered by a venetian blind beside the door. Inside were two chairs and various pieces of equipment. The window turned out to be a large mirror. A one-way mirror, she assumed.

When her escort closed the door behind them, she jumped.

"Where—where is Mr. Dorsey?"

"*General* Dorsey will be watching through the mirror.

The procedure works best if the operator and the subject are alone.''

"He's a general?"

"Retired. Sit down," Claymore said, indicating the far chair, which was equipped with huge armrests. Beside it was a machine with dials, a printer-like device, and a number of electrical leads.

She sat and saw her bloodless face in the mirror. She already looked guilty of something, she decided. Closing her eyes, she tried to keep her breathing even as Claymore attached a blood-pressure cuff and several monitors to her fingers. God, if the thing was measuring nerves, the reading must already be off the scale. When he tightened a rubber tube-like apparatus across her chest above and below her breasts, she cringed.

"Am I hurting you?" he asked, not sounding particularly sympathetic.

"No," she whispered, fighting the desire to rip off the connectors as he adjusted dials on the machine.

"Ready?" he finally asked.

She gave a tight nod, tensed, and ordered herself to relax.

"I want a baseline," he said, looking at the printout coming from the machine.

"Is your name Meg Wexler?"

"I don't know," she answered.

"Have you ever lied to someone who trusted you?"

She gave the same answer and heard him swear under his breath as he watched the bank of pens move across the paper. "I'd like yes or no answers."

"I wish I could give them to you," she retorted.

"Did you have an automobile accident on your way to Castle Phoenix?"

An image of the black Volvo filled her mind. "Yes."

"Did you kill the dog attacking Alex Shipley?"

"Yes."

"Did you come here to get information?"

"I don't know."

GLENN TOOK THE STAIRS two at a time. Four men had already stopped him to ask questions about Shipley, and he hoped there wouldn't be any more.

Ignoring the two guards at the entrance of the security center, he charged toward Hal, who moved his chair to block the door to one of the interview rooms.

"What the hell's going on?" he demanded. Through the mirror he could see Meg inside, facing Blake, her face as white as paper, telemetry equipment attached to her body.

When he reached for the door handle, Hal shook his head. "Don't. He's already pretty well into the session. Let him finish."

"She—"

"Glenn, we're giving her a chance to prove she isn't lying. Or are you afraid to find out the truth?"

Admitting nothing, he turned and faced the window.

"Did you come here to see Glenn Bridgman?" Blake asked Meg.

"I assume so."

"I said answer yes or no," the security chief snapped.

"This was your idea," she reminded, obviously trying to keep her voice even—and a leash on her nerves. "I told you, I can't remember anything."

"Are you telling the truth when you say you can't remember your name, your background?" Blake demanded, leaning over to mark the question on the graph paper.

Meg raised her head, watched him reading the machine. "Yes."

"Did you come to Castle Phoenix to seduce Glenn Bridgman?"

His heart skipped a beat, then started pounding in his chest. What kind of question was that, for Lord's sake?

"No," Meg snapped.

"Are you sure?"

"No," she answered in a lower voice.

"Would you like to seduce Glenn Bridgman?"

Her lips trembled. "I don't have to answer that."

"Are you using sex to get favorable treatment?"

His nerves screamed as he waited for the answer.

"No."

"Did you come here to spy on him?"

Meg made a small sound of frustration. "I don't know."

"Are you familiar with the Winchester rifle?"

"I must be."

He kept the questions coming fast now, not giving her time to think about the answers.

"Did you climb up to the bathroom window and see me outside?"

"Yes."

"Are you familiar with covert operations?"

"No."

"Have you ever killed a dog?"

"Yes."

"Have you ever killed a person?"

"No."

"You're sure about that?"

She raised her face to Blake's. "As I keep telling you, I can't be sure of anything."

"Do you want to have a personal relationship with Glenn Bridgman?"

"Yes," she whispered, then looked down at the hands twisting in her lap. "Please. No more."

"Have you already had sexual relations with Glenn Bridgman?"

Her face flamed. "Stop it!"

"That's enough," Glenn growled as he pulled open the door and surged into the room, his angry gaze fixed on the security chief.

Blake looked up, his face contorted. "I—"

"Get out," Glenn growled.

Claymore stood, then retreated.

When Glenn looked back at Meg she was tearing off the equipment that had attached her to the machine. He wanted to help her get the wires and leads off her body. Instead, he stayed where he was.

"Go away," she whispered, her voice thick, her face averted. "Just go away. Do you think I want to be anywhere near you now?"

He didn't move. Couldn't.

After several heartbeats, she lifted her eyes, and he saw that they were filled with tears. "That was—" She stopped, gulped. "How much of that did you hear?"

"The last ten minutes."

The color in her cheeks deepened.

"I'm sorry," he said again. "That session was...unforgivable."

"Did you order him to ask me those questions?"

"Of course not! You were with me when I told Blake I didn't approve."

"Well, for all I know, that could have been a little performance for my benefit," she said in an oddly detached voice. "If you were hooked up to the machine, I'd know if you were telling the truth."

"Meg—"

"I can't remember anything about my life. But I'd be willing to bet that was the most mortifying experience I've ever endured. Like being stripped naked." She sucked in a shuddering breath and expelled it in a kind of gasp. "I agreed to let them do the polygraph because I thought it would prove something—exonerate me. Now...is there some cell where I sit while you and General Dorsey and the chief of security decide whether to march me in front of a firing squad?"

"I had a room made up for you in the residential quarters. You can—"

She cut him off before he could finish. "Then let me go there. If you have to keep me in your castle like a prisoner, at least give me some privacy."

Chapter Eight

"The goons who brought me here can take me," she added in a barely audible voice.

Probably that was best, he silently told himself. He was getting too involved. But he couldn't stop himself from imagining how he'd feel if someone had asked him the questions he hadn't dared to ask himself—then checked to see that he wasn't lying about the answers.

Turning, he strode to the guard station. "Take her to the guest quarters. Room 24."

"And lock the door?" the senior man asked.

"Yes." There was no question about that. It was for her own protection—as well as the protection of Castle Phoenix.

He ducked into one of the other rooms so he and Meg wouldn't pass each other in the hall. Long after her footsteps receded down the corridor, he waited in the sparsely furnished cubicle, his hands clenched at his sides. When he felt calm enough, he went in search of Blake. He found the security chief showing the polygraph readings to Hal.

"I don't appreciate the two of you getting together and making decisions when I'm in the middle of an emergency," he said with deceptive composure.

"It was in your own best interests," Hal answered with no trace of apology. "We need as much information as we can get about Ms. Wexler."

Glenn silently conceded the point. He hadn't authorized the procedure, and he hadn't liked some of the questions, but he would be stupid to ignore the results if they prevented another unfortunate event like the attack on Shipley.

"You might as well fill me in."

Blake relaxed a notch. "Well, we don't know as much as we normally would. The fact that she can't remember her past is...inconvenient."

"So you've established that she's not lying about the amnesia," he clarified, feeling a weight lifting off his chest.

"Yes," Hal replied. "Unfortunately, it would be more definitive if the reverse were true."

"Want to explain that?" Glenn challenged.

"All we know is that she can't remember who she is and why she came here. That doesn't mean her intentions were honorable."

Glenn gave a curt nod, then said, "You didn't follow standard procedure."

"Which standard procedure?" Blake asked.

"I hardly think you went over the list of questions you were going to throw at her."

"Sue me," the security chief muttered.

"What the hell were you trying to do to her?"

"Put her under pressure. Get her to slip up."

He should leave it there, Glenn told himself. Instead he asked the question that had been tearing at him since he'd arrived at the session and heard her grappling with questions about the two of them. "Are you convinced she was answering truthfully to the best of her ability?"

"As far as I can tell."

"I wouldn't take that to the bank," Hal advised.

"What is that supposed to mean?" Glenn retorted.

"It means, keep your pants zipped."

"I don't need that kind of advice," he snapped. In fact, if anyone besides Hal had given it, he would have invited the man to step outside.

For a charged moment, he and Hal stared at each other.

Glenn turned away first, addressing his next comment to Blake. "Write me up a report."

"I want to talk to you about her," Hal said.

"Don't push your luck," Glenn muttered.

Hal ignored the advice. "I enjoyed talking to her. I can see why you're attracted to her—starting with that gorgeous body. Beyond that, she appears to be a warm, vulnerable young woman—until you start asking yourself the obvious questions."

"Drop it!"

The older man plowed ahead. "Her innocence is what makes her dangerous. That's what makes *you* vulnerable."

Without bothering to answer, Glenn pivoted on his heel and strode out of the room.

IT WASN'T A GUEST ROOM, it was a guest suite on the castle's top floor, Meg found as she wandered through the luxurious rooms, switching on lights. There was a bedroom furnished with antiques, except for the obviously new queen-size bed; a sitting room with similar appointments; a little kitchen alcove, and a bathroom that looked as if it belonged in a health spa. The only drawbacks were that the door locked from the outside and the windows were barred. But she wasn't really surprised by the security precautions. She had a pretty good idea how far they trusted her here at Castle Phoenix.

They. The men who ran this place. Claymore. General Dorsey. Glenn Bridgman.

Men. She made a small sound of frustration. There didn't seem to be even one woman who lived and worked here. Maybe if there had been, these guys would have had a slightly different perspective on life.

The thought brought back a vivid replay of the session with Claymore.

"Do you want to have a personal relationship with Glenn Bridgman? Have you already had sexual relations with Glenn Bridgman?"

The questions rang in her head, even when she pressed her hands over her ears—the questions and her answers. If she'd known Claymore was going to get into anything like that, she would have flat out refused.

A choking sensation rose in her throat, and she stared toward the barred window, knowing there was no escape—from either this place or her feelings.

The feelings were dangerous, she told herself. She'd been drawn to Bridgman for the wrong reasons; had imagined qualities that he didn't possess. If he'd let his security chief humiliate her like that, there was no telling what he'd do to her—and she'd better not forget that. If she dropped her guard with him again, she would be a fool.

JEROME JOHNSON PACED the length of the terrace, his hands moving restlessly at his sides.

Twelve hours ago he'd gotten a coded message from Castle Phoenix, and he'd sent his response at the designated time.

Unfortunately there was no real-time two-way communication, only prearranged codes to describe certain situations, because security at the castle was tight, and he hadn't been willing to risk his agent being detected.

All he knew was that something had gone wrong with the damn girl. She hadn't been following her part of the scenario, so he'd given the order to eliminate her before she spilled the beans to Bridgman. She'd served her purpose. They could get the biological-weapon samples without her. Then his lab team would get to work on the genetic engineering needed to increase the rate of cell destruction. That would make it a much better weapon—better than the original. And anybody who wanted the stuff would have to come to him.

But right now, everything was at a standstill until he got the "microbes" or whatever you called them. Too bad his technicians hadn't been able to extract it from the sick men. They'd tried, all right. And he didn't understand all the scientific mumbo jumbo they'd given him to explain why that didn't work. All he knew was that you couldn't get enough of the stuff to work with unless you started with a pure, laboratory sample.

He cursed under his breath, angry that he had to depend on other people. If he'd been able to go in there himself, it would all be over now.

He entered the house, his steps carrying him to the indoor firing range with its customized targets that bore various likenesses. His father. His chief competitor in the arms business. His high-school math teacher. And a dozen more, including Glenn Bridgman.

Bridgman had made a fool out of him in the eyes of the world, and the self-righteous bastard was finally due to pay the price. Not only was he going to provide a weapons-grade supply of a deadly biological agent, he was going to get the credit as the man who'd developed it.

Jerome laughed softly to himself as he checked his Browning automatic. Poetic justice. Very poetic.

Sighting down the barrel, he squeezed off six shots in rapid succession, smiling as neat little holes appeared in the target's chest.

BY THE TIME GLENN HAD strode a hundred yards across the grounds, he was feeling calmer. After opening the locked door to the level-four biohazards lab, he locked it behind him again and started down the stairs. Two flights below ground level, he stood in front of a massive door with Warning: Biological Hazards. Authorized Personnel Only emblazoned in eye-level, six-inch-high red letters.

This was where the real work of Castle Phoenix was carried out. Not in the greenhouses where he cultivated exotic plants for their medical value, but here, in his sealed-off multimillion-dollar underground laboratory where he worked under strict security procedures.

Only a few of the seventy-five men at the installation were cleared to come here. Usually Glenn called in one of them as a backup for safety precautions. Today he needed to be alone. And the lab was an excellent refuge.

He worked the keypad on the wall, punching in the access code, then pressing his palm to the scanner. When the lock disengaged, he stepped into the anteroom, then the dressing area, where he took off everything he was wearing, including his underwear, and stowed them in a locker before changing into cotton lab pants and a shirt. In the next room, he donned a one-piece positive-pressure suit ventilated by a life-support system, then mechanically went through the safety drill, checking the helmet, gloves and boots that would shield him from the lab's immediate environment. When he'd finished, he could have been an astronaut preparing for a space walk, except that the gravity here was normal. And the enemy wasn't the vacuum of space—it was the invisible virus particles that lurked beyond the final door.

After completing the procedure, he stepped into the air lock, and waited for the pressure to equalize before the system buzzed him through to the laboratory where he was growing one of the most dangerous viruses in the world. It didn't kill quickly, like the Ebola. Instead, this nasty little bug, which he'd named K-007 after having been appalled by the body count in a James Bond movie, took its victims on a slow, inexorable downward course, attacking nerve cells and bodily organs in a random pattern that was all the worse for its unpredictability.

Really, the time frame meant it wasn't even a good weapon. The army had snatched it when it was still in the development phase.

Yet, that didn't make it less deadly in the long run. And maybe, just maybe, he had figured out a way to stop it, he thought, as he crossed to the cell cultures bathed in the artificial heat of warming lamps. He'd started a new series of experiments three weeks ago, and they were more promising than anything else he'd tried. This was the third trial, and so far everything looked— He wanted to say "perfect." Instead, he stuck with cautious optimism.

Mentally crossing his fingers, he went over the notes Dylan had left on his last check of the cultures twelve hours earlier, feeling a surge of satisfaction as he compared the new data to previous results.

"Good," he approved, his breath puffing against the flat surface of his face mask as he put away the notebook and turned to the electron microscope. He was adjusting the focus when the lights flickered and went out, plunging the underground room into absolute darkness.

Softly he cursed under his breath. Now what?

For half a minute, he waited patiently in the blackness, expecting the backup systems to kick in. They didn't. After switching on his emergency oxygen supply, he moved cautiously in the darkness and found the wall phone. When he picked it up, he got only dead air.

MEG HAD DECIDED TO TAKE a long, luxurious bath. Why waste that wonderful Jacuzzi? Maybe the judicious application of hot water would even untie the knots in her shoulder and neck muscles. Returning to the bedroom, she kicked off her sandals and grabbed the robe she'd found in the closet.

After stepping out of her slacks, she tossed them toward the bed. She had just discarded her shirt and was about to unsnap her bra when the lights went out, and she was plunged into darkness.

For several seconds she stood stock-still, enveloped in silence. Then she heard someone shout and the sound of running feet.

It must be some kind of emergency. Hurrying toward the bed, she began to search for the clothing she'd carelessly discarded. Just her luck if a goon squad came charging through the door and found her like this.

TOO BAD HE HADN'T TOLD anyone he was coming down here, Glenn mused as he took stock of his options. Eventually, they'd find him. But by then he might well have run out of oxygen. The door lock was electrically controlled. And his only hope of escape was finding the emergency controls in the dark.

Allowing himself only shallow breaths, he stood in the absolute darkness, trying to get his bearings. From his present position, the door to the dressing area must be at six o'clock.

Hoping that he was correct, that he hadn't gotten turned around in the blackness, he carefully retraced his steps. When he made it to the door, he sighed his thanks. Working by touch, he began to search along the wall for the access panel. After wasting precious seconds, he realized he had to be on the wrong side and tried the far wall.

The small metal door turned out to be only two feet above the floor. Who had designed it? A team of midgets?

With the lights on, he'd felt perfectly at ease in the pressure suit. Somehow the darkness made his gloved hands feel as if they were encased in layers of bandages as he worked to free the crank on the emergency lock.

He should have enough reserve oxygen to get out of here, he told himself. Yet he could feel the air inside the suit thicken and his lungs begin to labor painfully.

His hands itched to reach up and open his faceplate. The rational part of his brain knew it would be a fatal mistake. He'd expose himself to K-007—and die along with the poor bastards he had sent off to Operation Clean Sweep.

That might satisfy the gods of cosmic justice. But it wouldn't do the men any good. They needed him working on the cure.

So he kept up his attack on the panel, his eyes closed as he tried to accomplish what should be a simple task.

It was getting hard to concentrate. Then in the dark, it seemed that someone was beside him—a woman—her fingers digging into his shoulder, focusing his scattered attention.

"Meg?" he whispered.

"Right here," she answered, her breath soft and cool against his hot skin.

But she couldn't be here now. Not in the lab. His mind was playing tricks. Yet, illusion was far more comforting than reality.

"Did you mean it about wanting a relationship with me?" he asked, holding his breath as he waited for the answer.

"You'll never find out unless you get out of here," she replied sweetly, with a teasing edge in her voice.

"If I take off the faceplate, I could kiss you," he said as he slowly cranked the lever.

"No! Later!" she warned, her voice high and sharp like a siren going off in his head.

"Okay."

He left the heavy, protective plastic in place, while his sausage-like fingers twisted the lever. It seemed as if he'd been doing it for centuries with no results.

He leaned his head against the wall, resting for a moment. Just a moment. Then he'd start working again. He promised.

"Hurry!" Meg urged, and it seemed that he could sense the light pressure of her lips against his.

"How much time do I have left?" he asked in a shaky voice as he lifted his head.

"Don't talk. Save your breath," she warned. "Do that for me, Glenn. I'll be waiting for you when you get out of here."

He didn't know how she could be in here with him and waiting on the outside, too. But he did as he was told, drawing comfort from the feel of her breast pressed against his shoulder.

Finally the lever wouldn't turn any further. Bracing his

hands against the wall, he pulled himself up and fumbled with the lock, falling through the door as it opened.

Somehow he remembered to seal it again behind him. Then he crawled toward the chemical shower and pulled the emergency chain, sending a decontaminating spray over the suit.

Meg was still with him. "Good. Good," she whispered.

He didn't have the breath to speak. Only when he'd stepped from the chamber and reached the changing room did he rip off the faceplate and gasp in air.

As his head cleared, he knew he was alone in the dark. Meg's comforting presence had been only a product of oxygen starvation. She wasn't here to help him—and he still wasn't out of the woods. He still had to open the outer door before he used up all the air in the sealed room.

MEG HAD EXPECTED Claymore to send in troops. So it wasn't exactly a surprise when she heard the sitting-room lock click softly open. She'd found her slacks. The knit top had eluded her frantically searching fingers. So she was barefoot, half dressed and cursing the timing of the blackout when she turned to face the bedroom door.

She almost called out to say she'd be with them as soon as she found her shirt. But the manner of the invasion stopped her.

No uniformed men charged through the entrance as if they owned the place. Instead, she heard the door ease open—quietly, stealthily, as if a burglary was in progress. Then the door closed again, and the lock turned, the small sound raising goose bumps along her arms as she realized that whoever had entered the suite had shut her in with him.

Was it one of the security men who'd looked at her with such malice? Or someone else?

Instinctively, she shrank back against the wall as she watched the beam of a flashlight play rapidly across the rug. Behind it, she could make out the vague shape of a man who moved quietly across the chamber, inspecting every corner, bending to check under and behind the sofa. When he knocked a vase off a table onto the rug, he cursed softly and kicked it out of the way before moving down the hall.

"Ms. Wexler?" he called.

The voice was familiar and brought a twinge of remembered fear. She'd heard that voice before. Been afraid of this man before. But where? And when?

"Don't hide from me. I'm here to help you," he said.

Somehow, she didn't believe him.

Shoulders glued to the wall, she considered possible hiding places. He'd find her under the bed or behind the drapes. That left the closet. It was long, taking up one whole wall of the room. From the outside, it looked like two closets—with two separate entrances. If she slipped inside, she could get closer to the bedroom door, get past him.

But then what? He'd locked the front door of the suite, which blocked that means of escape.

Cursing the bars on the windows, she moved along the wall, found the closet door and slipped inside. She had only a fifty-fifty chance of pulling this off, she knew as she moved quietly toward the far door. If he opened it first, he'd be on top of her.

Through the slit in the door, she saw him swing his light in an arc, then turn toward the closet door where she'd originally entered. When she saw the long-barreled gun in his hand, her heart leaped into her throat. For a moment she was paralyzed. Then she ordered her legs to take her through the door behind him and into the hall.

Sliding into the bathroom, she closed the door and turned the lock. There was barely enough light coming through the window for her to spot the vanity chair. Pulling it out, she tipped it backward against the knob, wedging the door closed.

Footsteps sounded in the hall, then the door rattled on its hinges.

"Come out of there!" a low voice growled. Apparently he'd given up any pretense of being friendly.

She didn't answer, and the next thing she heard was a spitting sound as something small and deadly slammed into the door. A bullet! From a gun with a silencer. With a little gasp, she shrank back around the corner to where the toilet was shielded by a tiled wall.

There was another spit. Another bullet.

In the dark she looked around for something heavy. There was nothing in the immediate area. Heart in her throat, she risked a dash for the dressing table, where she picked up a foot-high statue of a Greek girl with a water jug. Holding it by the feet, she flung it at the window. The glass shattered, and she jumped back around the barrier as more bullets hit the door. God, how many shots did he have?

What did it matter? He probably had a spare magazine. At this rate, the door was going to be Swiss cheese soon.

Cupping her hands, she turned toward the broken window. "Help me! Somebody help me! There's a man with a gun!" she shouted through the window.

No one answered, although in the distant darkness, she imagined she saw men running across the grass.

"Help!" she called again, pulling at the bars. They were cold and unyielding in her clenched fists. "Fire!"

There was no response.

Her eyes darted around the room, probing every shadowy corner—and spotted what looked like an access panel above the toilet. If she could get to it, maybe she'd have a chance to escape.

Sparing a few more precious seconds, she flicked the cold-water knob on the tub, then pulled the flexible shower spray so that it was dribbling a small stream of water onto the floor.

Another shot had her scrambling onto the toilet lid and then the tank. Barefoot on the cold porcelain, she stood on tiptoe and raised her hands toward the panel. It was too far above her head to reach, and she heard a small sob well in her throat.

Gritting her teeth, she jumped. Her outstretched hands hit the light plywood, which flew upward before crashing back into place. Again she jumped, trying to nudge the panel to one side.

This time it came down at an angle, giving her enough space to jump again and catch the molding around the edge.

Maybe she was really a circus performer who had come to Castle Phoenix to arrange a private show, she thought, verging on hysteria as she swung her legs, gathering enough momentum to propel her body upward. She pulled her feet through the opening, twisted to the side, and flopped onto a ceiling joist just as she heard the door splinter and crash open.

From her perch, she saw the assailant barrel into the bathroom like a freight train that had lost its brakes. When he hit the water spreading across the tile floor, he went flying, screaming as he crashed onto the slippery surface.

Meg slid the panel into place, leaving a tiny crack where blackness shaded into gray. Every ounce of concentration focused on escape, she began to crawl across the rafters, moving by feel, the rough wood beams her only guide.

It was darker than the inside of an elephant's belly and as hot as an oven. She had no idea where she was going. Dust filled her lungs, and splinters dug into her hands and through the fabric of her slacks, but she figured the pain was better than getting shot.

She had managed to put several feet between herself and her point of entry when she heard a voice call her name.

This time it was Glenn.

"Meg? Are you all right, Meg?" he called frantically, and she knew he was on the level below—in the suite. Or outside in the hall.

Her heart stopped. Oh, God. He had no idea of the danger.

"Glenn!" she shouted. "Get out of there! He's got a gun!"

"Meg! Who? What are you talking about? Where are you?"

She might have answered, but a bullet crashed through the ceiling only a few feet from where she crouched. The warning shout had given her away.

Quickly she shifted her position, almost losing her balance on the rafter.

"Meg!" Glenn's voice was strained. "Meg!"

Risking an answer was risking her life. But she took the chance—because she had to. "Glenn! Get away!" she screamed, then moved, estimating the distance between rafters, and hopped gracelessly to her right. She landed on the next beam with a jarring impact that sent her sprawling on her bruised knees.

Stifling a moan, she braced for another bullet. But it didn't come in her direction. It was fired below—aimed at Glenn.

Somehow she kept from screaming out his name. An awful silence stretched. Finally, to her relief, she heard him give an angry snarl—anger not pain, she told herself. The impact of one body colliding with another made her suck in a sharp breath. Then a piece of furniture thumped, followed by a grunt and a curse.

They were fighting—Glenn and the intruder. Somewhere below her. At least that was the way it sounded from her hiding place.

Going very still, she listened, trying to judge the direction and the distance of the noise.

To her left. And several feet ahead. As fast as she could, she crawled toward the sound of men engaged in hand-to-hand combat.

Carefully reversing her position, she braced her hands against the rafters. With as much force as she could muster, she slammed her heels against the ceiling of the room below her. Her feet punched through, sending up a cloud of dust.

When the debris settled, she found herself looking down into a large area—the sitting room, she realized as she made out the shapes of the furniture in the beam of a flashlight. Rolling in and out of the shaft of light were two male figures locked in mortal combat.

Chapter Nine

Tearing frantically at the edges of the hole, pulling with her hands and kicking with her feet, she enlarged the opening, ripping off chunks of gypsum board and scattering them on the carpet. Some hit the shoulders of one man or the other, but neither seemed to notice.

Dust rose in little puffs, making her choke. Her eyes watered, but she kept them fixed on the combatants, trying to determine which one was winning.

Glenn crashed heavily against a sideboard, his assailant gave a grunt of triumph and leaped forward, pulling back his fist for another blow. Before he could follow through, Meg jumped and landed on his back. Surprised, he exhaled sharply, and she clawed at his face, digging her fingernails into his flesh.

His roar was a mixture of anger and pain. With a mighty heave, he tried to throw her off, but she hung on, bent on doing as much damage with her bare hands as she could. She saw that Glenn had pushed himself to a sitting position. In a minute, he'd be back in the fight—she hoped.

The assailant must have seen the odds were going to change. Redoubling his efforts, he gave a mighty heave that loosened her hold. With a growl, he threw her backward onto the sofa. As she lay sprawled there, she saw Glenn spring at the intruder. Cutting his losses, the man dodged out of the way and ran from the room.

Glenn went after him, and she pushed herself up, straining her ears as she followed two sets of echoing footsteps. Moments later, she heard a door slam, then a curse. In the darkness, she waited tensely.

It was Glenn who returned, and she knew from his posture that the man had gotten away.

"He had an escape route all planned," he spat, his breath coming in gasps. "He must have taken the bars off one of the windows that had access to a roof. By now, he's probably somewhere on the grounds."

"Are you all right?" she questioned urgently, leaping from the sofa and hurtling toward him.

"Are you?"

"Yes," they both answered at the same time. Then his arms came around her, enveloping her in his warmth.

Tears swam in her eyes, but she willed them back.

"Did he hurt you? Tell me!" Glenn demanded.

"I'm fine. I'm fine now," she murmured, closing her eyes and holding on for dear life, needing the solid feel of his body, the safety of his embrace.

She was shaking with reaction, and so was he, his solid frame trembling like an oak tree battered by a windstorm as he wrapped her close.

"I—I called for help. Out the window," she quavered. "No one came."

He made a low, angry sound, then moved his hand across her bare back. "You're half naked. What did he do to you?"

"Not—not what you're thinking. He— I was getting undressed when the lights went out. I couldn't find my shirt."

She felt relief ease out of him. Then he demanded, "Tell me what happened."

"He came sneaking into the apartment and locked the door behind him."

"Lucky I had the key."

"Yes," she breathed, thinking about what might have

happened if the intruder had gone back into the hall and encountered Glenn there. He would have had a clear shot.

"How did you get away from him?"

"I barricaded myself in the bathroom." She gave a gulping laugh. "There's water all over the floor. We'd better turn it off."

"Later." His grip shifted to her shoulders, tightened painfully. "How did you get away?"

She shivered. "He kept shooting and shooting at the door. But there's a wall beside the toilet. I hid behind it."

"Thank God."

"Then I found an access panel in the ceiling and climbed up." She gave another hysterical laugh. "Try to get Claymore to believe that."

"The hell with Claymore."

"I was crawling across the rafters when I heard you calling my name."

"And you risked your hiding place to warn me."

"I had to."

"You don't owe me anything."

Her eyes widened. "I couldn't let you get shot."

"Why not?" He ended the question with a strangled sound. "You don't even know why you came to Castle Phoenix. But things keep happening to you."

"*You* happened to me," she murmured, lifting her hand to touch his face, no longer able to deny what she had felt from the moment she'd opened her eyes and he'd been there.

"Meg—" Her name sighed out of him like a plea. In the darkness, she couldn't see his face, but she could imagine the intensity of his features.

Honesty made her whisper, "We both know I came here to cause trouble for you."

"And we both know what kind of person you are," he said vehemently. "Everything you've done has shown me your true character."

He didn't give her a chance to argue about it. His mouth

swooped to take possession of hers. "You want the truth about us? I'll give you the truth."

Her own truth was a moan of surrender as he angled his head to take more complete possession, his lips parting hers so that his tongue could enter.

She twisted her fingers into his hair, clinging, possessing, desperate to hold him where he was. If he let her go now, she would shatter.

But there was no need to hold him in place. Not when blazing-hot need sprang between them like a forest fire out of control—sweeping everything away but the drive to be close, then closer still.

The kiss went on and on, pushing her further and further into the inferno. And when he lifted his head, they were both gasping for breath as if the fire had taken all the oxygen from the room.

"Do you have a better idea of the truth?" he grated.

She couldn't answer.

"You need more proof? Sweetheart, I'll be glad to give it to you."

At her back, his hands found the catch of her bra, slid it open, then pushed the cups out of the way so that her breasts could spill into his hands. Willfully, possessively, his fingers moved over her heated flesh.

Whatever she was going to say transformed itself into a moan of pleasure. "Please."

"This? You want this?" he growled, his fingers cresting across the hard, aching tips, then catching them between thumb and forefinger to make her gasp with pleasure.

She should have been terrified by the sudden flare of passion, frightened of her own out-of-control need. Instead she gloried in its possession. Had she ever felt this weakness and power clashing and raging inside her so that there was only one thing in the world that mattered?

"Glenn...I want—"

"I know, sweetheart. I know," he answered, his hands on her hips pulling her hard against his taut flesh. He kissed her once more, then moved her backward toward the couch, her feet alternately sinking into the rug and crunching over plaster, the sharp contrast in sensation causing another kind of stimulation.

She could hear blood pounding in her ears. In the background, she vaguely heard something else—something she should pay attention to, she realized.

"Glenn."

"What?"

"Someone's coming up the steps."

He raised his head, listening, then swore under his breath as he took in her state of undress. "Can you...get into the bedroom?"

"Yes."

She stumbled away from the couch and crashed into a chair, but she made it to the other room as feet came thumping down the hall.

Flinging the door closed, she leaned against the barrier while she pulled her bra back into place and hooked it. Instead of pawing over the bed for her shirt, she tried to orient herself in the room and locate her suitcase. When she found it, she pulled out a top, and in moments she had it on.

Without bothering to find her shoes, she pulled open the door and stepped back into the sitting room.

A flashlight beam hit her in the face, and she threw up her arm to shield her eyes.

"Lower that," Glenn growled.

The light flicked away from her eyes, and she blinked, trying to clear her vision.

"What happened?" a new voice demanded. It was Claymore. The cavalry to the rescue—twenty minutes too late to save the maiden in distress. Or was that the wrong metaphor?

Two of his men stood behind him in the doorway, holding handguns.

"Someone tried to kill me," she said, surprised that her voice sounded so steady.

"Who?"

"If we knew, we'd be way ahead of the game," Glenn answered for her. "She called for help," he added, moving beside her and slipping a protective arm around her shoulder. "Nobody came!"

"We were a little busy."

"You mean you heard her and didn't respond?" Glenn growled.

"No. I didn't hear her," Claymore retorted. "I'll find out if anyone else did." Turning to Meg, he said, "Tell me what you know."

Before she could answer, Glenn gave her a gentle push on the shoulder. "Sit down."

As she sank into the couch cushion, she saw Claymore looking at them. Glenn might have moved away, but instead he stepped closer so that he could keep his hand on her shoulder, his steady gaze daring the other man to make any comments.

Claymore kept his face neutral. "How long have you been here?" he demanded.

"Ten, fifteen minutes," Glenn replied. "If I'd been in better shape, the assailant wouldn't have escaped. At least I knocked the gun out of his hand."

Claymore's eyes narrowed as he swung the light toward Glenn and gave him a closer inspection. Meg turned to do the same. For the first time she noticed the tear in his shirt and the bruise forming on his jaw.

"He hurt you!" she gasped.

"I'm fine."

"Where were you when the lights went out?" Claymore asked.

"In the lab," he said tersely.

"Which lab?"

"Biohazards level four."

Claymore whistled. "How did you get out?"

"With difficulty," Glenn growled. "And don't worry—I went through the detox procedure."

The way he said it sent a shiver skittering across Meg's skin. She was staring at Glenn when the room's lights flickered, then came back on with full power. At first, no one did anything but blink. When Meg's eyes had adjusted to the brightness, she found Claymore looking around the room, taking in the tipped furniture and the chunks of plasterboard and white powder littering the rug. In the middle of the mess she could see the place where she and Glenn had been facing each other, locked in a clinch. Flushing, she hoped the area didn't speak so eloquently to Claymore.

"You were going to tell me what happened," he snapped, his gaze returning to her so that she was sure he could see even more damning evidence on her face.

She cleared her throat. "Uh—you'd better get one of your men to turn off the water in the bathroom."

Claymore nodded at one of the guards.

"The floor's wet. Don't slip," she called after him as he started down the hall.

Under the security chief's scrutiny, she repeated her story, trying to put in as many details as possible.

"Once again, you've proved you're very resourceful," Claymore muttered when she'd finished.

"Coming from you, that doesn't sound like a compliment," she returned.

Glenn's hand tightened on her shoulder. "Yeah, well, she'd be dead if she weren't resourceful. And so would I, if she hadn't shouted a warning when she heard me in here. She drew his fire to save me."

When Claymore started to respond, Glenn plowed ahead. "Don't try to imply that she was working with the guy. If you look at the bathroom door, you'll know he wasn't here to deliver flowers."

Her gaze swung to him. He hadn't even seen the door, but he was reporting the damage as if he had. The knowledge that he'd taken her word for the gory details made a warm glow spread through her.

Claymore gave a tight nod. ''Right. And I'd like to know why.''

''So would I,'' Meg whispered.

They were all silent for several seconds, since none of them had an answer to the question.

Finally Claymore cleared his throat. ''We're ignoring the fact that there's a weapon around here somewhere.'' He nodded at both guards. ''See if you can find it. But don't get any fingerprints on it.''

The men set to work, but nothing turned up immediately.

''What about the lights?'' Glenn asked.

''Somebody did a job on the power plant, after making sure the emergency generators wouldn't function.''

''Well, I think we've told you what we can,'' Glenn said. ''Keep me informed on the progress of the investigation.''

''What about Ms. Wexler?''

''I'll take care of her,'' Glenn replied.

They continued to face each other, each undoubtedly wanting to say more. It was the security chief who turned and left, the remaining guard following.

Finally, Meg was alone with Glenn once more. When she turned expectantly toward him, he made himself busy surveying the room.

''Obviously you're in jeopardy here. If you could crawl through the space above the ceiling on this floor, somebody else could. So I'd like to move you where I know you'll be safe.''

''Where?''

''To my quarters.''

The look on her face had him adding quickly, ''It's a large apartment. We won't get in each other's way.''

''Why not?''

''Because what happened a few minutes ago shouldn't have.''

She managed to speak around the sudden tightness in her

throat. "You didn't want me?" she asked. "Or you don't trust me?"

He made a low sound of frustration. "If I didn't trust you, I wouldn't be bringing you to my apartment where you could stab me with a kitchen knife while I was sleeping. And of course I wanted you. I think that was pretty obvious. But—" He stopped and ran his hand through his hair. "We haven't known each other long enough."

"You don't make love on the first date?" she challenged.

"Yes, that's exactly what I do. I go off to some swinging-singles resort where I can have all the women I want. Then I come back here and return to work."

"And I don't measure up?"

He answered with a muttered curse. "Stop being ridiculous. You more than measure up. But I don't want some kind of quick fling with you."

"What *do* you want?" she whispered.

"I want to make love with you. But you don't remember your past. You might belong to someone else. You might be married. Getting involved with me wouldn't be fair to you."

"Which part are you worried about most?"

When he didn't answer, she held up her left hand, inspected the third finger. "No ring."

"You could have taken it off."

"Why? So I could seduce you?"

He grimaced. "That's not what I meant."

"What do you mean?"

"That we should back off before one of us gets hurt."

"Which one?"

"Either. What about the things you said to me after the polygraph?"

She shrugged. "You're the one who had it right before Claymore interrupted us," she went on. "The truth between us is how we feel—what we want. From the moment I saw you, I knew." She waited for him to admit that feelings went deeper than any facts.

The look on his face told her he didn't think it was that simple—and that he didn't know how to cope with what he was feeling.

"I'll get my stuff," she whispered. "If you haven't changed your mind about inviting me to your quarters."

"I haven't."

Unable to cope with the grim look on his face, she fled into the bedroom and grabbed her suitcase. Then she sloshed through the water in the bathroom to get her toilet articles, her mind churning.

He was right. From a practical point of view, he'd assessed the situation pretty accurately. But he'd also been right earlier, when he'd taken her in his arms and begun to make love to her.

Those charged moments of passion had changed everything. He might be hiding his feelings now, but when all the barriers had been down, he'd shown her how he really felt. She wanted him to finish what he'd started. She longed to give him the comfort of her body. And she wanted to take what he'd been offering.

She could see that arguing wasn't the way to get there, though. In fact, if she pushed him now, he might change his mind about letting her sleep anywhere near him. And she didn't want to risk that.

When she returned, he was standing and looking out the darkened window, his hands stiffly at his sides.

"All ready," she said in a chipper voice.

His look of relief at her change in attitude cut her to the bone, but she only gestured with her hand for him to lead the way. They set off down the corridor to another flight of steps, then up half a flight to another level.

"How do you find your way around here?" she asked as they descended.

"You get used to it."

He brought her to another part of the castle that was probably closer to the original than the guest quarters she'd just occupied. Unlocking a door, he ushered her into an-

other sitting room where the walls were dark paneling, the
windows narrow and arched. In sharp contrast, the furniture
was teak, with leather upholstery. Off the living room was
a kitchen and a dining alcove with a square table and four
chairs. It was all very neat and orderly, as if the person who
lived here was hardly home, she decided as she set her
suitcase by the door.

"Did you have dinner?"

She shook her head.

"I can have some food sent up."

"Can we fix something here?"

He laughed. "I'm not much of a cook. But I get the
kitchen to freeze me some choice stuff. I think I've got
some beef-and-vegetable soup. Or some macaroni and
cheese."

Though his notion of "choice" didn't exactly match
hers, food wasn't her primary interest at the moment.
"Beef-and-vegetable soup," she said.

He rummaged in the freezer section of the refrigerator,
pulled out a plastic carton, and set it in the microwave.

"What would you like to drink?"

"Something hot might take the chill off," she replied,
sitting down at the table.

He gave her a look that told her he was trying to decide
if she was referring to more than just the air temperature.

Instead of enlightening him, she folded her hands and
looked down at them, while he ran water in a kettle and set
it on a burner.

When the bell on the microwave rang, he dished the soup
into two bowls. She let him fix the meal, let him get comfortable in his own surroundings—even though watching
the play of muscles in his arms and back made her remember the feel of his body under her hands as it responded to
her touch.

If he was having similar thoughts, he hid them pretty
well, she mused as she watched him begin eating with deep
concentration.

She tried the same tactic and even choked down a few spoonfuls of soup before giving up the pretense.

"I have to go back to the lab," he said when he'd managed to down about half his meal.

"Can't you give yourself a rest?"

"I was in the middle of a...crucial experiment. It was probably ruined when the electricity went off. I want to find out what happened."

"I'm sorry. I shouldn't have kept you away so long," she said stiffly.

"It was my decision. I wanted to make sure you were all right."

"I am. Physically." She gave a little shrug. "Emotionally, I'm on a roller coaster."

"I know the feeling," he muttered as he took a step away from the table and walked down a short hall. "I have to make a couple of calls. I'll be back in a few minutes."

She nodded.

When he returned, he was strapping on a holster and pistol.

"I haven't seen you wear a gun," she said.

"I've made it a point not to. Now—" he shrugged "—it seems prudent."

"Yes."

He carried another holster and gun, which he held out toward her. "Can you handle this?"

She stared at him, understanding the significance of the offer. To cover her reaction, she looked down at the weapon, checked it. It didn't feel as good in her hand as the rifle, but she was pretty sure she could fire it.

"Did you clear this with Claymore?" she asked.

"No. It's my decision. The man who came to your room was out to kill you. I won't leave you defenseless."

"Thank you," she whispered. "But giving me a gun creates other problems. What if I suddenly get my memory back and realize I was sent here to kill you?" She winced as she said it, hoping it wasn't true.

"I'm willing to take the chance," he answered, his voice calm and steady. They stared at each other, and she knew he had made the decision to trust her with his life. That had to count for a lot. The trouble was, he wasn't willing to risk his heart.

"I arranged to have guards posted outside," he told her. "But the door will be unlocked. I'd appreciate it if you stay in here. The men are pretty jumpy."

"I understand," she replied, remembering the way they had looked at her. Some of them thought she had brought trouble to Castle Phoenix. They might be right.

There was a knock at the door. A voice on the other side said, "Sir!"

"Thank you," Glenn called, then said to Meg, "That's your guard. I'd better leave."

"Be careful."

"Yes."

She wanted to hold him there—for just a little while longer. Instead she stayed where she was at the table, watching him walk out the door, leaving her alone again.

BLAKE CLAYMORE OPENED the top drawer of his locked file cabinet and removed the seven folders that he'd put there a week ago—before Meg Wexler had arrived. They were the personnel records of Chuck Fogerty, Steward Mac-Arthur, Bill Gady, Edmond Sparks, Duncan Catlan, James Oakland and Bruce Erdman. He knew all of them had been mouthing off about the discipline. And all of them were complaining about the extra patrol hours everybody was working because of Ms. Wexler. Maybe one of them had been unhappy enough to try and solve the problem by taking her out.

In Blake's opinion, it was too bad the guy hadn't succeeded in eliminating her, if that was what he'd been trying to do. She was dangerous. He wasn't sure yet what she was up to, or how she was causing the problems that had started with her arrival. But he was willing to bet the incidents—

from the attack to the druggings—were related and all tied to her. Even if they weren't, Glenn was entirely too wound up with the woman for his own good. He'd bought her story about a mysterious attacker. For all they knew, *she* could have put the bullets in the door.

Maybe Blake couldn't make his friend see reason. But he could maintain discipline at Castle Phoenix. Shuffling the folders, he opened each one and studied the contents. Catlan was the most recent addition to the security staff. He'd passed his psychological profile and come with a recommendation from Randolph Security, a good outfit. But maybe he wouldn't have been hired if there'd been some better candidates.

Oakland and Erdman had been around since the beginning, and they'd re-upped. Perhaps he shouldn't have pressured them to stay, since there were a lot of built-in stress factors associated with working here. But he'd given them a bonus for signing on again because finding the right kind of guy wasn't all that easy. They had to be dedicated. They had to be loyal. And they had to cut themselves off from friends and family for long stretches of time. That was a lot to ask.

Blake opened more folders, continuing with his ruthless assessment. Fogerty and Sparks had probably been bad choices from the beginning. They were too violent and too impulsive—even though they'd both gotten high marks from one of his old army buddies.

That left MacArthur and Gady. There was nothing Blake could put his finger on. Yet they'd been part of the group that congregated to complain when they weren't busy.

Stacking the folders, he pulled out the duty sheets and studied the entries. The dog could have been drugged anytime yesterday afternoon. But this evening the lights had gone off at exactly 7:45 p.m. MacArthur, Oakland and Catlan had all been on duty when that had occurred and when someone had subsequently attacked Ms. Wexler. None had been missing from their posts. So that let them off the hook.

His eyes narrowed as he shuffled the remaining folders. Gady, Sparks, Erdman and Fogerty. He'd made sure they were all working tonight. In a few minutes they'd be getting off and heading for the mess hall.

If there was a traitor in the lot, it was his damn fault. He'd signed off on all these men. Now he was going to flush the bastard out.

Pushing his chair back with a savage swipe of his hands, he rose, picked up the folders and locked them back in the drawer. Time to put a very dangerous plan into action.

GLENN STOPPED TO GIVE the guards instructions, then walked stiffly down the hall. Everything he had said to Meg was the truth, but it wasn't exactly the whole truth. He had said it wasn't fair to make love to her when she might belong to someone else. And that possibility was gnawing at him. He wanted to claim her as his own, but that meant more than finding out the facts of her past.

To keep things honest, he would have to tell her about himself, as well—about what he'd done before resigning his commission. And he didn't want to face the look in her eyes when she found out he wasn't Mr. Nice Guy.

Then there was the gun he'd just given her. Blake would have a cow if he knew. So would Hal, for that matter. But Glenn didn't give a damn what they thought about that. It was enough that he was carrying a weapon of his own. He'd vowed not to live his life with a holster strapped to his waist. Blake would notice that he'd been pushed into violating his principles again.

As he took the stairs to the office wing, he silently amended the opinion. He did care what Blake and Hal thought about his decision to give Meg a weapon—but not enough to change his mind.

He stopped short when he saw Dylan and one of the specially trained technicians inspecting the isolation suit he'd worn.

"I was going to take care of that," he said, as he stepped into the dressing area.

"I know," his friend answered. "But I thought I could handle it for you. I checked out the lab. Some of the virus samples are still alive."

"But now we have no way of knowing what killed them," Glenn finished for him. "The antidote or the drop in temperature when the heat lamps went off."

Dylan nodded. "Sorry."

"I can set it up again," he said wearily.

"I already have."

"Fast work." Glenn swallowed. "Thanks."

"I know what this means to you—and to the men from Operation Clean Sweep."

"Yeah." He paused, then plowed ahead with what had been on his mind since the power failure. "And you've got my notes. If something happened to me, you could finish the project."

Dylan's head jerked up. "Nothing's going to happen to you."

"We both know it almost did—when the lights went off, and I was trapped in the lab like a rat."

"Yeah."

"The way things are shaping up—something else could go wrong."

"Blake's working on it."

"Blake doesn't have a clue," Glenn growled. "So from now on, we're instituting new procedures. You and I will not go into the lab at the same time. And we will always have a backup working with us or stationed outside."

"Okay."

"I'll take the first shift," Glenn said. "You make a tour of the other labs and see that all our moneymaking schemes are still on track."

Dylan gave him a considering look. "Don't push too hard."

"I—"

"Cut the crap," his friend snapped. "I can tell from your face what you have planned. You're going to stay down here until you're ready to drop—which is hazardous to your health. You make a mistake in there, and you can die a very nasty death. In fact, you make a mistake, and you can spread the K-007 plague to every man and woman at Castle Phoenix. So I'm pulling rank and giving you a direct order. No more than two hours in this environment. Tops."

"Three," Glenn countered.

Dylan gave him a hard look, then turned and left the lab.

MEG WALKED RESTLESSLY around the apartment, touching furniture, picking up books, trying to get closer to Glenn through his environment. After half an hour, she decided it was a lost cause, since she might as well have been prowling around a motel room. There were no knickknacks, no pictures, no awards, no favorite novels. Apparently he read medical textbooks and journals for relaxation. The only personal information she gleaned was that he liked classical music. At least she found a pretty extensive library of CDs representing the great composers.

When she got to his bed, she paused, staring down at the neatly smoothed burgundy comforter. He hadn't told her where she was going to sleep. Maybe he'd planned on giving her the bedroom.

Easing onto the mattress, she rested her head against the pillow, then closed her eyes, trying to relax. But the bed carried his scent—the clean masculine smell of his body mixed with the soap and aftershave she'd come to associate with him. It stirred her senses, brought back the recent scene in the guest quarters. Her nerve endings tingled—especially certain intimate ones. And she knew she would never be able to relax if she stayed here. So she grabbed one of the extra pillows and lay down on the couch—with the gun beside her on the end table.

The weapon gave her a strange mixture of anxiety and comfort as she looked around the shadowy room. She

couldn't turn off all the lights, though. Two were still burning—in the hall and the bathroom—when she fell asleep.

BY PUSHING, GLENN GOT what he needed to get done in
two hours and grudgingly admitted that the experiment was
back on track. After going through the decontamination
procedures, he thought about falling into bed.

But Meg was in his apartment. So he got dressed again
and headed for his office. Unlocking the door, he checked
the answering machine hooked to his special line, a number
that gave the men from Operation Clean Sweep direct access to him, whenever they felt the need to call.

Sometimes they called to find out how he was doing with
the K-007 project. Sometimes they told him about their
symptoms and what their doctors were doing for them.
Against his better judgment, Glenn had let himself get involved in suggesting treatment strategies, although he knew
that any medication presently available was only a stopgap
measure.

Often the messages only jacked up his frustration level
and jabbed at his guilt. Tonight the red light wasn't quite
so daunting—until he pressed the play button and found
that the call was from Tommy Faulkner. Tommy had been
the Operation Clean Sweep team leader and a good friend.
Now he was one of the most urgent cases.

Sinking into the desk chair, Glenn listened to the message, which included a long, rambling report of Tommy's
symptoms and a vague reference to his sister. Apparently
he was worried about her since she'd gone out of town and
he didn't know how to get in touch with her. That was
typical of the guys. They called with problems that had
nothing to do with the operation and expected Glenn's
help—which he gave when he could.

He glanced at his watch. If he called Tommy tonight,
he'd probably wake him up. Tomorrow he'd get in touch
with him and see if the sister had turned up. If she hadn't,
he'd find out where she worked and see what they knew.

Chapter Ten

Blake stood in the mess-hall doorway watching the small group of men who had just gotten off the evening shift. Fogerty glanced up, saw him looking in their direction, and said something quick and low. The conversation died immediately.

When had he gotten to be the enemy? Blake wondered. Was he riding the men too hard? Or were they all just going through a difficult period? Maybe he was the one who should give the job a rest for a while. Indulge in some heavy R and R. The only problem was, he couldn't leave Glenn in the lurch, not when he was so close to a breakthrough on the K-007 problem.

Blake got himself a cup of coffee from the dispenser, then added cream and sugar, knowing the guys were waiting for him to leave so they could relax again.

Instead he brought his cup to the end of the table. Gady and Sparks stiffened. Erdman stayed elaborately casual. Fogerty pulled out a metal file and began using the end to clean his nails.

"How's it going?" Blake asked.

"Fine," everyone answered.

"Nothing unusual?"

There was a chorus of denials.

"Good," he replied, taking a sip of his coffee, knowing

some of them were counting the seconds until he cleared out again.

"Did anyone get a chance to check the light box up on Little Falls Summit—the one that was giving us trouble?" he asked.

"That wasn't part of the assignment," Erdman said firmly.

Blake snapped his fingers. "Right. Yeah. I forgot to put it on the list."

"Then maybe you should check it yourself."

To hide his elation, Blake scowled, waited a beat, pretending to consider. "Okay, I need to stretch my legs. I guess I'll take care of it myself as soon as there's enough natural light outside to see what I'm doing."

He finished the coffee, then stood and wished them a good-night as he headed back to his quarters, wondering which one of them was going to take the bait.

THE SOUND OF THE LOCK turning brought Meg to instant alertness.

Her eyes blinked open and she lay staring toward the door, calculating the seconds it would take her to reach the gun.

A large shadow entered the apartment, but she recognized Glenn in the semidarkness, and the rigidity left her body. He looked totally exhausted, she thought, as she took in the slump of his shoulders. What time was it? How long had he been up?

He stayed where he was, his eyes scanning the room until he found her on the couch, then quietly crossed the rug. Keeping her breath even and her eyes shaded by her lashes, she watched him watching her.

"Meg," he said, his voice so low that she wasn't positive if she'd really heard him or imagined it.

She ached to ask what he had intended to say. Instead she silently closed her fingers over the edge of a sofa cushion as he turned and walked down the hall. When he came back, he'd taken off his holster and revolver.

Crossing to the kitchen area, he opened the refrigerator, took out a carton of milk and got down a glass from the cupboard. Instead of pouring the milk, he simply stood there staring at it.

Leaning against the counter, he supported the weight of his upper body on his elbows while he cradled his head in his hands. He looked so totally worn-out and so totally daunted that she felt her heart turn over.

"Glenn," she called softly so as not to startle him as she climbed off the couch.

Instantly he straightened. Before he could move out of reach, she came up behind him, slipping her arms around his waist as she pressed her face against his back.

"Bad?" she asked softly, moving her cheek against the knit fabric of his shirt, breathing deeply.

"Bad enough."

She ran her fingers over his rigid muscles, feeling the tension and the strength. His shoulders were broad, but not broad enough for the weight of his burden—which she sensed was more than any human being should have to endure.

"Tell me about it," she urged, gripping him with gentle pressure, trying to make him understand with her voice, with her posture, with her touch, that it was safe to entrust her with his secrets.

"It's not your problem." His answer was automatic, and she knew he wasn't accustomed to reaching out for help.

"I know," she murmured. "But I think you'll feel better if you let me listen. Maybe it's not as bad as you think."

His reply was a brittle laugh.

"Don't."

For an endless moment, he didn't speak. Then she felt him shift, heard him sigh deeply. "I guess I might as well get it over with."

"It's not supposed to be a punishment."

"Yeah." He pushed away from the counter, opened another cabinet and took out a bottle of Scotch. Unscrewing the cap, he sloshed some of the amber liquid into the glass he had intended for the milk and took a quick swallow, then grimaced.

"Does that help?" she asked.

"Not really. I'm just stalling."

Taking her hand, he led her to the couch. She might have turned on some lights, but she knew he'd prefer the dark.

He set the glass on the coffee table and stretched out his long legs, resting them on its flat surface. She scooted closer to him, turning so that her knees were tucked under her and her head was against his shoulder. His hand moved to her hair, sifting through the strands, and she wondered if he had changed his mind about telling her anything.

Finally, he began to speak in a gritty voice. "We can start with the standard war criminal's defense—'I was just following orders.'"

"Were you?"

"In the beginning. Down the line, when I stole a deadly biological-weapons agent from a top-secret government laboratory, things got a little more complicated," he said.

She tried not to react, tried to let him say what he had to say, yet she couldn't prevent her body from stiffening.

"That's what I've got down in the level-four biohazards lab. I call it K-007. My little sick joke. The James Bond virus. Licensed to kill. A drop of the stuff would wipe out everybody at Castle Phoenix."

She gave a little nod, knowing he was going for shock value. "You want me to ask why you stole it?"

"That's the easy part," he replied. "See, the army found out that a certain African dictator was making the stuff, and they wanted to shut down the operation. So they sent in a special forces team to neutralize the laboratory. I was the physician assigned to review the data and make a judgment about whether to authorize the mission. One thing I had to evaluate was the level of safety for our men."

"And you cleared them for the mission—based on the facts you had," she guessed.

"I thought they could get in and out of there with no risk to their health. What I didn't know was that the army had an agenda besides shutting down the lab. Their top priority was to take home a sample of the stuff—so they could test its weapons potential."

Meg sucked in a sharp breath.

"I keep wondering what I would have done if I'd known in advance about the plan to help ourselves to the virus. Would I have gone along with the generals, or would I have tried to stop it?" He grimaced and went on. "Six months later, the members of the team who brought it back all started exhibiting a variety of strange neurological symptoms."

The self-reproach in his voice made her reach up and capture his hand. Folding his fingers around hers, she pressed his knuckles against her cheek. "The same illness?" she asked.

He moved his hand to her lips, stroking their softness for a moment before continuing. "I think it's the same illness, but the toxin attacks various parts of the body. The men were all given medical discharges, and they're all eligible for care at Veterans hospitals. But the doctors there can't really treat the illness because there's no antidote, and since the U.S. Army doesn't officially acknowledge stealing the K-007, they aren't working on a cure."

"But you are," Meg finished for him. "That's why you stole the virus from the army, so you could experiment with it."

"Yeah. I had to, because I couldn't grow any usable samples from the men. It's like the AIDS virus—only more tricky because it's genetically engineered. It hides in the DNA of the cells where you can't get at it. I resigned my commission so I could devote full time to research here. All the moneymaking medical projects we have go to pay for my K-007 experiments. Hal kicked in a lot of the initial investment. I'd like to pay him back, but we both know he won't live to see any profits."

"And the blackout today set back your progress with the K-007."

"I was testing an antidote on tissue samples. They died because the temperature in the growing area dropped dramatically."

"Don't beat up on yourself like this," she whispered.

He turned toward her, his eyes fierce. "If I hadn't sent those men in the first place, they wouldn't be sick."

"*You* didn't send them."

"I gave the approval."

"And you'd change places with any one of them if you could."

"Yes," he growled.

"Oh, Glenn, they need you. Working yourself to death isn't going to help them. Denying yourself any pleasure in life isn't going to help them. Locking yourself away like the beast in the enchanted castle isn't going to help them."

"How can I enjoy anything when I know how much they're suffering?"

"You can make some sort of balance in your life so you don't burn yourself out."

"It doesn't matter if I burn out. Dylan Ryder can finish for me. He knows as much about the project as I do."

"No."

"No, what?"

"The project needs *you*," she said with conviction. "Without you, it wouldn't exist. You looked at the data from every angle. You asked questions. You made careful judgments. And when you found out what happened to the men, you pushed to start a treatment program within the army."

His eyes widened, and he literally reared back. "How the hell do you know all that?"

Quickly she reached out a hand and gripped his arm. "I

didn't know for sure. I was making educated guesses based on what I've learned about your character.''

He relaxed a fraction, but the tension etched into the lines of his face was more than she could bear. "Did you think that if you told me your secrets, it would drive me away?" she asked softly.

He could only answer with a tight nod.

"You were absolutely wrong." Reaching up, she brought his mouth down to hers.

He fought against what he wanted for a few more heart-beats, then made a sound of surrender deep in his throat as her lips began to move against his, telling him without words how she felt about him now that he had made his terrible confession.

If she had wanted him before, it was nothing compared to now—knowing how much he needed her.

"I have no right to ask for anything from you," he gasped out when he'd finally wrenched his mouth away from hers.

She shook her head, her eyes soft and warm. "You're not asking for anything I don't want to give freely."

"But you're not in a position to make decisions."

She laughed softly. "I think I'm in a pretty good position. Or I will be, if I just lie back on this couch and bring you with me." Her arms came up to his shoulders, tugging.

He resisted the pull. "Be serious."

She looked steadily into his eyes. "I am serious. I could tell you I've never been more serious in my life, but I wouldn't know it was true. What I do know is that I've been drawn to you since I opened my eyes and found you standing over me with a look on your face that told me how much you cared. And the better I've gotten to know you, the more I've wanted to be closer to you. That's simply an impartial opinion from a woman who'd never heard of your background—a woman who drew her conclusions from direct observation."

"Lord, Meg, you make me sound like a saint."

"You're no saint. You're a man—who needs the same things other people need. And I'm a woman who wants you to make love with me."

"You're sure?"

"If you keep turning me down, I'm going to think there's something wrong with me."

"Never." He reached for her, brought his lips back to hers, slanting his mouth to get a deeper taste of her.

When he lifted his head, they were both breathing in hard, uneven gasps.

"Promise me we're not going to stop this time," she whispered.

He laughed. "You drive a hard bargain."

"Well, then, there's more."

When he looked at her inquiringly, she smiled. "I want to do this right. There's a nice big bed in your bedroom, where I think we'd be a lot more comfortable than on this couch."

He gave her a long look. Then, standing, he pulled her to her feet. As if he were afraid she'd change her mind, he led her quickly down the hall and into the bedroom, leaving the door open so that the light she'd left on earlier gave them enough illumination to see each other.

She followed him with confidence. This was what she'd said she wanted. It *was* what she wanted. But when they reached the side of the bed, she couldn't keep her nerves from buzzing. And when he pulled her into his arms and kissed her with what she recognized as unleashed hunger, she felt her body stiffen. As he became aware of her reaction, he eased away, his eyes questioning.

His voice was thick when he spoke. "We don't have to—"

"I want to," she answered before he could finish. Tipping her head up, she caught his gaze with hers. "But...one of the things I can't remember is what it's like to be intimate with a man." She made an exasperated face—half self-mocking, half serious. "I don't even know if I'm supposed to take my clothes off or if you're supposed to do it.''

His eyes had turned an intense liquid blue as he gazed down at her, then he lifted his hand and stroked his finger across her cheek. ''You don't remember this, but you're sure you want to do it with me?''

''Yes,'' she said, hearing the thin, reedy timbre of her voice. Because it didn't sound very convincing, she slid her arms around him, pulling his body tightly against hers so that she could feel the thumping of his heart and the un-mistakable pressure of his erection. This was so elemental, such a basic part of loving and being loved. Yet no mem-ories came to her. And that was good, wasn't it? Because she ached to belong only to this man.

He crooked his finger under her chin, tipping her face up so that she couldn't hide from him—or from herself.

''What am I going to do with you?'' he whispered.

''I think you know. At least I hope you do. Because if neither one of us remembers how to do this—then we're in serious trouble,'' she replied, making it sound like a chal-lenge.

To her relief, he took it that way.

''I think you're in good hands,'' he growled, his fingers moving in a sensual pattern across her back as his mouth covered hers, demonstrating his expertise with a kiss that had her blood singing. As she clung to him for support, his lips traveled lower, teasing her neck, her collarbone, the V of flesh at the neckline of her knit top.

But before going any further, he turned toward the closet where he searched for something in a suitcase. When he came back, he set a small box on the bedside table. Con-traceptives.

If she wanted him to stop, this was the time to tell him. Instead, she gave him a cocky grin.

''I guess it doesn't matter who takes my clothes off, does it? Just so we both end up naked.'' Pulling her top over her head, she tossed it away. Before she lost her nerve, she unhooked her bra and shucked it.

Fighting the feeling of vulnerability that swept over her, she stood tall, watching him take the measure of her size and shape.

"You're magnificent," he said thickly, his gaze on her as he discarded his own shirt.

"So are you," she replied, taking in the muscular contours of his chest, accented with a broad pattern of dark hair.

"Come here."

Was he still waiting for her to prove something—to both of them? Her eyes locked with his, and she took a step forward. With a growl of satisfaction, he pulled her to him. The feel of his hair-roughened skin against her breasts had her whimpering with pleasure. His hand moved between them, finding the snap of her slacks, opening it so he could skim them and her panties down her legs. Then the rest of his clothes were out of the way as well, and she could move her naked legs against his.

When she swayed on her feet, he eased them toward the bed, pulling aside the covers so they could slip between the sheets.

He looked slightly dazed, as if he couldn't believe she was really here—hot and willing in his bed.

But she was. Very hot and very willing. Caught by the same giddy sense of wonder, she wrapped her arms around his neck.

"You're shaking," he growled.

"You, too."

"I want—"

She managed a tiny laugh. "I think you want to stamp your brand on me."

"Oh yeah."

Whatever else she might have said turned into a long sigh of pleasure as his hands found her breasts, shaping them to his touch before capturing the hardened centers between his thumbs and fingers, drawing another exclamation from her.

He followed the caress with his lips, and she stared down in a daze at the top of his dark head, unable to quite believe that anything could feel so good. When he added his tongue and teeth to the caress, she discovered there was more—much more. And she knew that whatever she might have experienced with another lover, this man reduced any past encounters to insignificance.

He rolled her onto her back, and she reached to stroke his dark hair away from his forehead.

"I think you already have," she whispered, gazing into his smoky eyes.

"What?"

"Burned your brand into my flesh."

"We'll see about that," he promised, his hands moving over her, discovering places that brought pleasure—and need.

When he found the moist, throbbing center of her, all she could do was close her eyes and cling to him.

He showed her more, and then more, so that every cell of her being seemed to glow with a heat that turned from red to white-hot.

"Please," she begged. "Please. Don't make me wait any longer."

"No." He fumbled for the box on the bedside table, readied himself, then moved over her, his legs opening hers, the hard shaft of his erection stroking against her, driving her to a new level of desire. Then his hands cupped her hips, lifting her as he changed the angle of contact and drove forward—his body staking its claim on hers.

In one blinding instant, pleasure turned to pain. A scream ripped from her throat even as she tried to twist away.

"God, Meg. Oh, God," he gasped, going absolutely still above her.

Her eyes blinked open, and she stared up at him, seeing the tension and regret etched into his features. She knew he was struggling not to move, struggling not to hurt her again. "I'm sorry. I didn't know."

When he tried to pull away, her arms tightened around him, holding him where he was. "Oh, Glenn. Of course, you didn't know. *I* didn't know," she soothed, trying to comfort him, even as she struggled to cope with her own shock—and elation. She'd been a virgin. He was the first man she'd wanted to do this with. No wonder she'd had no memory of making love.

"But…"

She moved her lips against his face, kept her arms where they were binding him to her. "Glenn Bridgman, if you stop now, I'll never forgive you."

The look in his eyes took her breath away. "Meg," he whispered again. She felt some of the awful tension seep out of him as he began to kiss her, softly, tenderly. Shifting slightly, he found her breast with his fingers, caressing her, rekindling the banked fires.

When he moved his hips it was slowly, carefully, watching her face to make sure he wasn't hurting her again.

"How are you?"

"Good." Then, "A lot more than good."

Quickly he brought her back to the aching pinnacle of need where she'd been before. Then he carried her higher, further, until her hips were moving frantically against his and she was begging him to release her from the unbearable tension. His hand slipped between them again, stroking, pressing, bringing her to flashpoint.

A deep, throaty moan welled from the depths of her soul as an explosion of pleasure tore through her.

He gasped her name as his body convulsed above hers, and she held tightly to his shoulders, claiming him as her own for this night and forever.

When he moved to her side, she snuggled against him, drifting as her hands stroked tenderly over his slick skin.

"I—" he started to say.

She finished for him. "You wouldn't have done that if you'd known. Thank God you didn't know!"

He swore under his breath.

"You didn't like it?"

"Get serious!"

She laughed softly. "The man has such a poetic way with words." Then she did get serious. "Don't spoil my euphoria by acting like it was a mistake."

"It was the best thing that's happened to me in a long time."

Rolling onto her stomach, she propped herself up and looked down at him, trying to keep her expression serious but ending up by grinning. "At least we settled one important issue. We know I'm not married—or seriously dating anyone else."

"Yes," he breathed.

"Does that make you feel any better?"

"Yes."

"Good." She snuggled down again and closed her eyes, exhausted, triumphant and deeply contented.

Chapter Eleven

Meg woke in the dark, in the grip of sheer panic, a sheen of perspiration covering her skin. Her hands pressed against the mattress and she struggled for calm, trying to banish the nightmare that had awakened her. Although it was impossible to block the images, her breathing gradually returned to normal, and her heart stopped threatening to pound its way through her chest.

Quietly she swiveled her head and looked at Glenn—thankful that her panic hadn't transmitted itself to him.

Inching to the side of the bed, she slipped from under the warmth of the covers, crossed to the closet and grabbed the first thing she found to cover her nakedness. It was one of Glenn's shirts and miles too big. But with the sleeves rolled up, it served the purpose.

In the bathroom, she gulped a glass of water and ran a towel across her damp face, then moved to the window and stood looking at the spotlights illuminating the gray walls of the castle.

She wasn't sure how long she'd been standing there when a noise behind made her body go rigid. Whirling, she found Glenn crossing the carpet toward her—naked and formidable. And she couldn't repress a little shiver as he approached. To hide the reaction, she rubbed her hands along her arms as if trying to warm herself.

Though his face was in shadow, she knew that he was watching her carefully. "What's wrong?"

She shrugged. "Nothing."

"You remembered why you came here." He answered his own question in a gritty voice, and she knew he had picked up on her disquiet—but had drawn the wrong conclusions.

"No."

"But you felt the need to get out of bed—to get away from me."

"No!" she protested, even as she struggled against a kind of sick disloyalty. Pivoting toward him, she wrapped her arms around his waist and pressed her face tightly to his chest. "No."

She could feel the beating of his heart, the pace faster than normal. "I had a nightmare. It woke me up, and I needed a drink of water. Then I thought I'd wake you if I got back into bed."

"Nice try."

"It was just a dream."

"About what?"

She didn't want to tell him, but she sensed she was only making things worse by resisting his questions. "A man was chasing me across wide green lawns—with a castle in the background."

"The man who attacked you?"

"At first I didn't know who it was. I was just trying to get away. I was running and running, looking for you. Finally I saw you near the garage and I knew I was safe." She stopped, swallowed hard.

"And?"

She sighed. "I don't know. Something made me look back, at the man who was chasing me. And it was you, too," she finished with a hitch in her voice.

He didn't move away, but he shifted his body, staring over her shoulder into the night. "I guess we can figure out what it means," he said, his voice as flat as glass. "Even if you don't know why you came here, your subconscious is trying to let you know you're supposed to be afraid of me.''

"No!''

"Do you have a better explanation?'' he demanded.

"Glenn, don't jump to conclusions. I can't control my dreams, and I can't tell you where they come from.''

"Nightmares come from hidden fears and concerns. A child might dream that his parents have driven away from Aunt Sally's and left him there. That's because he's subconsciously afraid it might happen.''

"Are you playing psychiatrist?''

"It was part of my medical training,'' he countered.

"What did you have—one course in psychiatry?''

Though he shrugged, she knew she had hit the mark. Still, the victory was hollow. Taking him by the shoulders, she raised her eyes to his. "We don't know what my dreams mean. But we can make other inferences. Obviously I'm a woman who's very cautious about forming relationships with men. I've finally—'' She stopped, afraid to give too much away, yet desperate to make him understand how deep her feelings went. Risking everything, she went on. "I've finally fallen in love with someone wonderful, and I'm afraid that it's all going to blow up in my face. Like, maybe when you find out who I really am, you won't want me.''

When she stopped, there was absolute silence in the room. She stood there with her heart hammering, waiting for him to speak. When he didn't, she let her hands drop to her sides and took a step back.

Before she could get away, his muscular arms caught her and pulled her against his body, holding her so tightly that she had to struggle to suck in a full breath.

"Meg,'' he growled. "Don't you know I started falling under your spell that first night I took care of you in the medical wing? God knows, I fought it.''

"I know.''

"Fighting it didn't stop me from loving you." He swallowed hard. "I didn't have the guts to tell you. That's why I was glad to have excuses to stay away from you. Like the lab experiment." His hands stroked possessively over her back and shoulders, pulling aside the collar of his shirt so he could touch her naked flesh.

"You didn't trust me."

"I couldn't afford to!"

"I understand that. Thank you for trusting me now," she breathed, awed by the implications.

"Maybe it's too late. Maybe it was always too late."

"Don't say that. Our situation is complicated. But it's not impossible," she insisted. "If two people love each other, they can work it out."

"How?" He gave a short bark of a laugh. "Nobody is more cautious about relationships than I am. I've felt I couldn't have a personal life until I solved the problem with K-007. Then you showed up here—such a strange combination of strength and vulnerability, questions and wisdom. You were like no one I had ever met. And all the walls I'd built around myself—all my defenses—came tumbling down. Do you know how much that frightens me?" he asked in a tight voice.

"I think so. You're a man who needs to know he's in control. And there's no way to control this situation."

"I want to hold on to you—forever. I keep thinking that I won't be allowed to keep you." She heard him swallow again. "That something terrible will happen—that you'll wake up and realize this was all a mistake."

"Glenn, I'll always be here for you," she said, giving him the only answer she could.

"You can't know that. You have another life—somewhere." His hands clenched her shoulders. "Worse, you don't know what our relationship was supposed to be. You don't know who you are or why you came to my castle. Suppose we're sworn enemies?"

"How could we be, when...when we love each other?"

He ran a hand through his hair. "I don't know. That's the worst part—I don't know."

She had no answers to give him. All she could do was lift her head, find his mouth with hers.

He made a low sound of need as his lips began to move over hers and his hands began to stroke her body. When he pushed the shirt out of the way and cupped her breasts, she arched into his caress, wordlessly telling him how his touch affected her.

They cleaved to each other, ravenously taking and giving everything there was to give.

Swinging her into his arms, he carried her back to the bed. When he lowered her to the mattress and covered her body with his, she locked her arms around him and held tight—as if she could bind him to herself for all time by the physical act of making love.

They made love fiercely, passionately, desperately. But when it was over and they lay panting in each other's arms, she knew that they hadn't solved their basic problem. Though they might love each other, there was no way to deal with the unknown future—until it reached out and grabbed them.

BLAKE CAREFULLY CHECKED his Beretta. He also checked the special equipment in his pack. Then he strode out of his quarters and down the still-darkened corridor. He could have stopped in the mess hall for a cup of coffee, but he knew his face would give him away if any of the men he'd talked to last night were waiting for him. So he went directly to the main door of the staff quarters.

It was the end of the night shift, and the guard at the door snapped to alertness as he saw the security chief coming.

"Sir."

Blake acknowledged the terse greeting and strode through the door.

Outside, the sun was just a promise behind the wall of

eastern mountains. He turned in the opposite direction and started for Little Falls Summit, where he'd already been the day before, making preparations.

Resisting the urge to glance behind him, he walked resolutely forward. Yet his ears strained for any hint that he was being followed. He kept imagining a target pinned to the back of his jacket, and his body jerking as a bullet tore through his flesh.

But it wouldn't happen within sight of Castle Phoenix, he told himself. Whoever was out to get him wouldn't risk a shot where he could get caught.

Of course, his speculations could be all wrong, he suddenly realized. It might not be one of the overt troublemakers. There could be a mole who'd slipped through the security checks and gotten himself on staff. In that case, he might not want to give himself away by drilling a hole in the security chief's back.

Blake gave a mirthless laugh. He'd thought he was walking into certain ambush. But maybe it wasn't going to happen—which put him in the strange position of hoping somebody really was going to try and nail him when he rounded the first bend in the trail—or the second.

THE SHRILL RINGING OF THE phone penetrated Meg's sleep. Glenn's body was already shifting as he reached across her and snatched up the receiver.

This time through the window she could see streaks of dawn tinting the sky a brilliant pink.

"Bridgman." After listening for several seconds, she heard him make an angry exclamation. "That was taking a pretty big risk," he growled.

The person on the other end of the line kept talking, with Glenn's shoulders getting more and more tense as he asked brief questions and listened to the answers.

Meg's own anxiety level escalated as she did her best to interpret what she could hear. When Glenn hung up, she looked at him questioningly. "Who was that?" she asked, pretty sure she could guess the answer.

"Blake." He confirmed her guess. "He wants both of us to come to the security center."

Even though she'd been mentally preparing for some new revelation, Meg felt every muscle in her body go rigid. "He's dug up something about me?"

"No. He thinks he's captured the man who attacked you last night. He wants you to see if you can make an identification."

She forced her voice to steadiness. "How did he capture him?"

"He suspected that one of his own men was out to get him, so he set up a situation where the guy would come after him."

Meg tried to read between the lines. "He put himself in danger?" she asked, no longer able to keep a quaver out of her voice. "For me?"

"For the project," Glenn corrected.

Right. The project. How silly of her.

When she started to ask another question, he waved her to silence. "We're wasting time. There's another bathroom down the hall. See how fast you can get ready."

She gave him a quick nod, taking in the tightness of his jaw as he stood and started for the door. In the few minutes he'd been on the phone, she'd sensed him withdrawing from her.

And he had just walked out of the room as if the night before had never happened—save for the box of condoms that was still sitting on the bedside table. Quickly she stuffed them into the drawer, lest the orderly or whoever took care of his room found them. Then another thought struck her, and she pulled back the covers. A red stain marred the white bottom sheet.

Her face flaming, she was stripping away the evidence when a hand covered hers. Glancing to the side, she saw that Glenn was standing behind her, staring at the bed. Unable to meet his eyes, she pulled the sheet loose and rolled it into a ball.

He clasped her shoulder, then turned her to him and held her close, the sheet wadded between them. "I'm sorry," he whispered.

"For what? Are you sorry you let me seduce you?"

"The virgin seductress!" he said. "No, I'm sorry for being curt with you just now. I'm upset. And I'm not used to…to thinking about the effect of my words."

"I know. I saw your reaction to that call."

He held her more tightly, then all too quickly eased away and gestured toward the bed. "Let me help you."

Taking the stained sheet from her hands, he stood looking around the room, then crossed to the dresser and stuffed the evidence into the back of his bottom drawer. He disappeared again and returned with fresh linen. Together they remade the bed. When they had finished, he stood regarding her gravely.

"What are you thinking?" she asked.

For a moment he didn't answer. Then his hands spread in a helpless gesture. The look on his face melted her heart, and she moved toward him swiftly.

"You're worried about the guy Claymore caught, aren't you? You're thinking he's some kind of agent sent to infiltrate your security force."

His tight nod told her what she wanted to know.

"And you're afraid that it will turn out that he and I have something to do with each other. That we're part of some conspiracy to…to wreck Castle Phoenix."

He gave a shuddering sigh, his eyes searching hers. "How do you know I'm thinking all that?"

"Unfortunately, the idea leaped into my head when Claymore was talking to you on the phone. Of course, that doesn't explain why the guy in custody decided to kill me. But maybe he has an answer for that, too." She straightened her shoulders. "So let's go down there and face the music."

"Meg, you don't have to go with me," he said suddenly.

"Yes, I do. Because I want to find out his motives as much as you do."

"Thank you." He gave her hand a squeeze, then left her to get dressed.

She took a quick shower in the bathroom down the hall, dried her hair, and pulled on the first clothes that her hands encountered. Her reflection in the mirror over the sink caught her attention, and she stopped to study her face—trying to see if there was any evidence of the night's activities.

When another face appeared over her shoulder, she looked up and met Glenn's gaze.

"Do I look any different?" she asked.

"Yes. More beautiful," he said, his expression amorous and intimate.

The words and the way he said them brought a brightness to her eyes and a flush to her cheeks. The pleasure and the warmth faded as she saw his features harden. Trying to keep her own expression calm, she looked at him questioningly.

"Meg, you and I—" He stopped, swallowed. "What happened between us last night has to stay private."

"I understand," she said automatically, stiffly.

Catching her shoulders, he pulled her gently backward so that she was resting against his chest. Then he bent and moved his cheek against the side of her face. "No, you don't. If the two of us act like lovers, the news will be all over this place before lunchtime. And a lot of the men here will assume you seduced me. They're already worried that you're a danger to me—and to our primary mission. If they think you've got some hold over me, they'll be hostile to you."

"They're already hostile toward me. I saw that when I was outside with you—just before the dog attack."

"Yes. It's possible that could explain the motives of the man Blake has in custody." His hold on her tightened. "I don't want anything else to happen to you. So we have to pretend our relationship hasn't changed."

"Okay," she agreed, her voice cracking. She understood his reasoning, but she didn't like it.

As she turned toward the hall, he kept his hand on her arm. "I don't like playing games with my orderly. But I put a sheet and blanket on the couch and made them look like somebody had slept there."

"You or me?" she asked. "Just in case we need to keep our stories straight."

"Me. I'm always the gentleman." He turned her in his arms, and brought his lips down to hers for a quick but ardent kiss. When he drew back, she caught a flicker of indecision in his expression.

"You want to tell me something else?" she whispered.

He shook his head. She suspected he wasn't telling her the truth, yet she didn't press him. That would only make things worse.

Drawing in a deep breath, she made her expression flat. "We'd better go."

He looked relieved, then swung away from her. When he opened the door, she saw the wisdom of his advice.

The guards standing in the hall snapped to attention, yet she could tell they were looking at the two of them with keen interest. So she kept her head down and stayed several paces behind Glenn as he strode toward the security center—her chest tightening as they got closer. She'd told herself she could do this. Now she wasn't so sure.

Still, when a haggard General Dorsey wheeled himself around the corner, she raised her head and met his scrutiny with as much bravado as she could muster.

Glenn went quickly toward the older man and squatted beside the wheelchair, bringing himself down to his eye level. "How long have you been up?" he asked.

"Since Blake brought in Sparks."

Sparks. That was his name, she thought. At least it didn't sound familiar.

"You didn't need to come down here," Glenn was saying to the older man.

The general waved his gnarled hand dismissively. "I couldn't sleep, anyway."

Glenn sighed. "So give me your impressions."

"It looks like he's cracked under the strain of working for us," Dorsey said, his voice etched with regret.

Meg watched them talking in a kind of shorthand that left out nonessential details, watched the easy give-and-take and the affection between the two men.

When the general's head came up so he could give her an extensive inspection, she froze. His gaze swept over her, and she imagined he was assessing her posture, her expression, the color of her complexion—which deepened as his eyes lingered. She felt as if she had a sign on her forehead advertising the night's activities, and it took all her willpower to stop herself from moving closer to Glenn. Instead she stood where she was—alone.

"Did you sleep well?" the general asked.

"As well as could be expected," she answered, keeping her voice and her eyes steady.

"Let's stick to business," Glenn snapped.

Meg turned toward him, seeing the repressed anger in his face, in his posture.

"Fine," Dorsey agreed. "But we want to collect as much information as possible."

"Such as?" Glenn asked.

Dorsey held his gaze. "Such as whether you're retaining the proper perspective, here."

The jarring comment hung in the air, and Meg felt her stomach go into a painful spasm.

"I always maintain the proper perspective," Glenn said, punching out every word to emphasize the point.

The two men stared at each other, Glenn daring his friend to make another personal remark. Instead, he swung his chair around and gestured toward the interrogation room. "You might as well see what you think."

Meg stood immobile as Dorsey rolled himself away. The wounded look on Glenn's face made her want to scream at the man in the wheelchair to turn around and face them. He had hurt Glenn; she could see it in his eyes, and she couldn't stand to watch. Moving to his side, she risked a brief touch to his arm.

"I'm sorry," she whispered.

"Don't be." Stepping away from her, he followed the general.

Meg walked stiff-legged after the men, who were now standing in front of the one-way mirror that gave a view of the interrogation room.

Last time she'd been here, Claymore had been brow-beating her.

She could see the security chief inside again, his back to the mirror. This time the victim was a young man with short brown hair and angry-looking brown eyes. He was gesturing with one hand while he talked.

When Meg saw that his other wrist was secured to the table by a handcuff, she cringed.

Dorsey motioned Glenn and Meg to stand to the side. Then he knocked on the door before opening it. Claymore stood and came into the hall. The handcuffed man stared intently at the mirror—making it seem as if he could see through the glass. But he couldn't, she reminded herself as she remembered her own experience.

Claymore looked at Meg. "Do you recognize him?" he asked.

She switched her attention back to the prisoner. "I don't know. It was dark when the man came after me, and I never saw his face."

She heard Glenn let out a little breath and knew he'd been waiting for the answer.

"What about from before the other night?" Claymore pressed.

"No!" she said vehemently.

When the security chief continued to look at her, she turned to Glenn. "You had more contact with him than I did. Do you think that's the man you fought?"

He stared at the prisoner and finally shrugged. "I don't think so. His body type doesn't seem right. But I could be wrong."

"How did you know he was the right man to take into custody?" Meg asked.

The general replied: "Blake let a group of hostile men know he was going out on the grounds alone—to an isolated location where he couldn't call for help. Then he marched out there and waited for a bullet in the back."

She could tell from the way he said it that he thought Claymore had done something very brave—and probably very foolish—and that the blame for his desperate behavior rested on her shoulders.

"We'd like his reaction to you," Dorsey added.

"You don't have to go into the room with him," Glenn said quickly. "You could stand in the doorway where he can get a look at you."

"I didn't think the victim had to confront the assailant—until he was brought to trial, or something," she said, watching Sparks, who had slumped in his seat, letting his head roll forward onto his chest.

"I'm not the police. We don't have to follow any particular procedure," Claymore answered.

She had the right to refuse. But she could see that everybody else present would think she was dismissing Claymore's bravery—or worse, canceling the value of his actions.

A giant knot wedged in her throat, yet she managed to say to Claymore, "You and General Dorsey want to know if Sparks and I are working together."

"Yeah."

"You're even thinking that the attack on me could have been staged."

The security chief didn't bother to deny it.

Swinging her gaze to Glenn, she saw that he'd been informed of the planned confrontation. So that was why he'd been so stiff with her after the phone call. Did he think she'd been capable of working with a cold-blooded killer?

Claymore studied her. "You want to back out?"

"No."

"Good. Then I'll step into the room and get his attention. When I do, you walk to the doorway." Without waiting for a response, he turned and rejoined the prisoner.

Sparks looked up as Claymore reentered. Then the security chief stepped aside and glanced over his shoulder.

Feeling as if a 500-watt spotlight were focused on her, Meg stiffened her knees and stepped to the door.

Her heart leaped into her throat as the prisoner lunged toward her. Only the handcuff on his wrist kept him from grabbing her.

Glenn stepped behind her, placing his hands on her shoulders. "That's enough," he growled, trying to pull her back.

She leaned on him then, glad of his warmth and the solid feel of his body.

Claymore had a hand on Sparks's shoulder, pushing him back into his seat.

The prisoner's eyes never left her. "It's your fault," he spat out. "You were the last straw. Things weren't so bad around here until you showed up."

"What did I do to you?" she managed to challenge.

"If you don't know, I'm not going to explain it to you, bitch," he snarled.

"Did you attack me in the guest quarters?"

"No. But somebody had the right idea. You're bad news." He snorted. "You wanted that dog to get Shipley, didn't you? He was a good guy. Now he's messed up—because of you."

"What did I do to the dog?"

"I hear you fed him something to make him go crazy."

"No," she insisted, her voice strengthening. Then she tried a question of her own. "Did you?"

"Are you nuts? Why would I do something like that?"

he demanded, his voice low and angry. "What are you trying to do? Get me in worse trouble? You'd better stay away from me, because you're dead meat if I get you alone."

She recoiled from the words, and from the hatred in his voice. He wasn't rational, yet she couldn't help wondering if he knew something about her that she didn't know herself.

To her relief, Glenn drew her back from the doorway. "Come on, let's get out of here," he said.

"I want her to stay," Dorsey countered. "I want to know for certain what her role in this was."

Glenn's gaze drilled into him. "She had no role."

"Glenn, you're not—"

"I think you have as much as you're going to get," he interrupted. "Maybe Sparks has formed an irrational hatred of her because he needs somebody else to be responsible for his problems. But I think it's crystal clear that he wasn't working with her. And neither one of us thinks he's the man who came after her in the guest quarters. So he may have attacked Blake, but that doesn't mean he's the main source of our problems. The way I see it, all you've proved is that you've got two rotten apples in the barrel—Sparks and some other guy."

Without waiting for a response, he moved Meg around the corner and into the corridor.

She waited until they were alone before saying, "After the phone call from Claymore, we talked about what you were thinking. But you didn't tell me your security chief wanted me down there to get Sparks's reaction to me. Or that he and the general were hoping their prisoner would give away some secret relationship we had."

He turned and faced her squarely. "Yes, that was part of the message from Blake. If I'd confided in you, they would have assumed it invalidated the test. I wanted you to prove to them you had nothing to do with him!"

"You were confident of that?"

"Yes," he growled, then sought her gaze. "What would you have done in my place?"

"I don't know. I'm glad I didn't have to make the decision."

Before she could say more, the shooting started.

Chapter Twelve

Glenn pushed Meg to the tile floor, his body coming down on top of hers even as his right hand pulled the gun from his holster. From the depths of the security center, an alarm began to sound, echoing through the building and across the grounds.

Meg froze, expecting a hail of bullets.

When the fighting didn't move toward them, Glenn sprang up again and headed down the corridor.

Grabbing a handful of his shirt, she tried to restrain him. "Glenn, stay here."

"I can't. *You* get out of the area," he ordered over his shoulder as he pulled himself from her grasp and crept back the way they'd come, his gun trained on the door to the security center.

Wide-eyed, she watched as he reached the door and pushed it open with his foot, then snapped out of the way, keeping his body to the side. He was greeted by another round of fire and a sharp voice.

"Stay out!"

"Sparks? What's going on in there?"

"I don't want to hurt you, sir. My beef's not with you."

"We can work this out."

"Yeah. Sure."

"Put down your weapon, and everything will be all right," Glenn soothed.

The man answered with a bark of hysterical laughter. "Sure, and pigs can fly. We both know I'm in deep guano."

"Don't do anything stupid."

"I already have."

How stupid, Meg thought as she pictured bodies sprawled on the floor in the security center. The general was in there. So was Claymore. And Glenn cared about both of them.

Turning to Meg, he motioned frantically for her to return to the protected area around the corner. Knowing she was only adding to his anxiety by sticking close, she backed up, rounded the corner and crouched on the floor, where a low cabinet hid her from view.

"Sparks?" Glenn called.

"Right here, sir. I'm coming out. But we're going to play this my way."

"All right," Glenn agreed.

"I'm taking the general with me. Drop your weapon or I'll kill him."

When Glenn hesitated, the order came again, this time edged with fear.

Glenn obeyed.

"Kick the gun out of reach."

Glenn sent the weapon sliding across the tile floor.

Meg found she couldn't draw a breath into her lungs. Glenn had just made himself totally vulnerable to an armed madman.

When a figure appeared in the doorway, every muscle in her body clenched.

It was General Dorsey, out of his wheelchair, his fragile form clamped tightly against Sparks, who held his captive with one hand and a gun with the other.

The general's gait was stiff, and his face was drained of color, but his gaze drilled into Glenn as if he were trying to communicate a vital message through mental telepathy. Glenn didn't move as his friend shuffled ahead of Sparks.

God, what if the old man stumbled? What if he tried something heroic? Then Glenn would get shot.

Praying that Dorsey could stay on his feet for the next few minutes, Meg watched as Sparks backed up several steps and stopped with his back against the wall.

"Let him go," Glenn ordered.

"When I get what I want," Sparks enunciated carefully. "I want off the estate. I want a plane and a pilot."

"All right," Glenn said.

Meg was sure he would agree to anything to keep his friend from being killed. Did they really have an airstrip here? She wouldn't have bet there was enough flat ground for a takeoff and landing.

Her speculation was cut off by Sparks's next question. "Where's the bitch who got me in trouble?" he snapped, his eyes darting around the area, and Meg felt herself freeze in place behind the cabinet even as her pulse began to pound in her ears. God, what would he do if he found her here?

"I sent her back to her quarters—under escort," Glenn answered, his voice carrying a ring of conviction.

"I hope so. I hope you don't let yourself trust her."

"Why?"

"She's trouble."

"You have inside information?" Glenn inquired.

"No. And I don't have time for a chat, either. You've got a phone in your pocket. Take it out real slow. And don't try anything funny, because I know how the system works around this place."

Glenn obeyed, watching the general who was breathing hard with the effort to remain on his feet.

Sparks's arm tightened across his captive's chest. "You'd better work fast, 'cause Dorsey's getting tired. Call the units. Tell them the emergency's over and nobody's supposed to interfere with me." He paused and looked down at the watch on his wrist. "Tell them to stay exactly where they are until further notice. Nobody should come near this end of the building. Or the airstrip." He paused and thought for a moment. "Or the access road."

"All right," Glenn agreed again, quickly punching in numbers and issuing terse orders. Seconds later, the alarms stopped sounding, and they stood in deafening silence.

"That's better. Now call the hangar, and tell them to get the Cessna ready. And have a jeep waiting for us at the door. Tell the garage I don't want a driver. He should park the vehicle next to the door and leave the engine running. You'll drive."

The man might be desperate, but he was thinking through each step, Meg saw, planning all the details.

Glenn dialed another number and spoke into the phone. "The jeep will be waiting when we get there," he said.

Sparks nodded toward the phone. "Set it on the table. I'm not taking a chance on your activating some secret code while my back is turned."

Glenn gave a tight nod and complied. When he had gone back to his original position, the fugitive eased forward and asked the general to retrieve the phone.

Dorsey grimaced but obeyed, his gnarled hand shaking. Only when the instrument was in Sparks's pocket did some of the tension leave his face. "Let's go," he said to Glenn. "You first. Then the general and me."

They moved down the hall, Glenn half turning as he stopped to see if the general and his captor were keeping up.

"I'll worry about Dorsey," Sparks snapped. "You make sure that nobody tries anything stupid."

Glenn nodded, and they all disappeared around a bend in the corridor.

Meg waited with her heart pounding, knowing that if she moved too soon she could get the hostages killed. Staring in the direction they'd disappeared, she forced herself to stay where she was like a kid playing hide-and-seek, while she counted slowly under her breath. One one-thousand. Two one-thousand. Three one-thousand... With each number, her tension mounted as she waited for guards to come running around the corner or for Sparks to dart back into view minus his two prisoners. When she reached twenty-five hundred, she found it almost impossible to keep her position. But she managed it for another ten numbers. Then she stood and began sliding along the wall toward the security center. Slipping inside, she gasped in a choking breath, then let it out as she forced herself to look around the room.

It was empty. Her heart threatened to pound its way through the wall of her chest as she took one step and then another farther into the facility.

The first body was lying in a heap in the hallway. It was one of the guards, and she knew by the bullet holes in his back and the blood pooled on the floor that he couldn't possibly be alive. His partner was a little farther on, in even worse condition.

The victim's holster was empty, and Meg was pretty sure that Sparks must have gotten his gun, shot him and laid down a hail of gunfire. In the interrogation room, Sparks had also been handcuffed. Either they'd made the mistake of taking his cuffs off, or he'd forced them to do it when he got control of the situation.

Stepping carefully around the man, Meg moved farther back, peering into the little room. It was empty.

So were the rest of the rooms along the corridor. When she opened a steel door and stepped through into the cell-block area, she found Claymore. He was locked in a cell, sprawled on a narrow bunk. Again she saw blood, and drew in a quick breath. Then she saw his chest was rising and falling.

The door was locked, and she knelt near the bunk, stretching her hand toward him through the bars, but it was too far to reach.

FROM HIS VANTAGE POINT on the cliff above Castle Phoenix, another man watched the jeep pull away from the building. He guessed it was headed in the direction of the airstrip. He confirmed the guess when the vehicle took the right-hand fork in the road.

Bridgman was driving. Another man was sitting in the back—with a gun trained on General Dorsey. Early this morning, the same guy had been brought in under armed guard. Now it looked as if he was calling the shots.

Very interesting.

When the alarm had gone off, he'd thought that they'd somehow discovered his location on the estate. Now he knew that the crisis had nothing to do with him—yet.

He waited, expected to see troops moving quickly to head off the jeep. But the place was buttoned down tight.

The watcher's lips curved into a satisfied smile. He'd gotten onto the estate and he'd avoided capture. But he'd been forced to switch from plan A to plan B and then to C.

Now he was back to A again—and it looked as if he had just been handed the perfect opportunity.

Pushing himself up, he began to move cautiously toward the castle—toward the stairway where he knew he'd find the secure lab.

"CLAYMORE. BLAKE. CAN you hear me?" Meg called, trying to rouse the unconscious man.

At first there was no response. Finally, the security chief stirred, his eyes blinking open. When he tried to sit up, pain contorted his face. "Glenn? Hal?" he asked in a rough voice.

"Sparks took them as hostages. Where are the keys?" she asked.

"In a desk near the door. Top right-hand drawer."

She hurried back the way she'd come, found the desk and located a ring of keys. Then she began trying them in the lock.

"I don't know why he didn't kill me when he had the chance," Claymore growled. "That's what he started out to do."

"Maybe he thought two men were enough. Maybe he didn't want to take the time."

"Yeah. Or maybe he figured that humiliation was better than death." He writhed in discomfort. "Get me out of here!"

The way he gave the order made her realize she had a choice. He was her enemy, and she could simply walk out of the cell block and leave him there. Instead she said, "I'm trying."

"What happened out there?" he demanded, sitting up and gingerly touching the back of his head.

As Meg worked, she related the encounter between Glenn and the fugitive. It was punctuated by a sharp curse when she said that Sparks had Glenn's phone.

"Of course!" he raged. "The son of a bitch knows our procedures. If he's working for the enemy, we've had it. I've got to send someone after him."

She put down the keys. "No! I saw his face. I heard him. He wants a clear escape route. And if he doesn't get it, he'll kill Glenn and Dorsey. So if you're planning anything that's going to upset him, I'm not letting you out."

He glared at her for long seconds, then replied, "All right."

"I have your word on that?"

"Yes."

Picking up the keys, she tried another. It was the right one, and the lock clicked open.

"Thank you," he said gruffly when she entered the cell. She gave him a direct look. "I'm doing it for Glenn."

"I know." Pushing himself up, he grimaced with pain.

"You should get medical attention," she informed him.

He gave the answer she'd expected. "Not now." His eyes burned into hers. "I won't try anything that endangers Hal or Glenn. But I've got to find out what's happening. Okay?"

"Okay."

"First, I need a sling for this damn arm. There are sheets

in one of the cabinets near the door and a knife in the guard desk. Cut a strip off a sheet and bring it here.''

Meg found the sheets and the knife. Ripping off a strip of fabric, she brought it back to the security chief. When he started giving her directions, she shook her head. ''I know emergency medicine.''

''And what else?''

''Unfortunately, it seems I don't find out until I need the information.''

Claymore gritted his teeth as she bound the arm to his chest, trying not to cause any additional damage.

''If there's a bullet still lodged in there, you need to get it out.''

''Later.''

He stood, swayed, and caught himself against the bars. After several seconds, he pushed away and strode down the hall. Meg followed, watching him stop and stare at the man with the missing sidearm.

''Sparks got his weapon?'' she asked.

''I assume so,'' Claymore answered. ''I was on the phone or I'd probably be dead, too.''

Sitting down at the desk, he got a service handgun from a locked drawer, checked the magazine, and shoved it into his empty holster. Then he pushed a button on a control panel. Part of the opposite wall slid aside, revealing a bank of TV screens.

One by one, Claymore switched on the monitors, which provided a view of various parts of the estate, indoors and out.

Meg got a look at the cafeteria where men were sitting tense and silent, the main gate where the guard stood rigidly at his post, and several other locations. The airfield, which looked as if it had been carved out of a mountainside, appeared deserted at first. Then a plane taxied out of a hangar and stood ready for takeoff on the tarmac.

As she watched, a jeep pulled into view. Glenn was driving. The other men were in the back. The vehicle stopped on the runway.

Sparks got out, holding tight to the general, who was struggling on his feet.

"I can give the order to bring him down once he takes off," Claymore muttered.

"Won't you kill the pilot?" she gasped.

"The pilot will have a chute," he snapped. "So will Sparks, if he's smart. But we'll pick him up in the woods."

Meg lacked his sense of confidence. Praying it would all be over soon, she watched the fugitive drag Dorsey toward the plane. Before he reached it, the general stumbled and went down. Sparks sprinted away, and gunfire erupted from inside the hangar.

"Glenn! Get down, Glenn!" Meg screamed as the TV screen went blank.

Claymore cursed, then reached for the phone, barking orders for a vehicle.

Meg's terse, "I'm coming," was answered with a nod.

Claymore continued to speak into his portable phone, issuing more orders. By the time they reached the entrance, a jeep was waiting. As they sped toward the top of a hill, Meg saw a column of black smoke rising in the air and gasped.

"Pick it up," Claymore growled to the driver.

Her fingers digging into the edge of the seat, Meg strained forward. But they were too far away to see anything besides the smoke. In the front seat, Claymore was punching the buttons on the phone and cursing, so she knew he wasn't getting any information.

Meg didn't know if she was a religious person. She didn't know if she prayed to God on a regular basis or if she turned to Him in a crisis. But there was nothing else she could do, so she began to pray now, gripping the seat and bracing against the swaying of the speeding jeep.

Please let Glenn be okay, she silently begged over and over as the jeep careened toward the scene of the unknown disaster.

Chapter Thirteen

The sirens of emergency vehicles sounded behind them on the road, and Claymore's driver whipped onto the gravel shoulder as two fire trucks sped past.

The moment the pavement was clear, the jeeps followed in the wake of the vehicles, arriving at the airstrip minutes later.

As they screeched to a halt on the tarmac, Meg saw a small plane about fifty yards away—engulfed in flames and smoke.

A cry welled in her throat. "Glenn!"

Only the roar of the fire answered.

She was out of the jeep and rushing toward the conflagration when a large hand clamped her shoulder. "Stay here!" Claymore hissed.

"I have to find Glenn."

"If he's in there, you can't do a damn thing about it. But I'll bet he's not!" the security chief retorted.

"Then where is he?"

"I don't know."

She let him guide her back to the side of the vehicle, let him press her against the cold metal, the heat from the fire searing her face, even at this distance.

Smoke burned her eyes and choked her lungs as she watched in a kind of wide-eyed shock as firemen pulled their hoses toward the ruined aircraft and began spraying it with streams of water.

Oh, God, where was Glenn? He couldn't be in there. He couldn't! She wasn't sure how long she stood there. All she knew was that the ringing of Claymore's phone snapped her out of the trance.

Hunching his shoulders, he turned away from her as he listened, made another call, and received a third. He straightened as two ambulances sped past and screeched to a halt on the tarmac.

The other doctor, Dylan Ryder, jumped out of the lead vehicle, followed by two men with a stretcher.

"Who—who are they here for?"

"The general."

"How do you know?" she demanded. "Why are there two ambulances?"

"I was just talking to Dylan. There are two ambulances in case we encounter other casualties."

"Has anyone seen Glenn?" she demanded.

"Not to my knowledge. At least, there hasn't been a phone report to that effect," he answered stiffly.

"You've got to tell me *something!* Was he close to the plane when it exploded?"

Claymore gave a tight nod and she felt as if she'd been hit with a fist in the stomach. It was all she could do to keep from doubling over.

"Maybe Dorsey knows something," the security chief muttered.

"Let me go with you."

He considered the request. "Okay."

She followed as he moved closer to the fire, asking questions of his men and receiving clipped answers.

By the time they reached the stretcher, she knew part of what had happened when the TV monitors went black. Sparks had returned the gunfire from the hangar, and the fuel tank had taken a hit. So had one of the TV cables. Sparks had been blown up with the plane.

The last anyone had seen of Glenn, he'd been rushing toward the Cessna.

"Then what?" Meg asked the guard who was briefing Claymore.

The guard turned toward her, his expression apologetic. "There was too much confusion. We don't know."

She looked down at Dorsey, who was gazing up at her with a twisted expression on his face.

"I suppose you think this is my fault," she said.

"No. Mine," he replied, his voice thin and gritty. Exhausted from the effort of speaking, he closed his eyes.

She was about to ask him what he meant, when a flash of movement caught the corner of her eye. Looking up, she zeroed in on a tall figure coming through the smoke. His shoulders were slumped, and his head was bent so that she couldn't see his face. Yet her heart turned over in her chest as she recognized him.

"Glenn!" she shouted, pushing her way past several startled guards. Hands grabbed at her.

"Please. Let me go," she begged. "Don't you see? It's him. It's Glenn."

The hold loosened and she sped across the blacktop.

"Glenn!" she called again, her joy surging. Blind to everything but her own relief, she launched herself toward him.

"Meg." His face contorted as his arms came up to catch her, then banded her so tightly that she could scarcely draw a full breath. She cleaved to him, moving her hands over his back and shoulders, and raised her face to his. With a deep groan, he lowered his mouth to hers, kissing her as if she were the only thing in the universe that could save his life—his sanity.

When he lifted his head and gazed down at her, she gasped in air and tried to take stock of him.

"Are you all right?"

"Yeah."

She prayed it was true. His face was covered with soot,

his clothing was bloodstained and his eyes were red-rimmed. Worse, she could hear the air rasping in and out of his lungs.

"What happened?" she asked urgently. "Were you shot?"

"No."

The denial eased her a little. "Where were you? Nobody could find you."

"I was getting the pilot out of the plane. I made it to him before the engine went up. But—" He swallowed hard. "He's dead. He'd been hit in the neck, and I couldn't save him."

"I'm so sorry," she answered, her words sounding terribly inadequate.

Before he could say anything else, Claymore strode toward them. "Thank God. I thought...you hadn't made it."

"I lead a charmed life." Glenn's mouth curved ironically. Then he sobered, his gaze sweeping over the security chief. "What happened to your arm?"

The reply was lost to Meg as she looked over the chief's shoulder and realized with a start that the whole scene between her and Glenn had been playing to an avid audience.

Her gaze shot to him, and as if he read her thoughts, he said, "Don't worry about it." His eyes turned from her to the onlookers. She followed his gaze and saw a mixture of reactions—relief, bemusement and tinges of the hostility that had dogged her since her arrival. Some of the men looked as if they were willing to give her the benefit of the doubt. Others probably would never see her as anything but a threat.

With elaborate casualness, Glenn slipped an arm around her shoulder and pulled her against his side.

After a moment, he cleared his throat and addressed the crowd. "Ms. Wexler—" he began.

Before he could get any further, Claymore cut him off. "Ms. Wexler freed me from a cell in the security center where I'd been locked up by Sparks," he said, his voice ringing out in the sudden silence. "She acted with no thought to her own safety, and I'm grateful for her assistance."

"Thank you," Meg said.

"I owe you one."

Most of the men relaxed. A few looked as if they still weren't completely convinced that she hadn't put the two commanding officers under a witch's spell.

The drama was interrupted by the arrival of Dylan Ryder.

"Is Hal all right?" Glenn asked quickly.

"He's in pretty good shape, under the circumstances. But he's on his way to the medical center—where the two of you are headed—now."

When Glenn opened his mouth to object, Ryder waved him to silence. "That's an order, sir."

Both men nodded wearily, and Meg suspected that Claymore, at least, was probably secretly thankful that he could finally get his arm treated.

Glenn still hesitated.

"Do you want me to come with you?" Meg asked softly.

"Yeah."

Ryder hurried to open the door of the second ambulance. Glenn and Claymore climbed in and sank to the benches. Meg dropped down beside Glenn and wove her fingers with his, gripping his hand tightly. She wanted to be alone with him—for a long, long time. Instead, she settled for a whispered exchange as they rode toward the castle.

"I was worried," she murmured.

"I'm sorry."

"It's not your fault." Her fingers clamped harder to his. "You take too many chances."

"I do what's necessary."

She nodded, then raised her head to find Claymore looking at them intently. Shutting her eyes, she turned her face toward Glenn, trying to burrow into his warmth. For a long moment, he let her cling to him, his hand stroking across her shoulders. Then she felt his posture straighten. When she raised her head, she found that he and Claymore were staring at each other across the aisle.

"Am I keeping the two of you from talking?" she asked.

"No," Glenn answered. "Anything we have to say, we can say in front of you."

Before she could respond, a shrill ringing sounded.

Glenn reached for phone on the wall. The message from the other end of the line had him leaping to his feet, moving toward the front of the vehicle and banging on the window that separated them from the driver.

"Let me off at the lab area," he said.

"You should get checked out," Ryder objected. "I want to listen to your lungs."

"There's been a security breach in level four."

The two other men were instantly on the alert.

"When?" Claymore demanded.

"Probably about the time the plane went up."

"Somebody took advantage of the emergency," the chief growled. "I'll—"

Glenn shook his head. "I'll take some men down there," he said, the tone of his voice cutting off further argument. He turned to Meg. "I want you back in my quarters—with the same guard arrangement that we had before."

"But—"

He squeezed her fingers in a crushing grip. "I want to know you're safe. I want at least one thing I don't have to worry about."

"Okay," she agreed, feeling as if she'd been maneuvered into a corner. But she knew that following orders now was the best way to help him.

Vowing not to get in the way, she listened as he made more phone calls—ordering two guards to meet her as soon as they reached the castle, calling for special reinforcements at the lab, arranging to have a weapon brought to him, and issuing a terse bulletin to his unit commanders. Finally, he ordered five portable lightweight biohazard suits to be delivered to the lab entrance, along with guns designed to be used with gloved hands. He was all business—the way he'd been before when he snapped into combat mode. Yet this time was different. He kept his free hand tightly linked with hers until the ambulance pulled to a halt at the nearest castle entrance.

Meg forced herself to walk inside, then turned and looked over her shoulder as the ambulance lurched away. When she couldn't make out Glenn through the narrow windows in the door, an awful feeling of dread grabbed her by the throat.

I'm never going to see him again.

No, that was ridiculous. Insane.

Yet she couldn't shake the sense of impending doom hanging over her as she allowed the guards to escort her to Glenn's quarters. When they'd left her alone, she stood with her knees locked and her back braced against the door, waiting until she could stand on her own. Then she pushed away from the door and tottered to the bedroom—where they'd made love the night before. Climbing under the covers, she burrowed between the sheets, trying to will away the feeling of cold dread that had sunk into her bones. Even though she and Glenn had changed the sheets, his familiar scent clung to the pillows, and she clutched at the fantasy that he was there with her. Closing her eyes, she tried to calm her pounding heart. But there was no way to shake the premonition of disaster.

"YOU WANT ME TO GO IN there with you?" Blake asked as the ambulance sped toward the lab wing.

"I want you to get your arm fixed up," Glenn replied over his shoulder as he exited the vehicle and joined the contingent of six men waiting for him.

The door leading to the level-four biohazards lab was unlocked. A guard had found it that way twenty minutes earlier and immediately called security. Glenn posted two men at the door, then gathered the rest around him.

"There was an intruder alert at this location," he began.

"So I don't know if the integrity of the lab has been compromised. Anyone who goes with me will be wearing a full contamination kit." He gestured toward the suits that the team had brought. "Under ordinary circumstances, these would provide adequate protection from the virus I've been working with. But not if someone's down there—and he's stupid enough to start shooting. If your suit takes a hit, the seal is broken and you'll be exposed to the virus. Do you understand?"

All of the men nodded, but he still wasn't satisfied. "This has to be a volunteer mission. I'm not ordering anyone to go with me."

After a moment of silence, Lewis, the senior man, stepped forward. "I'm volunteering," he said.

The others signaled their agreement, and Glenn felt his vision film over. God, would they follow him to hell if he asked? He hoped he never had to put it to the test.

"Okay," he said, hearing the husky quality of his voice. Quickly he turned and began suiting up.

When they were all encased in the protective clothing, they double-checked their oxygen supply and communications equipment before opening the door.

After the whole team had entered, he locked the exit behind them and started down the stairs, his gun drawn and his attention focused on his surroundings as he descended to the restricted area. Listening to the sound of boots hitting the concrete treads—and the hissing of his own breath inside the suit—he imagined an intruder leaping out from around the next bend. But there was no one inside the stairwell.

Two flights below ground level, he and the men stood in front of the familiar massive door with Warning: Biological Hazards. Authorized Personnel Only emblazoned on it.

When he tried the door handle and found it locked, he breathed a sigh of profound relief. Then he bent to examine the lock. There was evidence that someone had tried and failed to pry the mechanism loose. Thank God the intruder hadn't succeeded.

With the guards on alert, he worked the keyboard on the wall, punching in the access code. When the lock disengaged, he took two men into the anteroom. There was nowhere to hide and no one in sight. The dressing area was also empty. Leaving the two guards on alert, he went through the procedure for entering the lab itself. Once inside, he checked his virus samples—the infected cells and the ones receiving the antidote treatment.

"Everything okay?" Benson asked when he returned.

"Yes."

He could feel some of the tension around him dissipate like fog burning off as the sun rose. Still, they were all on the alert as they returned the way they'd come.

"I want a four-man, twenty-four-hour guard on the door to the lab," Glenn said into his phone as soon as he'd climbed out of the contamination suit.

He longed to go straight back to his quarters—straight back to Meg. He imagined himself catching her in his arms, scooping her up and taking her back to bed. But they were still in crisis mode, and he wasn't going to retreat into the little world they'd created together. Somebody had broken into the outer layers of the biohazards lab, and he was going to find out who it was.

Back in his office, he put out an order for every available man and dog to search the grounds. As he recradled the phone, he caught sight of his reflection in a windowpane and grimaced. He looked as though he'd come out of a chimney stack. So he stepped into the private bathroom that was attached to his office and took a quick hot shower. Then he changed into clean clothes. He was just buckling on his holster when the phone rang again.

Striding to the desk, he read the name on the caller ID: Tommy Faulkner. Tommy had phoned yesterday, and he hadn't gotten back to him yet. Well, he could spare a few minutes for one of the men.

"This is Glenn," he said.

"I was waiting for you to call me," answered the weak voice on the other end of the line.

"I'm sorry I didn't get back to you sooner. I've had some problems to take care of."

"Anything serious?"

"Just nuisance stuff," Glenn lied. "But I couldn't pass it off to someone else."

"Good." There was a pause on the line. "I'm still worried about my sister," the young man blurted.

"You said she was missing?"

"Well, she goes on a lot of trips. For her job at Adventures in Travel. But this time…I can't find a phone number where I can reach her. Do you think I lost it?" Tommy asked, sounding plaintive and a little confused.

"Did you call her office?" Glenn asked.

"Yeah," Tommy replied slowly. "They said she had some personal business to take care of. But I don't get it. Meg didn't tell me anything like that. And she didn't leave a phone number where they could reach her."

Glenn felt a tightening in his chest that made it difficult to draw in enough air to speak. "Meg. Your sister's name is Meg?" he managed to ask.

"Sure. Meg. Didn't I say that?"

Feeling as if he'd been shot in the chest, Glenn collapsed into his chair.

Chapter Fourteen

Meg. Tommy's sister was *Meg*.

His ears were ringing so loudly that it took several seconds to realize Tommy was speaking to him.

"Glenn. Is something wrong, Glenn?" Tommy wheezed.

"No," he insisted, then made an effort to control himself while he dug for information. "Meg what?"

"Meg Faulkner."

"Not Wexler?"

"Where did you get that idea?"

"I guess I'm confused."

Tommy laughed. "Like me."

Cradling the receiver under his ear, Glenn scooted his chair to the file cabinet where he kept personal data on the men from Operation Clean Sweep. Pulling out the correct folder, he quickly flipped through and found several pictures. One was a formal portrait of Tommy in his dress uniform. The others were candid shots. One showed a young man and woman at a picnic table, smiling for the camera. Tommy and his sister. Meg.

Glenn's Meg.

His fingers dug into the edge of the file as he stared into her beautiful, innocent face. He knew now why she'd looked vaguely familiar. It was because of the resemblance to her brother. Except that her name was supposed to be Meg Wexler.

His heart was pounding so hard that he thought it might careen through his chest wall.

"You don't have to worry about her. She's here at Castle Phoenix," he heard himself saying.

"What's she doing there?" Tommy asked, sounding even more confused than before.

Glenn debated with himself, trying to come up with an answer that wouldn't stretch the truth too much. "She came here to talk about you," he finally said, hoping it was true. "On the way, she was in a car accident. She had a concussion. But she's fine now."

Tommy gasped. "She was hurt? You're sure she's okay?"

"She's fine."

"Thank God."

"I know you depend on her a lot," Glenn tried, making a reasonable assumption.

"Yeah, with Dad gone, she's all I've got. But..."

"What?" Glenn prompted.

"I wish she'd find herself a guy."

"Yes, she's some woman," Glenn agreed, then asked the question that had been in and out of his mind since he'd made love with her. "Why hasn't she married?"

Tommy made an exasperated sound. "It's partly Dad's fault. The colonel—"

"You called your dad the colonel?"

Glenn shuffled through the pictures and found a snapshot of a younger Tommy with a ramrod-straight military officer wearing a colonel's uniform. With his piercing eyes and firm lips, he bore a resemblance to both his children.

Tommy sighed. "Yeah. He ran our house like a military base. And when she got to be a teenager, he drummed it into Meg that guys were after her for her great body. Unfortunately, there were a few jerks who proved the point.

When she was in college there was a guy who…tried to rape her.''

A curse sprang to Glenn's lips.

"She fought him off."

"I can believe it."

"But that made her cautious."

Glenn closed his eyes for a moment, understanding Meg better. She'd been wary of men. Vulnerable. But she'd reached out to him. That had to mean something, didn't it?

"She's away from home so much," Tommy was saying. "When she's here, she's taking care of her sick brother, 'cause she's got this tremendous sense of obligation, you know? I guess we both got that from Dad."

"Meg loves you. That's why she takes care of you," Glenn answered, knowing in his bones that it was true. He could imagine exactly how she'd react to her brother's illness.

"She can do anything a guy can," Tommy said proudly. "Shoot. Jump out of a plane. Climb a mountain. That's why leading adventure expeditions is the perfect job for her."

Adventure expeditions! No wonder she could handle a gun and think so well on her feet.

"But sometimes I think she'd secretly like to settle down with a guy who'd appreciate her." He paused, then added, "You know, she'd be perfect for you, Glenn. You go on those trips to all sorts of remote places. She'd be a real asset to you."

"In more ways than one," he said before he could check himself.

"Are you saying you two clicked?"

"Let's not get ahead of ourselves," he cautioned, dishing out the advice for himself as well as Tommy.

"But you like her! Good. It would take a load off my mind to see the two of you end up together."

"Me, too," Glenn replied, knowing he was giving too

much away. Closing his eyes, he worked to clear away the lump in his throat. "I'll have her call you later."

"Thanks for letting me know she's in good hands."

"Tommy, hang in there. I'm almost ready for clinical trials. If you want to be one of my first guinea pigs, we can bring you up here soon."

"You mean it?" The voice on the other end of the line sounded stronger.

"I mean it." Glenn concluded the conversation, glad that he'd given one of his men new hope, glad that he'd managed to keep saying the right things even with his brain on fire.

When he hung up, he had to clasp his hands together on the desk to keep them from shaking violently. The answer had been there all the time. But he hadn't known where to look.

Meg Wexler was Meg Faulkner. Tommy's sister. So now he had a plausible reason why she'd come here. To help her brother. He clung to that by his fingernails—to the simple logic of it. The trouble was, he was pretty sure her motives hadn't been simple.

When a knock sounded at the door, he recoiled, then sat up straighter and cleared his throat. "Come in."

Blake stepped into the office, his arm in a more official-looking sling and his face drawn.

"You're supposed to be in the medical center," Glenn objected, glad to have another focus for his thoughts.

"So are you!"

"I discharged myself."

"So did I," Blake countered.

Before Glenn could point out that only one of them was a physician, the security chief handed him a piece of paper.

"What's this?"

"My resignation."

Glenn flicked his eyes over it. "I hope it didn't hurt your arm too much to write it, because you've just wasted your time.'' Tearing the paper into pieces, he dropped them into the trash. ''Care to explain your reasoning?'' he asked.

''If you were counting on me for security, I've been doing a pretty miserable job.''

''You've been doing your job as you saw it. I need you to keep doing that.''

''Even if I've screwed up royally?''

''Like how?''

''Pushing an amnesiac for information. Focusing on the threat from my own men.''

''You have a better angle?''

''Yeah. I had a hunch about the car that I wish had paid off sooner. I had it dusted for fingerprints. When I got back to my office a little while ago, there was a report from a friend in army intelligence. He can get access to FBI files. The prints are from a guy named Leroy Enders. Wasn't there an Enders in the Clean Sweep group?''

Glenn crossed to the cabinet and pulled out another file. ''Leroy is Paul Enders's father.'' He shuffled through the folder, found a picture of a tough-as-nails older man with a military haircut—not unlike Meg's father, actually. ''He's a former Green Beret.''

Blake took the folder and paged through it. ''Good training—for infiltration and dirty tricks. I'm thinking now that he came in in the trunk of her car, then had some sort of spray that drugged Lipscomb.''

Glenn's mouth tightened.

''I thought the prints might match the ones on the gun from the guest suite.''

''You found it?''

''I had guys combing the place. It was wedged under the credenza. Unfortunately, whoever shot the place up was smart enough to wear gloves.'' The security chief sighed. ''Too bad, because we could have avoided this whole mess with Sparks.''

Blake's gaze dropped to the folder again. ''Enders had

the training to cause a lot of trouble around here. And he's been in a couple scrapes with the law. Nothing major, but he did six months in a state prison for assault.''

Glenn sighed. ''I was going to give you the theory that his prints are all over the car because he helped Meg get ready to come here. That maybe they were just part of a support group for families of the men from Clean Sweep.''

''How did you come up with that?''

Glenn steeled himself. ''I found out a few minutes ago that Meg's name is Meg Faulkner. She's Tommy Faulkner's sister.''

The security chief's eyes widened. ''You've made a positive ID?''

''The guys call me when they've got problems. Tommy was upset because his sister, Meg, has been missing for several days.'' Glenn pushed the snapshot from Tommy's file toward Blake.

His friend studied the brother and sister, then nodded. ''It's her, all right. And now that I see the picture, I remember meeting Tommy. Nice guy. You and he were close, weren't you?''

''Yeah.'' Glenn swallowed. ''I'd like to think she came here to beg me to do something for him. But I'm not stupid. I have to assume there's more to it than that. Do you have every available man out there beating the bushes for Enders?''

Blake sighed. ''We had a perimeter alarm forty minutes ago. The fence was clipped in the south quadrant. I'm thinking that when our friend couldn't get into the secure lab, he decided to cut his losses and make his escape. Or maybe he had a deadline.'' His eyes narrowed. ''But I think your next step should be tell Ms. Wex—Ms. Faulkner her real name and some of her background and see if you get any reaction.''

''I intend to,'' Glenn retorted. He picked up the file and

started to step around Blake, but the security chief put a hand on his arm.

"Glenn, I know you've gotten in pretty deep with her. I'm sorry."

"Maybe you won't have to be," he said, still daring to hope for the best as he gathered up the Faulkner file and headed for his quarters.

HE FOUND MEG IN THE bedroom, huddled under the covers with her knees drawn up. She was sleeping, and she looked so sweetly innocent that his heart gave a painful squeeze. She had said she loved him, and he believed her. But that was the woman who thought she was Meg Wexler.

Meg Faulkner was another matter. She had come to his castle to lay open his defenses. Glenn didn't know what she'd had in mind—specifically. But probably she'd succeeded beyond her wildest dreams.

His hands clenched at his sides as he fought the need to sink down beside her and gather her into his arms. From the moment she'd awakened in the medical wing, something magical had wrapped itself around them. Now he longed for one more sorcerer's spell that would bind her to him.

He knew that if he reached for her, she would pull him close and give him anything he asked. But he couldn't ask Meg Wexler for any more favors. He could only ask Meg Faulkner.

He stood there for another few seconds, drinking in the sight of her, silently praying for everything that had happened between them to be true. Then, pulling a chair from the corner of the room, he sat down and gently touched her shoulder.

She woke, and her incredible green eyes blinked open and focused on him.

"You're back. I tried to stay awake...." Her smile faded when she took in the grim look on his face.

"What's happened?"

"I've found out who you are," he said, watching her. Hope, fear, uncertainty all crossed her features in rapid succession. He was certain they were all genuine, the mix too complex to fake.

"You're sure?"

"I talked to your brother. He was worried about you."

Again he saw perplexity. "My brother?" She shook her head. "Do I have a brother?"

"Yes, he's one of the men from Operation Clean Sweep. Come into the dining room. Let me show you some pictures."

Reluctantly she followed. But when he moved toward the folder that he'd laid on the dining-room table, she grabbed his hand.

"Wait."

"Meg, you need to find out who you are."

"I don't want to know!" Her voice was edged with desperation. Darting around to face him, she took him in her arms and held him as if she never intended to let go. When she raised her head and found his mouth with hers, he was helpless to stop the rush of emotion that surged through him. Not simply desire or wanting, but need—at the most basic level.

Her mouth moved over his, urgent, demanding, desperate, and it was impossible to hide his response from her or from himself.

She kissed him with the same passion, the same greedy fury, her hands stroking and pressing, then sliding down to his waist so that she could mold her body to his.

He needed no urging to lean into her, bond himself to her like honey dripping over the bowl of a spoon. And when she found one of his hands and brought it to her breast, he groaned his approval as his fingers began to stroke her stiffened nipple.

"Come to bed, Glenn. Love me. Please love me," she begged, her words vibrating against his lips.

They were moving down the hall when sanity finally overtook him. God, he couldn't think when he had her in his arms, her body all soft and yielding. But he had to think.

"Meg, we can't."

She lifted her large green eyes to him. "Of course we can. We love each other. I realize we haven't known each other very long. But what happened between us happened fast!"

"That's why I owe it to you to stop."

She searched his face for truths. "What do you mean?"

He forced the words out of his sandpaper throat. "When you remember who you are, you may think I've been taking advantage of you—that I pushed you into something you weren't ready for."

She gave a high, broken laugh. "Is that what this looks like to you? From my point of view, I'm trying to drag you into the bedroom—only you're stronger than I am, and you're digging in your heels."

Searching for the right words, he struggled to make her understand. "You're not dragging me. Don't you think I want you as much as you want me? But you're trying to prove something in bed. And that's the wrong place for certainties."

Her eyes flashed. "All right. I get it. You've found out why I came here, and you think you've made a mistake."

"No. I only know you're connected with one of the men who got sick because I sent them to raid a biological-weapons plant. I don't know your motives for showing up here, probably with a man in the trunk of your car."

"*What?*"

He held his hands palms outward. "Okay, Blake thinks there was a passenger hidden in your trunk. He found fingerprints that belong to the father of another one of the men. A guy who's been in jail for assault."

When she sucked in a strangled breath, he was immediately sorry he'd given her more information than either one of them was equipped to handle. "This isn't getting us anywhere." He sighed. "If you look at the pictures, maybe you'll remember your past. Then you can tell me what you know—if you still want to."

"Stop it!" she cried. "Stop casting my motives in the worst possible light." After giving him one long look, she turned, marched toward the dining-room table, and flipped the folder open.

He wanted to withdraw to another room and give her some privacy. But he found he was unable to move, unable to do more than stand frozen in an airless bubble where it was impossible to draw oxygen into his lungs.

He watched her brow wrinkle as she read about Tommy Faulkner's background.

She glanced at him, her face stony. "Sorry. This doesn't ring a bell."

"Look at the pictures," he suggested, marveling that he could speak around the golf ball blocking his windpipe.

Lips pressed together, she shuffled through the papers and picked up the photo of the brother and sister at the picnic table.

He watched her body go rigid, and he knew to the instant when memory came slamming back to her.

She gasped as if she'd been pierced by a sword, the blood draining from her face as her eyes shot to him and filled with a look of such horror that his throat felt suddenly full of acid, his belly with fire. When she swayed on her feet, he wanted to go to her and help her. But the panic on her face stopped him.

"Meg, sit down," he said, his tone low and flat because putting out more volume was impossible. Pride and determination kept him standing there, facing her. "Sit down before you fall down."

The sound of his voice made her flinch, and perhaps that

was the worst of all. A few minutes ago she'd been warm and pliant in his arms. Now she was like a robot as she put her hand on the chair back and pulled it away from the table. Melting onto the seat, she cradled her head in her hands.

Stiff-legged, he crossed the room to the sink, filled a tumbler with water and set it on the table in front of her.

"Drink."

Again she followed directions, then gagged and began to cough. The agonized sound released him. But when he rushed to her side and rubbed his hand across her shoulders, her whole body stiffened and he snatched his hand back.

"It's okay. I won't…won't touch you again." God, what was wrong with him? All the evidence showed that she'd come here to spy on him—probably even steal from him. And he'd do well to keep that fact in mind.

Moving to the counter, he leaned his hips against the solid support and braced his legs to keep himself steady. He should haul her down to the security center. But he wasn't going to put himself through that. They could keep this private, between the two of them.

His hands clenched and unclenched as his traitorous mind served him up images of the way she'd clung to him, pulled him down the hall toward the bedroom.

"I guess you've been sleeping with the enemy," he accused, then wondered why he'd needed to say it. One last chance. One last hope against hope that he'd hear a denial. None came.

"Was it the Jackal who got to you?" he demanded.

"Who?"

"The millionaire arms dealer Jerome Johnson," he clarified. "Or did you and your friend Leroy Enders hatch this plot?"

"It was Johnson," she whispered. "Is he an arms dealer?"

"What did he tell you about himself? That he worked

for the International Red Cross or something? Did he tell you *I* was a moneygrubbing bastard who sent men to their deaths? Was that why you were willing to do it?''

Her shoulders hunched, and she kept her eyes trained on her hands. ''Something like that.''

He heard himself make a derisive noise. ''Yeah, well, he's not a very nice guy. He'll do anything it takes to get his hands on a laboratory-pure sample of the K-007 virus. He wants to sell it back to the country where the Operation Clean Sweep team wiped out production. And to anybody else who has the money for weapons of mass destruction. Of course, I don't expect you to take *my* word for any of that now. Except that maybe you're wondering why good old Enders tried to kill you.''

She didn't answer, didn't move. As he watched her, a chilling thought struck him like a sucker punch, and he cursed under his breath as the full impact hit. Wondering why he cared, he said, ''I was going to hustle your butt out of here, since you're a serious security risk to me. Now...I'm afraid that could be writing your death sentence.''

MEG HUDDLED ON THE CHAIR, fighting the sick feeling rising in her throat, struggling to string one coherent thought together with the next one.

Meg Faulkner. Meg Wexler. Fraud. Liar. Cheat.

The realization brought shame, sadness, a sense of utter desolation. No wonder she'd fought so hard against regaining her memory. She'd made a pact with the devil, and no matter how hard she'd tried to convince herself she was doing the right thing, she'd regretted her decision to the bottom of her soul. Her unconscious mind had understood that and had taken the only course available. When she'd awakened in Glenn Bridgman's emergency room, she'd forgotten all about her secret mission.

''I can't stay,'' she whispered.

"It's not going to be too good for Tommy if Johnson kills you."

An image of her poor, sick brother zinged into her mind. Glenn was right—Tommy needed her. If she got herself killed, he'd have no one—except Glenn Bridgman. The man she'd thought was a monster. The man she'd fallen in love with. The monster image had been so compelling. She had bought into it so strongly that it still flickered at the edges of her mind; like the shadows in Plato's cave, it had taken on the shape of reality, yet now she knew it had no foundation in truth.

Mr. Johnson had handled her like a master manipulator—sketched in a bogus image of the reclusive Glenn Bridgman—because he'd wanted her cooperation. It hadn't been so difficult, because she'd already blamed the master of Castle Phoenix for all her brother's troubles.

But that was before she'd found out that no one could paint a more damning picture of Glenn Bridgman than the portrait he carried around in his own head. It was totally wrong, of course. Like the picture of Dorian Gray—only in reverse. She'd learned that well enough for herself when her defenses were down.

Instinctively she'd trusted Glenn. And he'd responded to that trust. She was the one who had lured him into a physical relationship. She was the one who had made him admit that he had the same need for closeness and love as other men. She'd told him she wouldn't hurt him, but that was exactly what she'd done.

He'd opened himself to her, because she'd pushed hard to make it happen. Now he knew the truth about her. She was a spy who'd come here to do whatever damage she could.

She clenched her hands together until she thought the bones would snap. Now that she understood the depths of her duplicity, knowing how badly she'd betrayed him, she couldn't look him in the eye. Still, as he pushed himself away from the counter, she risked a quick glance at his face. The pain she saw was like a hot poker stabbing into her vital organs.

Trying not to moan, she squeezed her eyes shut and covered them with the heels of her hands, pressing with such force that she saw flashing lights.

"Are you all right?" he asked, his voice gritty.

She got out the syllable, "Yes," hating the lie, hating the hollow feeling in her chest.

Sitting up straighter, she cleared her throat. "I can tell you Johnson's scheme—or at least what he told me I was supposed to be doing. The plant specimens in my trunk were from South America. I was supposed to be posing as a biologist."

He gave a bark of a laugh. "Kind of inconvenient having Enders curled around them."

"Lee... He told me his name was Lee," she managed. "He—he reminded me of my father. I always did what my father told me."

"Yeah."

"He had some kind of spray that would make any of your guards who looked in the trunk forget they'd seen him." She shuddered. "I—I guess that's what happened to your man who was drugged."

"Did you know he was planning to go after the guard dogs?" Glenn pressed.

"No. Honestly, I didn't know!" she said, wondering if he believed her; if he'd ever believe her again.

"Did you know he was after the virus that infected your brother?"

She gave a violent shake of her head. "I thought he was here to steal some kind of pharmaceutical—with highly commercial value."

Glenn's gaze bored into her. "Lucky for him he didn't manage to break into the lab."

"Yes," she wheezed.

"It looks like Johnson didn't care who got hurt if it increased the odds of success. The first surprise he had for you was the rockslide—so you'd need my help. He didn't know the accident would wipe out your memory. Maybe that's why Enders decided he had to eliminate you. No telling what you'd do if you suddenly got with the program."

She swallowed hard, then forced herself to look him in the eye. "Maybe you won't believe me, but I'm sorry I agreed to go along with Johnson."

"How was all this supposed to help Tommy?"

"Johnson was going to pay me a million dollars—for Tommy's care."

Glenn whistled through his teeth. "A lot of money. I can see why you were persuaded."

"I did it for my brother! He's falling apart before my eyes. I wanted him to have the best medical care, and he's not getting that from the army."

He gave her a tight nod. "I told him you'd call later this evening. I also told him I'd put him in the first group of human trials."

"You'd do that for him? After what I did to you?"

"The two things aren't connected. I like Tommy. I know he's in bad shape. I'm hoping I can turn him around." He stopped, gave her a direct look. "I'm not trying to win your approval."

"I know," she managed. Never that. He was too proud.

She was wondering what to say next, when his phone rang, and he pulled it from his pocket. She'd come to hate the way the emergency phone dictated his life. This time she was thankful for the interruption.

After listening for a moment he asked, "How is he?" then answered, "Good." Again he listened, muttered something under his breath, and hung up. When he raised his head, his eyes bored into hers. "Hal—General Dorsey is okay. He wants to talk to both of us."

"About what?" she asked, her stomach tightening with apprehension.

"That wasn't part of the message. I can tell him you aren't available, if you want."

She shook her head. She'd face the general the way she'd just faced Glenn.

"Give me a minute to get ready," she said.

"Don't take too long."

HE LISTENED TO HER footsteps recede down the hall, feeling relief as much as anything else. God, why had he asked her to go back to his quarters? Anywhere else would have been better.

Now the scent of her would linger here hours longer. And he didn't want to be reminded of anything they'd done, anything they'd said. Anything he'd felt.

His nails dug into his palms, and he told himself to unclench his hands. When he was sure she was out of earshot, he smashed his fist against the table—grateful for the jolt of pain.

It was better than the raw burning of acid eating him from the inside out. Ruthlessly, he turned the gnawing pain into anger. At her. At himself.

God, what a jerk he was. He was still trying to protect her. Mr. Nobility. Keeping her here so Johnson wouldn't kill her.

He snorted. Feeling compassion for her was dangerous. *She* was dangerous. Not just to him—to everyone at Castle Phoenix.

Send her away! his anger screamed at him. *Before she does something else to damage you—to damage the mission.* But he couldn't do it. Not now. Because if something happened to her, he'd have one more death on his conscience.

MEG WOVE HER WAY INTO the bedroom, her breath coming in painful gasps. There were no bars here. She could be out the window in moments. Across the lawn. Into the woods. Away from the man she'd hurt so badly.

She wrapped her arms around her shoulders, fighting for control. If she ran, she'd only confirm his worst assumptions about her. If she stayed, maybe she had a chance to...

To what?

Regain what they'd had together?

Impossible.

But perhaps there was some way to earn his respect again.

She didn't allow herself to hope as she mechanically pulled on fresh clothes.

Going quietly back down the hall, she caught Glenn standing with his hands rigidly at his sides as he stared out the window into the darkness. The tight set of his shoulders made her vision blur. By force of will, she kept herself from crossing the room and slipping her arms around him. He wouldn't want that. Not now. Not ever.

Instead she only called out softly, "I'm ready."

His posture changed abruptly. Without looking in her direction, he started for the door. She stayed several paces behind him, unable to meet the inquisitive gaze of the guards who fell into place behind them.

Nobody spoke on the way to the medical wing. Glenn checked a chart, then led her down the hall to a hospital room that was much like the one she'd occupied.

Hal Dorsey was propped up in bed, an IV line attached to his left arm. When they stepped through the door, he pushed himself up straighter, grimacing with the effort. His gaze went from her to Glenn and back again.

"You've gotten your memory back," he said.

She nodded.

"And you've found out you were sent here to—"

She swallowed hard. "Help Mr. Johnson—the Jackal, I guess you call him—steal a sample of K-007."

"How much was he paying you?"

"A million dollars. But it wasn't for me. It was for medical expenses for my brother, Tommy Faulkner," she answered, her voice low and flat. Quickly she filled him in on a few of the details she'd already given Glenn.

"And now you're feeling like hell—wishing you'd had better judgment," Dorsey muttered. "Well, you were misguided—but honest. That's more than I can say for myself."

She stared at him, wondering what he could possibly mean. Before she could ask, he swung his gaze to Glenn. "I've let you think you were responsible for giving the okay on Operation Clean Sweep."

"I was!" Glenn replied.

"Yes. You had the data. You made the decision. But I had the same data. I reviewed it at the same time. I had questions in my mind about the mission, but I made the determination that we needed to get our hands on that virus, and the risk was acceptable. I'm the one who didn't tell you the entire plan."

"You? I thought it came from…higher up."

"I know. I never gave you all the facts."

They stared at each other for several silent seconds. "Why are you telling me now?" Glenn finally asked.

Dorsey's gaze turned inward. "Because, at first, I could keep fooling myself that the price we paid was acceptable. We got control of the K-007, and a squad of men suffered for a few years. I thought that if I pumped enough money into your research, you could cure the men. And that would make it come out all right. But some of them have already started dying." He stopped, as a wheezing sigh trickled out of him. "Even if you get the antidote on-line in the next few weeks, the sickest ones will never regain their health. When I thought Sparks was going to get me killed a few hours ago, I realized I couldn't go to my grave with that on my conscience."

"I know you had the final say," Glenn admitted. "That doesn't take any responsibility away from me."

"You don't know that General Tallfield tried to scrub the operation. I insisted that we go ahead."

Glenn shrugged. "Does that really make a difference?"

"I think so." He turned to Meg. "Tell him what you think."

"Don't bother," Glenn interrupted. "I can't imagine that I'd get an honest answer."

She felt her throat close as she struggled to keep her tears from spilling over.

Glenn turned and walked out of the room, and she was left alone with Hal Dorsey. The old man's eyes were moist, and he seemed to be waging the same struggle as she.

Neither of them spoke for several moments.

She went to the bedside table, grabbed a tissue and blew her nose. When she felt more in control, she turned to the man in the bed. He'd been her enemy. But now...?

"What should I do?" she asked him.

"What do you want?"

Taking a chance, she whispered, "I want him to trust me again. I want him to...love me."

"You love him?"

"Yes."

"Love at first sight, was it?"

"Don't mock me."

"I'm not. I'm trying to help you."

"Why should you?"

"You were good for him. I could see that." He gave a raspy laugh. "You may not believe it, but secretly I was rooting for you. I still am." His face contorted. "Glenn doesn't give his trust lightly. He gave it to you. Now he feels betrayed."

"Cheated. Used," she added.

"At the moment. But maybe he's smart enough to get past that. Don't give up on him," Dorsey whispered.

The old man's vote of confidence meant a lot to her. But she knew it would never be enough. And it was obvious the conversation had worn him out. "I should let you rest."

When she slipped from the room, two hard-faced guards were waiting for her by the door. She cringed when she recognized one from the group at the garage. He looked just as menacing now, and she supposed the rumors about her were flying again.

But he wouldn't do anything to her here. Not with so many people around, she told herself, as he and his partner followed her down the hall to the central station where Glenn and Dr. Ryder were discussing Dorsey's condition. They stopped talking when she approached.

"You told Tommy I'd call," she reminded Glenn. "I should do that."

"There's a phone around the corner in the lounge. Dial nine to get an outside line," he answered brusquely, then addressed the guard. "Gady, keep an eye on her."

She saw the guards take in Glenn's demeanor, and the obvious tension between them.

"Yes, sir," he answered smartly, and he stayed only a pace behind her as she turned and hurried away.

She should have asked Glenn what he'd said to Tommy, she realized after she'd dialed the number. But that would have meant getting into conversation, and he'd made it clear he didn't want to talk to her.

As the phone rang, she clamped her hand around the receiver, her nerves tightening as she waited for her brother to answer. Sometimes he was slow, but after ten rings, she felt panic rising in her chest. Twelve. Fifteen. Twenty. Something was wrong.

She pictured him lying on the floor, struggling to get to the phone, or in bed, unable to raise his arm, and a violent shudder racked her body.

God, she never should have left him alone in his condition. She should have arranged for someone to stay with him while she was gone.

The tears she had been struggling to control welled in her eyes and trickled down her cheeks. She'd kept herself from crying for Glenn, but she couldn't hold back her anguish over Tommy.

Jumping up, she ran from the alcove and made a frantic dash toward the area where she'd left Glenn. The man named Gady grabbed her arm and pulled her to a halt, his face angry and challenging.

"What was that? Some kind of code call?"

"No!" She tried to wrest herself from his grasp, but he held her fast. "Please. I have to leave!" she gasped out, frightened now as well as desperate.

When she pushed frantically at him, he twisted her arm behind her back.

"That's enough crap out of you," he ground out, slamming her against the wall with enough force to make her head ring. She screamed in pain and terror, then gasped as he pulled out a pair of handcuffs and grabbed her wrist.

Chapter Fifteen

Heavy footsteps sounded in the hall.

With her face against the wall, Meg could see nothing. But she could hear Glenn's angry voice as he skidded to a stop behind the guard.

"Back off, Gady!" he ordered, moving into her line of sight, so that her terrified gaze collided with his.

For heartbeats, there was no response from the man who held her against the wall.

Glenn's hand slid to the pistol at his waist. "Back off," he repeated, "before somebody gets hurt."

"Yes, sir," Gady wheezed.

The menacing hands dropped away from her, and she twisted to the side, fighting the need to slide to the floor and curl into a ball.

Instead, she turned slowly, her eyes riveted on Glenn as he stood over the guard.

"What the hell were you doing?" he growled.

"I thought she was going to attack you, sir."

"She's not going to grab a gun and shoot me, if that's what you're worried about."

"Sir—"

"Leave us alone," he ordered. "Both of you."

There was a moment's hesitation, and Meg wondered if the guards were deciding whether Glenn was competent to make a decision about his safety where she was concerned.

Finally they complied and her gaze rose to Glenn's, willing some kind of understanding. When his eyes remained hard and flat, she pushed away from the wall. She thought she could stand on her own, but when she started to pitch forward, he caught her. A sob welled in her throat as she wrapped her arms around him and held tight.

She felt a surge of hope when his hands came up to cradle her shoulders. Then, perhaps realizing what he was doing, he let his arms fall back to his sides.

"Are you okay? Did he hurt you?" he asked gruffly.

Always the gentleman, she thought. He'd kept her from falling on her face, but that was the extent of it. Her eyes swam, but she held back the tears by force of will.

"He didn't hurt me," she lied, controlling the impulse to flex her arm so she could judge the extent of the injury.

He lifted her wrist and looked down at the place where a bruise was forming. "You should put some ice on that," he said, his face a strange mixture of concern and medical objectivity.

With a little nod she stepped back, then turned her head and quickly swiped her hand across her eyes.

Once again, the impact of what she'd done to him hit her like a runaway freight train. And with her shame came the overwhelming need to make him understand.

Perhaps the general's words had given her the courage she needed. When Glenn took a step back, she grabbed his sleeve.

"Wait!"

The plea stopped him.

"Up in your quarters, I was too shocked to tell you what I was feeling. Too shocked to sort it all out. Now I want to explain—" Trembling, she raised her gaze to his again.

His eyes were glacial. "I don't think that would be productive."

His frigid stare cut through her flesh to her bones, turning them brittle. He was silently telling her to back off. Risking everything, she tightened her hold on his arm and kept talking. "I know it's difficult for you to give your trust to me again. I worked hard to get close to you, and you learned that everything about my background was a lie. You found out I came here to—to subvert your mission. Now you think my feelings for you couldn't be real. But you're wrong."

"I don't appreciate having someone else explain to me what I'm thinking," he ground out, the delivery like a slap in the face.

She felt her cheeks burn, wondering why she'd harbored any hope of reaching him again.

She couldn't look at him now, but she still couldn't turn away—even if there was nothing left to say but goodbye. Taking a small step closer and then another, she rested her cheek against his shoulder, feeling him stiffen in reaction.

While he was still within her reach, she moved her hand, stroking his forearm, feeling the rigid muscles clench under her touch. On a sigh, she closed her eyes and pressed her lips against his collarbone, absorbing his physical presence, memorizing the fit of his hard body against her softer curves.

"Glenn," she murmured. "You gave me something I never dreamed I'd have—something to cherish. I'm willing to admit that it might not have been possible for the two of us to get so close so quickly in the real world. But that closeness wasn't an illusion, and while it lasted, it was the best thing that ever happened to me."

She swallowed, willing to bare her soul, because honesty was the only thing she could give him now. "I want what we had back. But I understand why you don't."

He stood like a marble statue about to shatter. Yet she could see a pulse beating wildly in his neck. She gave herself a few more seconds of contact, her own pulse pounding. Then she stepped away, the shock of cold air against her body like a frigid wind against her flesh. Stiffly, she turned so that he couldn't see the anguish on her face and gave herself a few moments to regain her composure.

But then, perhaps she was still standing there with her

heart pounding because she hoped against hope that he'd reach for her.

Seconds stretched—each one a year of her life dragging by. When she couldn't bear it any longer, she started stiffly down the hall.

"Meg—"

Dimly above her footsteps echoing on the tile floor, she thought she heard him call her name. But she knew she had conjured it up from her own wishful thinking.

Swiftly, she approached the desk where Dylan Ryder was still working.

"I have to go back to Baltimore. Something's happened to my brother," she told him.

"What did he say to you?"

"Nothing. He didn't answer the phone. That's how I know something's wrong."

"He could be out," Ryder suggested.

"In the middle of the night?"

The physician blinked. "The middle of the night?"

"It's been a long day," she said wearily, then continued, "Tommy doesn't go out of the apartment. A nursing service brings in groceries—or I do. He's always there. That means he's too sick to answer the phone. Or he's fallen down or something. I have to go see what's wrong."

"The Jackal will come after you," Glenn said, and she realized he had followed her around the corner.

She kept her eyes away from him. "That's not your problem."

"Maybe not. But Tommy is my problem. We can fly to Baltimore. If he's too sick to be on his own, we'll bring him back here by medevac."

"You'd do that for me?" she whispered.

"I made a commitment to him a long time ago," he replied, sidestepping the direct question.

She was about to thank him, when the phone interrupted once again. Ryder picked it up. As he listened, his brow wrinkled.

"Meg tried to call you," he said. "She was worried."

"It's Tommy?" she asked, her mood swinging wildly again.

"Yes," he mouthed, giving her a reassuring look. It faded as he kept listening to the voice on the other end of the line.

"Let me talk to him," Meg demanded.

Ryder handed over the phone, and she spoke into the receiver. "Tommy? Are you all right, Tommy?"

"Meg! Thank God," he gasped.

"What's wrong? What's happened?"

"I was taking a nap...and men burst in," he said, his voice slightly bewildered. "The guy who has me, he says his name is Mr. Johnson, and he hired you to do some work for him. What were—?" Tommy's voice stopped abruptly.

Frantically, Meg called his name.

Someone else answered. "Ms. Faulkner. I see you're coping with life at Castle Phoenix. Congratulations."

A chill stirred the hair at the back of her neck.

"Ms. Faulkner, are you there?"

"Mr. Johnson," she said. "What are you doing at Tommy's?"

"I'm not at your brother's. I have him with me—in custody. If you don't do exactly what I tell you, I'm going to kill him."

"No!"

"Oh, yes. Let me speak to Bridgman," he ordered.

She raised her eyes to Glenn and handed him the phone.

"Tommy Faulkner had better be all right," was the first thing out of his mouth as he pushed a button on the console.

Meg heard a loud static buzz as a speaker leaped to life and began to broadcast Johnson's voice. "You're not in a position to make demands," he was saying. "And I'm aware that your automated system has initiated procedures to trace this call. I don't mind in the least. In fact, I'm going to tell you where I am, because you're coming here, with a laboratory-pure sample of the virus you call K-007."

"The hell I am!"

"You don't have any options. I have Tommy Faulkner with me. And twelve other men from Operation Clean Sweep. If you're not here in two hours with the sample, I'm going to start killing them—one every hour, beginning with Faulkner."

"No!" Meg breathed.

"I need time to think about it," Glenn answered.

"In case you need further incentive," Johnson continued, "I have a man on your estate. He's set explosives at various strategic locations. If you don't comply with my orders, he'll blow up your whole operation."

"And then you'll never get what you want," Glenn growled. "So I think you're going to give me some time to consider your proposition. I need a few hours."

"One hour."

"Three."

"Two. I'll call you back then," Johnson said before slamming down the receiver so hard that the noise reverberated through the hallway.

Meg couldn't move, couldn't breathe.

But Glenn was already considering his options. "I can't give the virus to Johnson."

"But what about Tommy?" Meg pleaded. "He's going to kill my brother and the other men if you don't."

"I won't let him." He looked at his watch. "It's 2:32," he announced. "We need to be prepped to deploy a code-D action by 4:32."

Meg didn't have a clue about what that meant. But Ryder's eyes brightened. "Code D," he repeated.

"And we've been assuming that the intruder escaped," Glenn went on with lightning speed. "Now we can't take a chance on his still being on the estate and still being active. I want a bomb squad with dogs at the level-four biohazards lab on the double. Next I want other teams equipped with night scopes at the power plant, the water-treatment plant, the barracks, the office complex."

"We can't cover all of them at once," a voice answered. It was Blake Claymore, who looked as if he'd run all the way from the security center—with his arm still in a sling, his face slick with perspiration. "We've traced the call," he added. "It's from his compound on Long Island."

"Get me a map of the location—and a map of the grounds. A schematic of the building would be good, too."

Meg expected to hear that the request was impossible. Instead Blake said, "We're already on that."

"What's a Code-D action?" Meg asked, allowing hope to seep into her.

"A little something Glenn cooked up for just such an emergency," Claymore told her smugly, then launched into a quick explanation.

When he finished, she shook her head. "No."

Glenn's angry gaze focused on her. "What do you mean—no? You don't have a vote on this."

"Your plan involves a face-to-face confrontation with Johnson. I say you're too valuable to risk." She raised her chin. "If someone has to take him what he thinks he wants, then it's going to be me," she said.

"That's crazy. We've practiced the drill half-a-dozen times. You can't just come in cold."

"I'm a quick study."

"You'll screw it up!" Glenn growled.

"I don't think so," Claymore chimed in. "Not from the way she's reacted to every situation we and Enders and Sparks threw at her."

She gave him a grateful look. Glenn shot him an angry scowl.

Ignoring them both, Claymore plowed on. "Don't overlook the most compelling factor of all. If you go, Johnson will be prepared for you to pull a fast one. If she goes, he'll think you're giving her exactly what she deserves. And since he's already tricked her into cooperating once, he'll think he has the upper hand with her." He gave Glenn a direct look. "But more important, she keeps you out of the line of fire. Whatever happens, you can finish the research, because you're the best hope for the men of Operation Clean Sweep.''

"Dylan can do it," Glenn snapped.

"As a backup, I'm okay," Ryder answered. "But we both know I'm not as good as you are in the lab. I'm a hands-on medic who's best with patients. With me in charge of the K-007 project, we'd have delays. And delays could be fatal—to Tommy, for example."

Meg felt her teeth clench. In the end, everything she'd sacrificed to save her brother could be for nothing. When she turned to face Glenn, he was staring at her—and she saw a tiny spark of compassion in his eyes. His arm jerked, and she thought he was going to reach for her. She was already swaying toward him when she saw his palm was pressed to his side. Warning herself not to wish for the impossible, she grasped the edge of the desk with a steadying hand and hung on.

"We're wasting time arguing," she told him. "I suggest you start briefing me on what I need to know to pull this off."

THE TICKING OF THE WALL clock seemed to dominate the briefing room. That and Claymore's voice. It was flat and precise, going over details, clarifying points. Meg tried to listen closely, because she knew her life depended on following instructions. Even so, she found her thoughts straying to Glenn.

He'd coolly turned her over to the security chief and gone off to make other preparations—leaving no opportunity for any more personal discussion.

But then, what had she expected from a man who was a master at pushing his emotions to some corner of his mind where they were barely a distraction?

At 4:32 when a buzzer rang, she jumped. It was the warning signal that Johnson was calling Glenn.

"Stay here," Claymore ordered as he surged to his feet

and stepped into the next room, closing the door behind him.

Meg had no intention of obeying. Moving to the door, she opened it several inches and listened to the conversation being broadcast over a speaker.

"Your time's up," Johnson was saying, the speaker giving his voice an eerie quality as he asked, "Should I start killing the hostages? Or should I detonate the bombs?"

There were no bombs. At least, that was Claymore's opinion after he'd received reports from the teams he'd sent to search the grounds. Still, he could be wrong.

"No. I'll trade the virus for the hostages," Glenn retorted.

At the sound of his voice, Meg pushed the door wider, but the security chief was the only occupant of the room. Glenn was somewhere else.

"A wise decision," Johnson said. "You will bring it immediately."

"Not me. Transporting the sample involves a certain amount of risk," Glenn told him. After a pregnant pause, he added, "I'm going to let the woman you sent here do it. Ms. Faulkner. If anyone gets shot 'by accident,' it will be her—not me."

The stinging words brought a choking sensation to Meg's throat. If Glenn was acting, he was doing a superb job.

"I don't want her back."

"Too bad. She put us in considerable jeopardy by coming here. So it's only fair she be the one to take the risk of bringing the samples to you."

"Very interesting logic," Johnson answered. "You more than live up to your reputation, Bridgman."

"So do you. Why did you decide to have her killed after she brought your saboteur in here?" Glenn asked, his tone conversational.

"My man sent a message that she was cooperating with you. The longer you had access to her, the better the chances that she'd reveal my plans."

"What she knew of them," Glenn said.

"I don't take chances."

"Neither do I. What guarantee do I have that you'll play straight with me?"

"I could ask the same question," Johnson observed.

"I want the men back—unharmed."

Numbly, Meg listened to the exchange, wishing she could see the expression on Glenn's face.

"I'll release the men when I get the virus," Johnson replied.

"I want Tommy Faulkner out of there before she comes in."

"Why?"

"He was the team leader. I feel a special responsibility toward him."

"I thought you did," Johnson said with satisfaction. "Which is why it was so amusing to subvert his sister."

She stood with her hand curled around the edge of the doorjamb, holding herself erect by sheer force of will. It was a relief when the two men turned to logistics.

As if he didn't already have the information, Glenn pretended he needed to consult his computer for a location where he could set down a helicopter near Johnson's house.

When they'd agreed on the landing site, he added, "I'll have the woman send me an electronic signal when her brother is out."

"I will be monitoring all local channels. I don't want any two-way communication between you and her, in case you have something funny planned."

"I'm playing this your way!" Glenn snapped. "All she'll be able to do is send an electronic pulse."

"You can have Faulkner first. When I get the virus, you can have the other men."

"I suppose I'll have to take your word on that," Glenn growled.

"Afraid so."

"Well, I'll give you some additional incentive to keep

your part of the bargain. Fighting you for so long has cost me considerable resources. If this goes okay, I'll take your cooperation as a sign that we'll come to some sort of accommodation in the future.''

There was a moment of stunned silence on the other end of the line. Then a noise that was half incredulous, half yearning. ''You'd work with me?''

''It was General Dorsey who was so set against you,'' Glenn said. ''He was the moneyman, so I had to dance to his tune if I wanted research funding. As you may know, he's failing fast. When he's out of my hair, I won't have to bow to his wishes.''

''Yes. I understand,'' Johnson murmured, his silky voice making Meg's skin crawl. ''Perhaps I haven't fully appreciated the fact that you've been working under a handicap.''

''Exactly. If the two of us joined forces, no one could touch our operation. You've got the distribution and I've got the biological expertise. But we can discuss our mutual interests later.''

When the call ended, Claymore pressed a button on the phone, then turned. Finding her standing in the doorway, he scowled. ''You weren't supposed to hear that.''

''So I gather.'' She swallowed. ''It looks like Glenn has Johnson convinced. That—that part about the general was a brilliant touch.''

''Yeah.'' He cleared his throat, watching her. ''Meg—''

''What?''

''We're all doing what we have to.''

She gave him a tight nod, wanting to beg for more crumbs. But he pressed ahead. ''I want to check on the special equipment Glenn ordered. Then you'd better leave. If you're late, Johnson will be suspicious.''

''Yes.''

''I'll take you to the helicopter.''

She followed him out of the room and downstairs.

IN HIS OFFICE, GLENN watched on the TV monitor as Meg marched down the hall and descended the steps.

One eye on the screen, he placed a call to Long Island, then made a couple more within the castle complex. Then he went to the closet where he kept emergency-combat gear and pulled out a camouflage shirt and pants.

After arming himself, he took a considerable amount of cash from the safe in his office. There had been times when he'd been annoyed by practice drills designed to keep the facility on semi-alert status at all times. Now he silently thanked Blake for emphasizing readiness.

Crossing to the window, he stared in the direction of the chopper, watching for the first glimpse of Meg. When he was sure that something had gone wrong, she finally appeared, walking between two guards, her shoulders back and her head up, until she automatically ducked as she came near the whirring blades.

Lord, the woman had guts. More than he. She'd told him how she felt about the two of them, even when she'd thought he wasn't capable of listening.

Acid churned through his vital organs as he watched her climb aboard, her golden hair catching the first faint rays of light from the rising sun.

He was sending her off to Johnson's hideout thinking she understood his strategy. But she didn't. She had no idea what was really going to happen. Neither did Blake. Because Glenn wasn't asking permission from his chief of security. He'd already made too many mistakes in his life. Now he understood what needed to be done, and he was going to do it.

He was about to exit the office when he stopped short, scribbled a second note—to Hal. It was brief and to the point. But he was sure his old friend would read between the lines.

His goodbyes said, he grabbed a windbreaker that would conceal his Beretta. Then he took the steps two at a time, heading for the ground floor. As he ran, he pulled the phone from his pocket and called the additional helicopter pilot that he had on standby. The jeep he'd ordered was already at the back entrance. It took off for the airstrip as soon as he leaped into the passenger seat.

Chapter Sixteen

Glenn was in the air, in a small high-speed copter, taking a route that would bring him to a location where he could land without being detected—even as he reviewed the data Blake had brought him on Johnson as well as the supplemental information he'd gotten from the computer databases. Together with what he'd already collected on the man, it was a sizable amount of material. But was it enough? Was there some trap waiting for a foolhardy lone assailant?

The Jackal's summer home in the Hamptons was well guarded. And there was an electric fence. But there was also a crumbling, unused boat dock jutting into the Long Island Sound.

Nobody could safely electrify water, which made the sound the one possible point of entry. But not by boat. Johnson would be on the lookout for that.

MEG SLIPPED HER HAND into her pocket and fingered the remote control that Blake had provided.

Back at Castle Phoenix, she'd acted as if she had nerves of steel. She'd made them think she had everything under control, because that was the only way to convince them to send her. But there hadn't been much time to review her hurried instructions—or to test the special equipment that the security chief had provided. It might literally blow up in her face or it might function perfectly. Unfortunately, there was no way of knowing which until the moment of truth.

Harrison, the pilot, had said almost nothing since she'd climbed aboard. Sliding him a sideways glance, she found he was watching her speculatively. For a moment, their gazes locked. Then she swiveled her head toward the back of the chopper. It was a large troop carrier, and she wondered for a moment where Glenn had gotten it. Probably Dorsey had pulled a few strings.

The rest of the seats were empty. If everything went the way Claymore had planned, the seats would be filled with sick men on the return journey.

A CALL CAME FROM CASTLE Phoenix when Glenn was a few miles from the Hamptons. Blake might have figured out he'd gone, but it wasn't going to do him any good. He hesitated, aware that his pilot was waiting for him to acknowledge the call. As he debated his options, he imagined Hal on the other end of the line. Or Blake. They'd tell him he was crazy. He'd say that a lone man could slip past Johnson's defenses more easily than an assault team.

But there were good reasons for not answering. He didn't want to explain his motives. And he didn't want to be distracted by any more bad news. If Blake was calling to say a bomb had gone off on the estate, it was better not to find out about it until later.

So he turned off the radio, then instructed the pilot to land on a large vacant tract where he'd arranged to have a rental car meet him. At this hour of the morning, there was no traffic on the road. But his car was waiting for him— parked at the edge of a sandy field. Lucky for him that you could buy anything you wanted in this plush New York enclave if you were willing to pay the price.

Grabbing his knapsack, he exited the chopper. After paying the sleepy driver with the wad of cash as promised, he had a quick consultation over the map he'd brought, then headed in the direction of Johnson's estate. He pulled into a patch of underbrush a quarter of a mile from his destination and ditched the car. Then he made a quick dash across private property and started along the water's edge toward Johnson's house.

As he expected, it was a low-slung wood-and-stone structure that looked as if it had been up-to-the-minute "modern" architecture in the sixties. Holding his gun above his head, he slipped into the water, and began moving cautiously toward the house, using as cover the gray boulders that had been spread out to reinforce the eroding shoreline.

It had been a long time since he'd functioned in a combat situation, but he found he slipped easily back into the role—perhaps because thinking about his next move kept his mind from turning to more disturbing topics.

When he saw a two-man patrol sweep by, he ducked below the edge of the bank until they'd passed. After determining he was in the clear, he climbed the water-slick rocks and began to circle toward the back of the house, congratulating himself that everything was going smoothly.

He was fifty feet from the cover of a low hedge surrounding the rose garden when he heard a helicopter overhead.

Meg.

God, he'd thought he had more time. Glancing at his watch, he sprinted toward the hedge, then prepared to advance to the next available cover. Before he could move, he felt the barrel of a gun at the small of his back.

"Hold it right there. And raise your hands," a gritty voice ordered. "One wrong move, and you're dead."

HARRISON DIPPED THE CHOPPER low over a rambling stone-and-wood house, circled, and set down on a wide stretch of deep green lawn enclosed by an iron fence with sharp, spearlike points.

As they came down gently on the grass, Meg wished the copter were outside the enclosure. The fence was a reminder that escape might be impossible.

Still, as she unbuckled her harness, she told herself that landing so close to the building would make it easier for Tommy to walk to the copter—if he was still able to walk.

The thought brought a strangled feeling to her chest, and she had to pause for a moment before lowering herself to the ground. Grabbing her carrying case, she started purposefully toward the house. She hadn't taken a dozen stops when six armed, hard-faced security guards materialized from side doors and formed a circle around her, halting her before she reached the building. They made Glenn's clean-scrubbed recruits look like Boy Scouts.

"TURN AROUND SLOWLY," the man with the gun ordered.

Keeping his face impassive, Glenn obeyed the gruff command and found himself facing a haggard-looking man wearing a camouflage outfit almost identical to his own. The clothing wasn't half as interesting as the chiseled features and the wild, desperate look in the mud-brown eyes.

In an even voice, Glenn asked, "Have you switched from dirty tricks to guard duty?"

The man shifted his weight from one foot to the other, but the gun stayed steady in his hand.

"Bridgman," he rasped. "I'll ask the questions. Suppose you tell me why you left Castle Phoenix, where you'd be nice and safe."

"Not so safe," Glenn countered. "Not with an intruder running around trying to wreck the place, trying to get himself killed."

A muscle in the gunman's cheek ticked.

"I'm surprised Johnson didn't terminate you, after you muffed your last assignment," Glenn said, searching for the right way to reach this guy, aware that while they talked, time was ticking by.

"Not likely."

Glenn evaluated the words, the tight features, the glittering eyes—and decided to take the chance of his life.

"Wouldn't it be interesting if we turned out to be on the same side?" he prompted.

THE GUARD TOOK AWAY Meg's carrying case and hefted it, obviously surprised by the weight. Setting it down, he stared at the lock.

"I wouldn't try to open it if I were you," she warned.

"I've been advised of that," he snapped, turning and looking her up and down, his gaze coming to rest on her breasts. "Let's find out what else you've got. Spread your legs."

Resisting the urge to clamp her lip between her teeth, she widened her stance and kept her eyes downcast as he began to frisk her for weapons—his touch straying where it would be impossible to conceal so much as a thimble.

But she endured his pawing and managed not to react when he emptied her pockets. They were full, to convince someone like him that she thought she'd be leaving directly after her mission. He checked the compartments of her wallet, shuffled through two hundred dollars in bills, ran his finger along the teeth of her comb, unwadded the tissues she'd balled into a crumpled mass on the flight down—then held up a small, cylindrical electronic device Claymore had given her.

"That's your signal device?"

She nodded.

"I'm gonna test it."

He pushed the button, and though she'd been prepared for something like this, her stomach dropped to her feet.

From her perspective nothing happened, but back in the helicopter, Harrison raised his hand, indicating that he'd heard the signal.

"Okay," the guard muttered, handing back the cylinder.

Meg gave him a tight nod, keeping her gaze steady.

Within the next few minutes, the pilot would press an activation sequence, changing the function of the device.

But neither one of them would know whether she was holding a full house or a bust hand—until the moment of truth.

Tensely, she waited while her captor spoke into a portable phone.

Before the call was completed, the front door of the house opened and a thin gray-haired man stepped onto the porch. It was the same man who'd hired her to invade Glenn's estate. She hadn't fully trusted him then, but she'd gone along with his scheme. He'd been slick and cunning and deadly. Now she understood why Glenn called him the Jackal. He was studying her with sharp black eyes, and she hated herself for letting his lies about Glenn fool her. She'd been gullible because she'd wanted to blame someone for her brother's illness, and Glenn had been such a logical choice. Then she'd discovered that Glenn would give anything—even his own life—if he could make Tommy and the other men well.

Hoping that none of the thoughts swirling in her head showed on her face, she picked up her case and started walking carefully forward, still flanked by guards.

Stopping a few feet away from the man who had gotten her into so much trouble, she raised her chin. "I want to see my brother."

"What, no friendly greeting?" Johnson retorted.

"You and I were never friendly. We had a business arrangement. Then I found out you ordered me killed."

He let the statement hang in the air for several seconds. "Is that what Bridgman told you?"

She fought to keep her expression neutral. "I think the evidence is on his side."

"What else did he say?"

"Not much. He plays his cards close to his vest," she replied.

"Is his friend General Dorsey still running the show?"

She shrugged. "He didn't confide in me."

Johnson studied her critically. "I hope you haven't developed any loyalty to Bridgman, because he doesn't care what happens to you.''

She let some of her anxiety seep into her face, using her fear to enhance the role she'd rehearsed. Unfortunately, there hadn't been much time to learn her cues—much less her lines. "I can tell you a few things. But—" She stopped and eyed their audience. "I'm not sure you want it to go any further than the two of us. Why don't we go inside?"

She waited for his answer, feeling her heart pounding inside her chest as he considered their mutual fate.

"All right," he said, looking toward the guards. "Crane and Butler, come with us. The rest of you, stay here."

Better than six against one, she thought as she clutched the handle of the carrying case and stepped across the threshold with the two designated men at her back.

They were in a wide entrance hall, as big as a master bedroom in a normal house. There were three doors leading from it, and all of them were closed. Perfect for her purposes.

Still, everything depended on what happened in the next few minutes. Letting Johnson see her raw nerves, she eyed the two remaining guards.

"These men are accustomed to hearing confidential information and keeping it to themselves," Johnson snapped. "So there's no problem about speaking in front of them."

She remained silent for several more seconds, then shrugged. "Okay. I'd say that Bridgman is at the end of his resources. It looks like he had a costly operation going. But it's getting shabby around the edges."

"Where?" Johnson demanded.

"Second-rate staff, old vehicles, damage all over the castle."

Johnson nodded in satisfaction. "So making a deal with me would be to his benefit."

"I don't know about any deals—except the one about my brother. You're supposed to let Tommy go, and I'll give you the material you requested from Bridgman."

Johnson's face turned flinty. "I'm sorry you came all this way for Lieutenant Faulkner," he said. "You see, since you've put yourself under my control, I don't have to deliver anybody to you.

"Take the package from her, Crane."

The man who'd searched her stepped forward and wrenched the carrying case from her left hand, stinging her flesh as the hard plastic handle whipped against her skin.

She rubbed her palm against her leg. "Bridgman was prepared for your trying to double-cross him. He told me I'd be able to force you to comply."

Pulling her other hand from her pocket, she held up the remote control, her fingers curled around the cylinder and her thumb tightly on the button.

"I now have my fingers pressed on a trigger device that will blow the cover off the case if my hand goes limp for a second. You understand?" she demanded, her head swinging toward the two men who had drawn their guns and pointed them at her.

Johnson's face had drained of color. "Hold your fire," he said, his voice thick. "Do you understand? Hold your fire."

"I tested it," Crane growled. "She's lying."

"We knew you would," Meg countered. "The helicopter pilot gave the signal for the activation. So drop the guns, unless you want to put it to the test," Meg said, feeling a surge of power as she waved the hand with the device.

"Do it," Johnson ordered.

Two pistols clattered to the marble floor, and she breathed out a little sigh.

"Send for my brother and the other men," Meg commanded.

"Bridgman said—"

"I'm making the rules now," she retorted, keeping her voice steady, half amazed that he hadn't called her bluff.

"You don't know the risk," Johnson hissed. "In that case is a pure sample of the virus that infected your brother.

It's in the contagious form. If you blow the lid, we're all dead."

She forced a smile. "Then you'd better get the hostages before my hand gets tired."

"How do I know you won't blow it anyway?"

She gave him a parody of a smile. "And commit suicide? You just have to hope I'm not that angry at myself for trusting you."

Johnson pulled the phone from his pocket, punched several keys, and began speaking as soon as someone came on the line. "Send the hostages to the front hall, at once," he said, then added, "all twenty."

"There aren't twenty!"

"Right. My mistake," he murmured.

She looked into his eyes, seeing a jackal's cunning, and knew where he'd gotten his name. Was he using some kind of code? Too bad if he was, because there was nothing she could do now besides follow the course she'd set.

When her tongue flicked out to moisten her dry lips, she saw Johnson watching with satisfaction. Angling away from him, she studied Crane and his buddy. They both looked pale and damp. "Move over toward your boss," she said.

They hurried to comply, and she backed up. The spacious entryway had become stifling, making it difficult to draw in a full breath. She longed to escape into the fresh air, but that was out of the question, since her effectiveness depended on staying close to Johnson.

On the other hand she still had to deal with the private army outside, she remembered with a sudden jolt. With her free hand, she opened the front door wide enough to give the remaining guards a view of the scene inside, then swiveled her head to address the master of the house.

"Tell them the plans have changed," she said in a voice loud enough to carry. "Tell your security force that I've got my finger on the trigger of a bomb, and that when the hostages get here, they are to be allowed to go directly to the helicopter. Tell them to drop their weapons."

The men on the lawn reacted to her sharp words by reaching for their guns, even as Johnson's face darkened.

"No!" he shouted. "Don't shoot! She's telling the truth."

His eyes bored into her, and she knew he was only waiting for his chance to get even.

"Drop your guns," he snapped.

Meg relaxed a notch as a small arsenal hit the ground, but she knew she wasn't out of the woods yet. Too much could still go wrong.

"Where will the men come from?" she asked.

Johnson jerked his shoulder behind him. She trained her eyes in that direction, then heard several sets of footsteps. Everyone was watching when a door opened and Tommy stepped through, his face pale and his expression puzzled. He and another man were leaning on each other, like two drunks staggering out of a bar.

There were more men behind them—a ragtag group who looked as if they'd been invited to a come-as-you-are party.

Relief flooded through her, and she realized with a jolt that she hadn't expected to get this far. Not really. But now it was almost over. All she had to do was get the hostages out of here.

"Meg," Tommy quavered. "What are you doing here?"

"It's okay. We're both leaving soon." She wanted to hug him. All she could do was ask urgently, "Are you all right?"

He looked ready to keel over, and she wondered if he could make it as far as the helicopter—even with his comrade's support.

When he started toward her, she held up the hand with the remote control. "Listen carefully, Tommy. I have a bomb," she said, using the same simplified explanation she'd given the security forces.

She saw from the way his eyes widened that he got the message. "What bomb? How?"

She showed him the controller clamped between her

thumb and finger, then gestured toward the carrying case. "If I ease up the pressure with my hand, that thing will go off. Which is why Johnson is going to let all of us go."

Raising her voice, she addressed the rest of the men, making a quick explanation. Some of them looked too confused to understand. Others straightened, their faces registering the implications of the situation. A couple in the back stood hunched over and unmoving so that she couldn't tell if they'd understood or not.

"Get the guns," she said, addressing two men who looked relatively fit and gesturing toward the weapons on the floor.

When they'd complied, she spoke to the entire group again. "There are more weapons outside on the ground. Get them, too. Then walk directly to the helicopter. It will take you to Castle Phoenix."

From the corner of her eye, she saw Johnson edging along the wall. But there was nowhere he could go, so her main focus stayed on the prisoners.

"Go on. Get out of here while you can," she told them.

Some of the hostages began moving eagerly toward the front door. One of the men in back stepped toward her.

When she realized who it was, her fingers froze on the controller in her hand.

Chapter Seventeen

"Glenn!" she gasped, hardly able to believe what she was seeing.

"In the flesh," he said dryly, stepping forward as if he'd planned to take charge all along.

His words elicited a laugh from the remaining prisoners and a low sound from Johnson, who now had his shoulders pressed to the wall.

"Gotcha," one of the hostages chortled, leering at Johnson before turning to Meg. "You like the way your brother played dumb? I guess he's still got some smarts left," he added, then let loose another wild laugh that teetered on the edge of hysteria.

"What the hell are you doing here?" Johnson growled at Glenn.

"Making sure everything goes according to plan." Glenn shouldered his way through the remaining prisoners and moved to Meg's side, gesturing toward the carrying case she'd brought from Castle Phoenix. "I'll take over the controller for the virus canister," he said. "When you feel my pressure on the button, slip your fingers out from under mine."

She shook her head, struggling to comprehend what was going on. "You're...you're not supposed to be here," she managed, echoing the gray-haired man's shock.

"That's what I wanted you to think, so you'd play your role. But I wasn't going to let you do this alone. Give me the controller. Go with the men. I'll catch up in a few minutes."

She was almost too stunned to answer, but she managed to reply. "No. I can't leave you here."

His eyes burned into hers, before flashing back to Johnson. "I didn't come all this way to argue with you. Go on! I'll follow as soon as you and the men are safe."

The commanding tone of Glenn's voice made her reconsider, until she got a look at the man behind him. Long scratches marred the skin of his face, and she realized with a start that she'd given them to him—when she'd leaped on his back in the guest quarters and clawed at his face. She'd forgotten about that till now.

"Glenn," she warned. "Watch out. That's Enders. He's the one from the trunk of my car—the one who tried to kill me—"

"I know," he interrupted. "He and I met up when we were both sneaking in here. He's changed sides."

"'Changed sides'? Why?"

She studied the man who had shot her bathroom door full of holes. He'd been energized then; on a rampage—or a holy war. Now he reminded her of a balloon with a slow leak.

Still, when his angry gaze focused on Johnson, some of the old fire came back into his eyes. And when he spoke, it was as if he and the Jackal were the only two people in the room. "When I heard Bridgman and his men talking at the biohazards lab, I realized you didn't give a damn about what happened to me—even though you'd been talking like you were going to make me your partner or something so we could use the money from your arms deals to set up a foundation to cure diseases. If I'd gotten in there like you wanted, I would have ended up with the same damn virus that's just about killed Paul.''

"No," Johnson countered. "You've got it wrong.''

Enders shook his head. "Cut the crap. You fooled me once. But never again. You don't care who gets hurt working for you, just so you get what you want. You brainwashed me into thinking Bridgman had to go. And the girl.'' He shot Meg a raw look, then swung his gaze back to Johnson.

Transfixed, Meg stared at Enders. Could they really trust this man who'd tried to kill her? Or was Glenn just teamed with him now because he had no choice?

She slid Glenn a questioning look. Before he could respond, Enders gave a frantic shout and dodged to the right. "No!''

Her head snapped around, and she saw that in the few seconds their attention had been focused elsewhere, the wall behind which Johnson was standing had slid noiselessly open, revealing a secret escape passage. All along, he'd been planning to get away, she realized with a surge of anger.

Enders threw himself through the doorway, grabbing at Johnson—who had slipped into the darkness.

Glenn drew his gun, but he couldn't get off a shot without hitting Enders.

There was only one thing Meg could do. "Duck!" she shouted at Glenn as she hurled the canister after Johnson, then eased the pressure on the trigger.

With a loud report, the top blew off the carrying case, and an obscuring white cloud poured out, even as Johnson shrieked in terror and tried to scramble away.

"What are you doing? We're all dead!" he screamed, above the sounds of kicking and clawing.

As they'd hoped, he thought he'd been doused with the deadly virus. But the small explosion and the vapor were only a special effect. Really, there was nothing in the canister besides a chemical fogging agent.

Glenn plunged into the passageway where the mist blocked Meg's sight and muffled sound. But it didn't hide the booming of two shots in the confined space.

"Glenn!" Meg screamed. "Glenn!"

"Stay back," he called, and she thought she saw his head and shoulders disappearing into the mist-filled tunnel.

"Glenn, no!"

She stayed where she was, knowing that if she went into the passageway after him, she could make things worse. But when two more shots sounded in the fog, she rushed toward the opening. She slammed into Glenn, who was getting to his feet.

"Are you all right?" she breathed, starting toward him, then stopping. She ached to hold him, to touch him, but she couldn't read his expression, so she stayed where she was.

"I'm okay," he answered.

"What happened?"

"I don't know." Blocking her entrance into the passageway he called, "Enders?"

There was no answer, no sound from the darkness.

"Stay here," Glenn ordered. Cautiously he crept forward. When she tried to follow, he turned and glared at her. "Back up."

She retreated to the front hall, waiting with her heart pounding while he advanced into the tunnel. Ahead of him, she could see a flashlight beam. When he made a grunting noise, she tensed.

"Enders is dead," he called. Moments later he issued another news bulletin. "So is Johnson. It looks like he had a gun stashed in there, and they shot each other."

He was just returning to the hallway when the front door burst open, and armed men poured inside. Meg recognized the Castle Phoenix uniforms. Each man had a canister that looked like a small fire extinguisher attached to his belt. When they saw the mist hanging heavily in the air, they began to spray the room. Under the barrage, the vapor dissolved.

Claymore, his arm strapped to his chest, stepped through the door.

"What the hell are you doing here?" Glenn demanded.

"The same thing you are—coming to lend Ms. Faulkner a hand. If you'd turned on your radio, you would have known I wasn't going to throw her to the sharks, either."

When Glenn opened his mouth, Claymore plowed ahead. "Don't give me an argument about it. If you can play Sir Galahad, so can I." Before Glenn could muster a comment, he turned to Meg. "I see you blew the top off our canister. Weren't you supposed to be out of the room when you did it?"

She nodded. "Johnson was getting away. Glenn couldn't get a clear shot at him. Pressing the trigger was the only thing I could do to slow Johnson down."

"He's dead," Glenn informed Claymore. "And so is Leroy Enders. You were right. He was causing all the trouble at the castle. When he realized that Johnson was just using him, he got mad." Wearily he gave the details to his security chief.

Claymore made a hurried inspection of the tunnel, then ushered them out of the house and toward the gate where another helicopter had set down just outside the fence. Before they reached it, Glenn pulled Meg to a halt. "Wait here."

Still numb, she watched him take off his gun belt and hand it to Claymore. The two men had a hurried consultation before Glenn returned to her side.

"Why did you take off your gun?" she asked.

"Because I don't need it. I hope I never need it again!"

Before she could ask another question, he announced, "You and I are leaving by car."

"Why?"

"Because we need to talk—in private."

She gave him a little nod, then turned to the security chief. "What about Tommy?"

"He's on his way to the castle."

Claymore went back inside and there was nothing Meg could do but follow Glenn to the gate.

It was over. Johnson and Enders were dead—no longer a threat to Castle Phoenix. Glenn would walk away from her now. But it seemed there were things he wanted to say first.

She was afraid to hear them. Afraid not to hear them.

On the trip down, she'd been pumped full of adrenaline—ready for anything. Now she simply felt a great weariness. Slipping her hand into her pocket, she found the wallet with her fake credit cards and money. At least she could rent a car and make it home. Or maybe one of her Light Street friends would be willing to come here and pick her up. Right now she needed her friends.

But Tommy was going to Castle Phoenix, her leaden brain suddenly remembered. Would Glenn let her see him?

After all the trouble she'd caused, she didn't feel as if she had the right to make any demands. At least she'd know her brother was in good hands.

Glenn had started up the road at a fast clip and was several paces ahead of her. Quickening her stride, she hurried to catch up, her breath coming in little puffs.

He stopped, turned to make sure she was still there, and she saw her own tension and uncertainty mirrored on his face.

"Why are you in such a hurry?" she asked as she drew abreast of him.

"I wanted to get the hell out of Johnson's territory."

Slowing, he looking up and down the blacktop. "Come to the car. It's up there." He pointed to a stand of windblown trees. As they drew closer, she saw a dark sedan half hidden under low-hanging branches.

Reaching the side of the vehicle, he turned and faced her. His expression had gone from tense to grim, and she felt her stomach knot in anticipation of a goodbye speech she didn't want to hear. God, why didn't he just get this over with?

He scuffed up a spray of gravel with his booted foot. "Communication isn't my strong suit. So let me say what I've got to say and get it over with."

She swallowed painfully. "Okay."

"When I fell for you, it was like stepping off a cliff. I had no control, no safety net, and it scared the hell out of me. Then I found out you'd come to Castle Phoenix to help Enders steal the virus—and I felt like everything that had happened between us was a lie."

"No!" She couldn't stand it then; couldn't stand his thinking she had been cold and calculating about the two of them. "Glenn, I didn't lie to you," she gasped out. "All my feelings were real. I fell in love with the Glenn Bridgman I met when I had no memory of what I'd been told about you. And when I got my memory back, the shock of finding out that Johnson had tricked me was so terrible that I couldn't...cope."

When he took a step toward her, she couldn't move; she could only whisper, "Oh, Glenn, try and forgive me for hurting you so badly."

"I don't have to," he said, his voice gritty. Then his features contorted as he caught the pain in her eyes. "I didn't say that right. I mean, there's nothing to forgive. Johnson was slick. He knew how to press the right buttons—with you, with Leroy Enders. He set you up. Then you lost your memory, and you were left trying to cope with an impossible situation. You were as honest with me as you knew how to be. Now I owe you the same honesty." She saw him swallow. "Meg, I don't want to lose you. "

She'd been so prepared for dismissal that all she could do was stand and stare at him in a sort of dumb-eyed confusion. "But I brought Enders onto the estate. I almost got you killed. I—"

He took another step forward and pressed his fingers to her lips. "And when you realized the part you played in that, you did everything in your power to put things right. God, it killed me to let you keep the appointment with Johnson, but I couldn't say anything—because I knew it would make your job more dangerous. If he'd thought I cared about what happened to you, he would have used that against me. So all I could do was let you go—then follow you down here."

"Oh, Glenn." She threw herself against him, wrapped her arms around him and held tight.

He hugged her close, and she clung, molding the contours of her body to his. When he began to speak, his voice was stronger. "You were right. I've been afraid to live in the real world since Operation Clean Sweep. I didn't know how to deal with what I was feeling, so I walled myself off in a castle like a monster. But you marched in there and shook up my life. Then you got your memory back, and the worst part was knowing that what you'd been told about me wasn't so far from the truth."

"Weren't you listening to anything General Dorsey said? Don't you know why he and Blake and all the rest of them are so loyal to you? They know you're a good man fighting for what he thinks is right. Fighting for other people's lives. That's why they were all so hostile to me. They thought I wanted to hurt you. And they wanted to protect you."

He stared at her, stunned, as if none of that had ever occurred to him.

"But you have to let yourself live, too. You have to do that for me and Tommy, and everyone else who—who loves you and needs you to be there for them."

"I'm not exactly lovable," he said, his voice thick.

"That's not your call." Tipping her face up, she clasped the back of his head and brought his lips down to hers. She thought she'd lost him; now she tried to tell him with her mouth and with her body what he meant to her.

"I love you. I love you so much," he gasped when he finally lifted his head.

"And I love you, too."

One hand moved possessively up and down her back while the other tangled in her hair, and again he covered her mouth with his. His hand crept under her shirt, splaying across the heated skin of her back, kindling raw need inside her.

She made a frenzied sound, moving against him, suddenly frantic to get as close as she could. When the kiss finally broke, she was giddy enough to contemplate pulling him into the back seat of the car and ripping off his clothing.

Before she could do it, a helicopter swooped low and circled them. Looking up, she saw grinning faces pressed to the windows.

"So much for privacy," Glenn muttered. He made a chopping gesture with his hand, and the spectators sped away.

Again he wrapped her close, but she sensed he was making an effort to control himself now.

"There's got to be a motel around here," he muttered.

"Probably. And undoubtedly some very nice country inns."

"Will you go to one with me?"

"I'll go anywhere with you," she answered from the

bottom of her heart as he opened the door and ushered her into the car.

He slipped into the drivers' seat but didn't immediately start the car. "You said things happened between us fast."

"That's because we both knew we'd found our soul mate," she replied.

He turned toward her, his eyes sparkling like a sunrise. "Then it's not too soon to ask you to marry me? I—I don't want to waste any more time."

Joy bubbled in her heart. "Yes. No. I mean you're not moving too fast. Well, actually," she amended, "my head is spinning. But I'll adjust."

"If the 'beast' of Castle Phoenix can adjust to being happy, I think you can."

"I'll thank you not to talk that way about my future husband."

She gave him a brilliant smile, then snuggled close as he backed the car out of the woods and headed for a place where she could show him how happy she truly was.

Epilogue

Meg stood in the doorway of the recreation room, watching the men who had gotten the medication Glenn had developed. They were all on the road to recovery—even the ones who had been in the worst physical and mental shape.

In the bright, cheery space washed with afternoon sunlight, some of them were playing board games. Some were watching television. Some were simply laughing and talking and getting used to feeling normal again.

When Tommy spotted her, he excused himself from the card table where he'd been sitting and came over.

"How are you doing, Miz Bridgman?"

She gave him a wide grin. "I'm doing very well. And you?"

"Never better."

It wasn't quite true, she knew. He still needed to gain back another thirty pounds along with considerable muscle tone. But she'd never dreamed she'd see him this healthy again. And for that she was profoundly grateful.

Glenn, who had been bending over the only man in a wheelchair, straightened and came over. It was Hal Dorsey, who was still fighting the insidious effects of his arthritis. But he seemed to be holding his own.

He watched with approval as Glenn moved to Meg's side

and slipped his arm around her. After a brief chat with Glenn, Tommy went back to his poker game.

"I have some notes on the Nepalese mountain herbs you wanted," she said, holding up a blue folder.

"Fast work." He took the papers from her and shuffled through them.

Before their marriage six months ago, Meg had left the Light Street offices of Adventures in Travel. Now she was working for Glenn, planning the details of foreign plant-gathering expeditions and directing some of the physical activities for the Operation Clean Sweep team. Her expertise was in rock climbing, hiking, fishing and a host of other outdoor skills that the guys seemed to like a whole lot better than their more regimented physical-therapy sessions.

With the Jackal out of the picture, Glenn had reduced the security force at the castle. The men who'd stayed on staff were also in her program, and there was a friendly rivalry going on to see who could climb to the top of Little Falls Summit the fastest. So far, she still had the best time. But she suspected that Blake Claymore was going to claim the championship soon.

"So, can we get away for a few minutes to discuss this stuff?" she asked, gesturing toward the folder.

Glenn's lips quirked, and she smiled into his eyes, giving silent thanks for the changes in his life. He was able to relax, able to enjoy the life they were making together. As their gazes held for a few more seconds, she was sure he knew that the report was only an excuse to be alone for a few hours.

They slipped around the corner, stole a kiss, and started toward their private apartment, arm in arm—two lovers still on their honeymoon.

And if Meg had her way, they always would be.

And there's more 43 Light Street!
Turn the page for a bonus look at what's
in store for you in the next
43 Light Street *book by Ruth Glick
writing as Rebecca York,*
NEVER TOO LATE

Only from Harlequin Intrigue!

Chapter One

"The police are in town—asking questions about you."

Mariana Reyes froze in front of the old porcelain sink where she stood with her hands plunged to the elbows in hot, soapy water. "Are you sure they're police?" she asked, struggling to keep her voice steady.

"They have the uniforms. The guns."

Mariana nodded. Maybe they were police. Maybe they were imposters. But what did it matter? Word had reached her that Benito Lopez and three others were dead. And now the killers were coming for her.

She felt the chill of fear sink into her bones. It was all starting again—the running, the hiding, the endless terror that was too much for any human being to endure. She didn't know how they'd found her; she only knew that it was true.

In this high mountain village far from Santa Isabella, where the air was cold and clear, she'd lulled herself into believing that she was finally safe. For six months, she'd worked here as a teacher, made a home for herself. Yet all the time, in her soul, she'd been waiting for this moment to come.

The old woman behind her must have seen her defeated posture. "You have to go," she said. "Quickly. For the *niña.*"

Mariana straightened and dragged in a steadying breath.

"Yes. For Alicia," she said, knowing that she had to hold on to her sanity—for her daughter. Because the innocent child sleeping in the next room was the only thing that mattered.

Reaching for the rough towel hanging from a hook beside the sink, she dried her hands. A long time ago, washing her own dishes would have been unthinkable for Mariana Reyes. She'd lived in a huge white house full of servants who'd washed and fetched and carried according to her whims. She'd taken it all for granted, unaware how lucky she was—until the life she'd known had been snatched away.

She looked down at her rough, reddened hands, wondering if that time had only been a dream.

"Tonio is talking to them," the old woman said. "He knows what to do. He's sending them in the wrong direction to give you time to get away."

"I don't want him to be in trouble because of me."

The old woman laughed. "He won't. He knows how to act the fool when it's convenient. He's been doing it for years. Remember when your father used to get so angry with him when the oranges disappeared from the trees?"

A smile flickered on Mariana's lips. "Yes," she replied, even as she rounded the dark wooden table and headed for the little bedroom where her daughter slept, curled under a bright wool blanket that the women of the village had woven—the kind they had woven for hundreds of years.

Crossing to the bed, she stood looking down at her child, seeing the long, reddish hair. Her father's hair.

The mouth was her father's, too—well shaped, sensual. Quick to break into a smile. Incredibly, her eyes were like his, also. Not the deep brown of her own Spanish heritage, but an impossible sea green that grew dark with strong emotion.

For an endless moment she stood very still, fighting the stab of pain that always pierced her heart when she thought of the man she had no right to love. Then she stirred herself and began to move around the room, taking clothing from the shelves that lined the wall, pulling rough wool travel bags from under the bed. Her belongings were meager. Still, she couldn't take everything.

"Mama?"

The quavering voice stopped her hand. She hadn't wanted to wake Alicia. Not yet. Quickly she crossed to the bed, knelt at her daughter's side.

Alicia sat up, looking from the empty shelves to the bags. "Are we leaving in the night? Like the last time?"

"Yes," she whispered, hating the admission, hating the knowledge that her five-year-old daughter already possessed the wisdom of a hardened fugitive. "I've put out clothes. Can you get yourself dressed while I make some arrangements with Tía Susanna?"

"I'm a big girl."

"I know." She managed a smile, then returned to the only other room in the cinder-block cottage.

The old woman was waiting. "I've packed some food. You can go in the truck that's taking produce to the market."

"Please, you've done enough."

"No. Not for you." Susanna hesitated. "Will you take some advice?"

"Always."

"Write the letter. The one you should have written years ago."

Mariana felt her heart stop, then start again in double time. "I...can't."

"You must. This time, my child, you must swallow your pride."

"I—"

"Don't tell me no. Tell me you want to save your own life and the life of your child."

She gave a tight nod, then whirled away. Before returning to the bedroom, she dried her clammy palms on her skirt and tried to wipe the look of sick panic from her face.

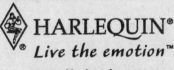

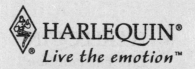

HARLEQUIN®
INTRIGUE®

BREATHTAKING ROMANTIC SUSPENSE

Shared dangers and passions lead to electrifying
romance and heart-stopping suspense!

Every month, you'll meet six new heroes
who are guaranteed to make your spine tingle
and your pulse pound. With them you'll enter
into the exciting world of Harlequin Intrigue—
where your life is on the line
and so is your heart!

THAT'S INTRIGUE—
ROMANTIC SUSPENSE
AT ITS BEST!

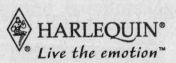

HARLEQUIN®

Super Romance®

...there's more to the story!

Superromance.
A *big* satisfying read about unforgettable
characters. Each month we offer *six* very different
stories that range from family drama to adventure
and mystery, from highly emotional stories to
romantic comedies—and much more! Stories
about people you'll believe in and care about.
Stories too compelling to put down....

Our authors are among today's *best* romance
writers. You'll find familiar names and talented
newcomers. Many of them are award winners—
and you'll see why!

If you want the biggest and best
in romance fiction, you'll get it
from Superromance!

Exciting, Emotional, Unexpected...

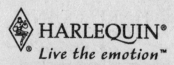

HARLEQUIN®
® *Live the emotion*™

HARLEQUIN®
Presents

The world's bestselling romance series...
The series that brings you your favorite authors,
month after month:

Helen Bianchin...Emma Darcy
Lynne Graham...Penny Jordan
Miranda Lee...Sandra Marton
Anne Mather...Carole Mortimer
Susan Napier...Michelle Reid

and many more uniquely talented authors!

Wealthy, powerful, gorgeous men...
Women who have feelings just like your own...
The stories you love, set in exotic, glamorous locations...

HARLEQUIN®
Presents

Seduction and Passion Guaranteed!

Harlequin® Historical
Historical Romantic Adventure!

*Imagine a time of chivalrous
knights and unconventional ladies,
roguish rakes and impetuous
heiresses, rugged cowboys
and spirited frontierswomen—
these rich and vivid tales will
capture your imagination!*

*Harlequin Historical . . .
they're too good to miss!*

passionate powerful provocative love stories

**Silhouette Desire delivers
strong heroes, spirited heroines
and compelling love stories.**

Desire features your favorite authors,
including

Annette Broadrick,
Diana Palmer,
Maureen Child
and Brenda Jackson.

**Passionate, powerful and provocative
romances *guaranteed!***

For superlative authors, sensual stories
and sexy heroes, choose Silhouette Desire.

passionate powerful provocative love stories